THE DEAD LETTER DELIVERY

THE GLASS LIBRARY, BOOK #4

C.J. ARCHER

WWW.CJARCHER.COM

CHAPTER 1

LONDON, SUMMER 1920

*N*othing captures a woman's attention quite as well as two muscular men who've dispensed with their shirts to perform a physical activity. Daisy and I couldn't take our gazes off the sight of Gabe and Alex as they changed a tire on the Vauxhall Prince Henry. Almost three hours into our journey from London to Ipswich, a puncture had forced us to pull over. Gabe suggested we use the unscheduled stop to have our picnic lunch, so Daisy and I found a shady spot on a gently sloping grassy bank where we laid out the blanket. We didn't get any further than opening the basket lid.

The sharp nudge of Daisy Carmichael's elbow drew my attention from the basket to her. My friend's heated stare drew my attention to the men shedding their shirts. We sat as one on the blanket, stretched out our legs, and watched on in silence, the picnic forgotten.

From a distance, we couldn't hear everything they said as they chatted while they worked, although I was quite sure I caught Alex's booming voice say the words "she" and "nurse". Gabe spoke and Alex's response was to shake his head and glance at us. Or, rather, at Daisy. Gabe stopped cranking the jack and followed his gaze.

Daisy and I dove into the picnic basket, clunking our foreheads together. By the time we stopped laughing and looked up, Alex was crouched beside the tire, wrench in hand.

Daisy leaned back, propping herself up on her elbows. The wisp of a smile touched her lips as she watched Alex remove the tire. I focused on Gabe lifting the spare from its storage position on the side of the motorcar. He may be a little shorter than his giant friend, but he certainly wasn't lacking in any way. I couldn't help but admire the bulge of his biceps, the stretch of his cotton undervest across his broad back.

Once the tires were swapped and secured, the men returned the toolbox to the motorcar and wiped their hands on rags. They put on their shirts before sauntering over to us.

With twin sighs of disappointment that the show was over, Daisy and I made ourselves look busy by emptying the contents of the picnic basket, but I bungled my attempt to appear composed by dropping one of the sandwiches. The carefully wrapped package came undone and slices of boiled egg and lettuce spilled onto the blanket.

"I'll eat that one," I said, laughing off my fumble. I glanced up to see Gabe smiling at me. It was very similar to the one Daisy had sported as she watched the men.

I redoubled my efforts to look busy with the picnic.

Alex peered into the basket and smacked his lips. "God bless Mrs. Ling."

Gabe's cook was indeed a marvel. Aside from four different types of sandwiches, she'd packed rabbit pies, a potato salad, sliced ham, chicken, scotched eggs, and mince pies. There were also pastries and fruit, with bottled beer to wash it all down. It was more of a survival kit than a picnic lunch.

"Mrs. Ling knows how much you eat." Daisy handed him a sandwich only to draw it back suddenly. "Are your hands clean?"

He inspected his hands. "As clean as can be under the circumstances."

Gabe sat with his back against the tree trunk. "Thank goodness for fine weather."

"I'll say," Daisy murmured.

Alex frowned at her, the sandwich halfway to his mouth.

"I wouldn't want to be changing a tire in the rain," Gabe went on.

"Or eating a picnic," I added.

"Nooo," Daisy said. "But it would have added an extra *something*."

"Yes, it would have," Alex said, matter-of-factly. "We would have got wet."

Daisy smiled at him around her mouthful, which only confused him more. He sensed she was teasing him, but he wasn't sure how.

Gabe must have been more aware of being watched while changing the tire than his friend. He pretended to inspect his sandwich, giving it far more attention than ham and buttered bread deserved. I had the sinking feeling he was drawing out the moment to tease us. "You seemed to be watching closely."

Daisy was quicker and more composed than me. While I tried to think of something clever to deflect from my embarrassment, she blurted out an excuse that seemed quite plausible, and did it with all the breezy charm of a young woman without a care in the world.

"I was watching closely because it might come in useful one day."

Gabe chuckled and ate his sandwich, but Alex gave her his full attention.

"You want to know how to change a flat tire on a motorcar that you don't even own yet?" he asked.

"Thank you for assuming I *will* one day own a motor. But no, it's for research. I'm going to be an author of novels."

Alex shook his head as if trying to loosen a thought. "Setting aside the fact you were going to be an actress last month and an artist before that, what does changing a tire have to do with writing novels?"

"I may need to describe how to do it if my character is presented with the problem of a flat."

He grunted. "You'll only succeed in boring your readers."

"You have no idea what goes into writing a novel."

"And you do?"

She sniffed. "Yes. I've written a chapter already."

"May I read it?"

"Certainly not. No one can read it until it's finished."

"Is it an adventure novel? I used to like adventure novels, but I haven't finished a book since before the war. I used to read a lot but can't seem to concentrate anymore."

"There'll be some adventure in it. That's why I came on this visit. I want to experience new things so my stories can have a more realistic flavor. I've never been to Ipswich before, let alone met a silver magician."

"We may not meet one this time," I told her. "From the information we've been able to find so far, it seems the Folgates were the last of their kind and they've possibly died out. With my brother gone..." My throat suddenly closed and my eyes filled with unshed tears. I hadn't thought about James for some time, and for that I felt guilty. He deserved at least a passing thought every day from his sister.

Gabe placed his hand over mine on the blanket. "Are you all right?"

I nodded. "With James gone, the survival of silver magic rests on the shoulders of the mysterious Marianne Folgate, and whether or not she had children."

"You're convinced your brother was a silver magician, related to Marianne in some way?" Alex asked.

"I am. James was convinced, and I now know that a magician is aware of their talent, deep within."

"But not you?"

"I have no affinity for silver, just paper."

Daisy had been frowning, and she now finally spoke what was on her mind. "But if your brother was a silver magician, then the line continues through you. You and James are from the same bloodline."

I plucked at a loose thread on the blanket. "I'm not sure…"

"You don't think he was your brother?"

I shrugged. "I don't know anything anymore. What if he wasn't? My mother was so secretive about our father, our past…I honestly wouldn't be surprised at this point to find out that James and I are adopted."

"You said he looked like her," Daisy pointed out.

"There is that. But, although I have gray eyes like her and am similar in height, there's really nothing else we have in common. I'm blonder, my face is narrower, and our characters are different." Perhaps James was her only natural child. Perhaps *I* was the adopted one.

Gabe remained silent, listening intently. He'd heard this argument from me before. We'd discussed it when I learned I was a paper magician and ruled out the possibility of silver magic.

Since that discovery, I'd met a paper magician family who operated a manufacturing business in London. Brother and sister, Mr. and Miss Peterson, had been welcoming. They'd kindly offered to answer any questions I had about my newly discovered ability. As far as we knew, I wasn't related to them, but it was possible our lineages merged further up the family tree than records showed. With access to his parents' catalog of magicians, Gabe had also given me a list of known paper magicians outside of London, in case I wanted to write to them. But I'd set the task aside for another time. I wasn't ready to expand my horizons. Yet.

For now, we wanted to investigate the Folgates, the last known family of silver magicians in the country. Whereas paper magicians were relatively common, silver ones were rare. If both magics were in my lineage, it seemed an easier task to begin with the Folgates to hopefully add more branches to my rather sparse family tree.

Gabe offered me a bowl of strawberries. "Hopefully we'll have a clearer picture after today."

We exchanged smiles as I plucked a strawberry from the bowl.

Daisy topped up her cup with more beer. "And if we discover nothing, at least we would have had an adventure to Ipswich. I've never been anywhere except Marlborough and London."

Alex held out his cup for her to refill. "Adventures are over-rated. Believe me, home is the best place in the world."

"You mean London?"

"I mean wherever home may be for each of us."

Daisy opened her mouth to say something, but shut it again and poured beer into his cup. It was impossible to argue with a man whose sense of adventure had been shaped and shadowed by war.

I watched Gabe through my lowered lashes to see if he agreed with his friend. Oddly, he suddenly broke into a grin.

He raised his cup to Alex. "You and I shall just have to be content with experiencing further adventures via Daisy's novels."

Alex touched his cup to Gabe's. "That's good enough for me."

Daisy pulled a face. "That's a lot of pressure. I'm not sure my writing talents are up to it."

"Since when has that stopped you doing something?"

In my mind, Alex was complimenting her, saying she possessed a carefree spirit unencumbered by doubt, but Daisy stiffened. Her lips thinned.

"So I'm a talentless hack, am I?"

Alex's jaw dropped before firming again. "You're putting words into my mouth."

Daisy tipped out the contents of her cup and shoved it into

the bag Mrs. Ling had provided for the rubbish. "Am I?" She stood and strode off to the motorcar with a toss of her scarf-covered head.

Alex collected the rest of the leftovers and rubbish and placed them in the bag. "Seems my mind has been made up for me." He slammed the basket lid down and hefted it as he stood. He stormed off in the direction of Daisy, who had her back to us as she put on her driving coat.

"What does he mean?" I asked Gabe as we watched them ignore one another. "Made his mind up about what?"

"I can't say, sorry."

"Does it have something to do with a nurse?"

He glanced sharply at me. "You heard that?"

"Who is she?"

"I can't break a confidence."

"Very well, but in the absence of more information, I'll simply have to go with my first thought—that Alex has been considering whether to pursue a pretty nurse who has perhaps shown an interest in him, or whether to explore his feelings for Daisy further."

Gabe gave no reaction. None at all. Based on that, it was safe to say my assumption was correct.

"And Daisy just made the choice an easy one for him." I sighed. "She's her own worst enemy."

He picked up the blanket and shook it out. I took the opposite corners and we folded it. Our fingers brushed as we came together, a small current of heat passing between us. I let go and quickly stepped back. As much as I desired him, I didn't want to explore my feelings. Not yet. Not when he was still raw from ending his engagement to Ivy Hobson, and not when he'd admitted he wasn't ready for another relationship.

And not when he could have no interest in me beyond friendship.

I cleared my throat. "Please tell Alex that Daisy is sensitive about her lack of formal education and skills. I know she seems confident, but she's really not. Particularly where he's concerned."

"I'll pass it on. Don't worry about them. They'll sort themselves out when they're both ready."

He wasn't the only one who wasn't ready for commitment, it seemed. It was understandable that Alex was also unsure of himself now, and the future he wanted, or thought he did. Where life had taken on a rhythm of certainty before the war, a new world had risen from its ashes; a world full of restlessness and doubt.

But it held possibility, too, and a sense that life was for living, not merely for existing. The combination was somewhat chaotic and confusing, but I felt as though the chaos and confusion would clear soon and we'd be left with something fresh. I suspected the new decade would bring about changes that none of us could yet fathom.

We traveled the rest of the way to Ipswich without speaking. Daisy was moping, Alex was ignoring her, and it was difficult to have a conversation over the wind and noise of the engine anyway. As we drove into the town center, Gabe slowed the vehicle while Alex used a map to guide him to the address we'd been given for the Folgates.

If Ipswich were a novel, it would be brimming with tales of adventure, romance and intrigue as befitting an ancient settlement that had both thrived and suffered at different points in its history. Smoke from the factories and iron foundries smothered the town, and a steady stream of lorries clogged the streets near the port. The municipal buildings stood proud and sturdy, as magnificent as anything found in London. There was no evidence of the two zeppelin raids that had damaged the town during the war. Although I'd read about the bombings in the newspaper at the time, censorship had forbidden them from reporting the locations. Until recently, only locals had known.

From the archivist at Ipswich's Silversmiths Guild we'd learned the address of John Folgate, father of Marianne. The archivist had done considerable research into the family over the years and traced the line back to the time of the Medicis in Florence. It had been a Medici who'd kidnapped a member of the silversmith family who worked for the powerful Ottomans, and then centuries later, a descendant had moved to England and changed their name to Folgate. The archivist couldn't find anything more about Marianne after she left Ipswich. Thanks to Gabe's parents, we knew she and a man named Cooper had briefly lived in a house in Wimbledon that was owned by Lord Coyle. We couldn't definitely say whether they'd married, as there was no record of their union, but that didn't mean they hadn't married somewhere else.

A jeweler now occupied the address the archivist gave us for John Folgate. The quaint shop amidst a row of shops with matching bow windows reminded me of those flanking the entrance to Crooked Lane where the Glass Library was located. The jeweler knew nothing of John Folgate and directed us to his neighbor, a tailor by the name of Mr. Dowd who'd occupied the same shop for almost forty years.

Mr. Dowd frowned when Gabe asked if he knew the Folgates, but he finally admitted that he did. "I knew them well." He clasped the measuring tape draped around his neck in both hands, capturing his jacket lapels, too. He squinted at each of us in turn through thick spectacles, looking somewhat over-whelmed with so many people in his small shop.

"Them?" Gabe prompted.

"John, Juliette and Marianne, their daughter. Why do you want to know about the Folgates?"

"You knew Marianne personally?" I asked. "What can you tell us about her? What did she look like?"

My eagerness startled him a little, but he soon recovered. He didn't immediately answer me, however. "Who are you? Why are you asking about the Folgates?"

Although Gabe had already introduced us, he did so again, this time explaining that I might be a relative of the Folgates, but was trying to find out for certain. Mr. Dowd leaned forward to study me closely.

"You could be related, yes. There are some resemblances."

My heart leapt into my throat. I tried to keep a lid on my excitement so as not to startle him again. "What resemblances?"

"You're the same height and build as Marianne, and there's something about your eyes that seems familiar." He adjusted his spectacles. "But that's all. It may mean nothing." He frowned and tapped a finger against his lips in thought, but didn't go on.

"What can you tell us about her? What was she like? How old was she when she left? Where did she go?" So much for keeping a lid on.

The fingers clutching the tape and lapels tightened. "Slow down, Miss. One question at a time. Marianne was just a girl of about seven or eight when I first met her. She was quiet, and rarely spoke to me. She was only eighteen when she left Ipswich. Very young. Too young for a girl to be out on her own." He clicked his tongue, disapproving. "I know things are different nowadays, since the war, but back then, girls didn't leave home until they married. But Marianne couldn't wait to leave. Then her parents died shortly after in an accident."

"After?" Gabe asked. "Not before she left?"

"Definitely after. Mere weeks, I think it was."

That was at odds with what we knew about the silverware Marianne had sold in London. The pieces were engraved with her father's initials and, according to the buyers, she'd inherited them. It was possible she'd come back to Ipswich after their deaths to claim her inheritance, but when Gabe posed that question to Mr. Dowd, he shook his head.

"She never came back. I wondered if she'd died. John and Juliette's possessions went into storage after their deaths to wait for Marianne to reappear, but as far as I know, nothing was ever claimed. I'm not sure if they've since been distributed to charities. If you are related to Marianne, perhaps you have an inheritance awaiting you, young lady." He let go of the tape to poke a finger into the air. "I've just thought of something that might help. Wait here. Mind the shop. If anyone comes, I'll only be five minutes."

He shuffled off to the back and disappeared into an adjoining room, leaving the door open. He headed up a staircase, his steps slow but steady.

We filled our time by inspecting the fine suits on display and the one being cut to size on the counter. Alex was placing different ties to his chest and admiring the effect in the mirror, although I caught him glancing at Daisy from time to time in the reflection. She sat in a leather armchair and watched the passing traffic through the window.

Mr. Dowd returned with a photo album, already opened to a page in the middle. He placed it on the counter and turned it to show us. He stabbed a finger on a photograph depicting one man and two women standing in front of the shop next door. The painted sign on the window simply read Ipswich Silversmith.

Mr. Dowd pointed to the younger of the two women in the photograph. "That's her. That's Marianne."

I didn't need him to tell me. I knew instantly it was Marianne because I recognized her. She was younger than I remembered, but it was definitely her.

My mother.

CHAPTER 2

Gabe touched my shoulder. "Sylvia? Are you all right?"

I'd covered my mouth with my hand without realizing it. My face must have shown my shock, because he told me to sit down, and suddenly everyone was making a fuss, guiding me to the chair Daisy had vacated.

Mr. Dowd offered me a glass of water, but I shook my head. I couldn't speak to tell them I felt fine, that I just needed a moment. All I could do was rummage through my bag to find the photograph I always carried with me. It was the only photograph I had of my mother with James and me. She hated her photo being taken, but had given in just before James went off to war.

I held it out with shaking fingers. Gabe took it then handed it to Mr. Dowd.

"It's her!" Mr. Dowd placed my photograph beside his and pointed to Marianne. "I must say I am pleased. I was worried you were a fortune hunter, like that other fellow."

I hardly heard a word he said. I doubted Gabe did either. He was crouching beside me, frowning and asking again if I was all right. It was left to Alex to ask.

"Other fellow? Has someone else been making inquiries about the Folgates?"

"Didn't I mention him earlier? Yes, there was another man here recently who asked similar questions. I didn't tell him much. He unnerved me. There was something too..." He clicked his tongue. "I don't know. Too eager, perhaps. Too desperate. I pegged him as a fortune hunter who'd got wind of an unclaimed inheritance. Not that I think John Folgate left much, but there must have been *something*."

"What did you tell him?" Gabe asked.

"Only what I've told you. That Marianne left when she was eighteen, shortly before her parents died, and she hasn't been back since."

"How did he react?"

"Unsurprised, and somewhat annoyed. He continued to pepper me with questions I couldn't answer—do I know where Marianne lives now, has she been back, were there other family or close friends she might have turned to? He became quite agitated when I couldn't tell him more. It was a relief when a customer came in and he left."

Alex removed a notepad and pencil from his inside jacket pocket. "What did he look like?"

"A small man, around my age, balding." He shrugged. "Rather insignificant to look at."

Alex's lips flattened in disappointment at the vague description, but he wrote it down anyway. "Did he give his name?"

"He gave no personal details. He simply stated that he was a friend of Marianne's and needed to find her."

"Does the name Cooper ring any bells?" Gabe asked.

Mr. Dowd shook his head.

Gabe gave the tailor a card with his telephone number on it. "Thank you. You've been very helpful. If the fellow comes again, please try to get his details then let me know. Don't inform him of our visit."

Mr. Dowd accepted the card and leveled his gaze at me.

"Leaving so soon? But you haven't told me what happened to Marianne after she left home. How did her life pan out? Clearly she had children." He picked up my photograph and returned it to me. "Two, am I correct?"

"Yes. My brother James was a few years older than me. He died in the war. My mother died of influenza."

"Oh, dear. I am so sorry, Miss Ashe. But at least she had you to care for her in the end." He offered a sympathetic smile. "I often wondered what happened to her after she left in such a rush and wondered why she never returned." He winced. "Well, perhaps that isn't such a mystery." From the way he watched me closely, I suspected he was trying to gauge how much I knew.

Considering I knew nothing, his hints drew me like a magnet. "Why? Did she have a falling out with her parents? Is that why she left abruptly?"

"She never told you?"

"She told us nothing of her childhood."

He pulled over a stool and sat. "Everyone has a right to know where they're from, who their people are, so I'll tell you what I know. It's very little, I'm afraid." He clutched his lapels along with the measuring tape around his neck. "Marianne was their only child, much to her father's disappointment. He wanted a son." He offered an apologetic smile to Daisy and me. "Some men are like that. Anyway, he wasn't a good father. I'd hear him berate Marianne, harp on every little mistake, order her to help him in the shop at all hours, even when she was supposed to be at school. I'd see her sneak a few minutes reading when he wasn't looking, but if he caught her...well, he wasn't physically violent, from what I saw, but he was cruel in other ways. He called her useless, often reminding her that he'd wanted a boy. John was very controlling of both Marianne and Juliette. They weren't allowed friends. They had to account for their where-abouts at all times, so Juliette once told Mrs. Dowd."

Gabe came to stand beside me and placed a hand on my shoulder. Daisy sat on the chair arm and tucked my hand into hers. But as awful as Mr. Dowd's account was to hear, it didn't affect me as much as it should. In a way, I couldn't connect the Marianne he knew to my mother. I hadn't fully digested the fact that Marianne Folgate and Alice Ashe were one and the same person. I'd also half-expected to discover that my mother's fear of men stemmed from her childhood experiences. It made sense that her anxiety around men could be explained by deep-seated trauma. Mr. Dowd couldn't say for certain whether John had physically abused Marianne and Juliette, but it wouldn't surprise me if he had. My mother had made sure that I knew how to fight if I were in danger. It had taken years of training that few girls were given. That sort of dedication and determination had its roots somewhere.

"Did Marianne ever fight back, do you know?" I asked. "Could her father have thrown her out as a result of her retaliation?"

"I can say that I never saw her so much as talk back to him, let alone shout or fight. John made her anxious. I could see it in the way she tried to avoid him. She'd avert her gaze and shrink in on herself, trying to make herself smaller whenever he was near. I suppose she fought back in the only way she knew how, by leaving the moment she was old enough. In some respects, that was probably the most devastating thing she could have done to John. It was the ultimate revenge, if I may be so bold."

"How so?"

"She was a silver magician, too, like him. As the only child, she was the last of the Folgate line. John was an only child and his father before him was an only child, too." He adjusted his fingers around the tape. "I wasn't aware he was a magician at the time, of course. Back then, magicians kept to themselves out of fear of persecution. The Silversmiths Guild would have revoked his license and then where would he be? Without a trade, no income. Dreadful business. Anyway, as I said, I knew nothing about their silver magic, but I did know that John saw Marianne as the future of his little business. In his kinder moments, after he regretted berating her, he'd tell her she was special and that's why he was so hard on her. He wanted her to be the best she could be, to learn everything about silver-smithing that he could teach her. According to Mrs. Dowd, who spoke to Mrs. Folgate about it, John had arranged a marriage for Marianne to protect her, as he put it."

"Protect her from what?"

"I wasn't sure at the time, but now I believe it was to protect her from unscrupulous persons who might use the Folgate magical lineage for their own benefit. Silver magic was valuable. It probably still is." He eyed me carefully then lifted his gaze to Gabe, still standing at my shoulder. He didn't need to say it, but he was suggesting Gabe needed to take care of me, too, if I were a silver magician.

I hurriedly assured him I was not.

"Ah. Well, then. That's that. But silver magic must run through your veins, Miss Ashe, and some people will presume your children will inherit it and they might want your children to be their children, if you understand my meaning."

"I do. And thank you for your concern."

"It's the least I can do." He sighed. "Sometimes I wish I'd done more to help Juliette and Marianne. Mrs. Dowd used to tell me I should say something to John, tell him not to speak that way to his wife and daughter, but no man likes to meddle in another fellow's business. It's not the done thing. Anyway, Mari-anne ran away so..." He shrugged, as if her departure absolved him from responsibility.

"How did John and Juliette react to her leaving?" Gabe asked.

"They were devastated. Both of them. Juliette cried all the time. John ranted and raged, said someone must have lured her away. He reported her missing to the police, but they couldn't do anything."

"You said they died in an accident shortly after her depar-ture. What sort of accident?"

"There was a fire. Fortunately, it was contained to the flat above the shop, but sadly, they both perished. Horrible day, it was."

"You claimed John never told you he was a silver magician," Gabe said. "How did you find out?"

"I guessed, but not until after he died. No one admitted to being a magician in those days. It was too dangerous." He laughed softly. "I was so naive, I didn't even know magic existed. I was quite in the dark. It wasn't until later, after the existence of magicians became public that I began to wonder if John was a silversmith magician. Of course, he was dead by then, so I couldn't ask, but Mrs. Dowd and I came to the conclusion that he must have been. His work was very fine. People came from all over the country to purchase his wares. Years later, the archivist of the Silversmiths Guild came here and asked a few questions about John. He was doing a family history of the Folgates. Guild members had long suspected John was a magician, you see. In all the years since his death, no other silver magician had come forward, so the archivist was quite sure the Folgates were the last of their kind. He had an interest in finding out more about the history of such a unique family."

"Did he ask about Marianne?"

"He wanted to know if John had any offspring. I told him as much about Marianne as I could."

The local Silversmith Guild's archivist had been very helpful when we spoke to him over the telephone. We'd not told him about my possible connection to Marianne, but he was aware of our search for her, as well as the other man also searching for her. It was very likely that man was the same one who'd questioned Mr. Dowd about Marianne, and who'd been a suspect in our investigation into the murder of a bookbinder after he impersonated a Scotland Yard detective over the telephone. We were no closer to finding out who he was, and why he wanted to locate Marianne.

We thanked the tailor and made to leave when he stopped us.

"I've just remembered something. Not that long ago, I was chatting to the postman about all the letters he can no longer deliver." At our blank looks, he elaborated. "The war and influenza took so many of the intended recipients, you see. Any post addressed to a deceased person is usually returned to the sender, but not all letters have a return address. Those that don't are kept at the post office in case someone comes forward to claim them. They don't keep them forever, of course, but if there's a chance a relative of the recipient is found, then they're more likely to hold on to them. I asked him about the Folgates' mail, knowing Marianne could one day return to claim an inheritance. I thought I could inform her that there was mail waiting for her at the post office if she ever stopped by here. The postman said it was likely there was, and told me to tell her, if she should ever appear, to present at the Ipswich Post Office and ask to see if there were any dead letters addressed to her parents."

"Dead letters?" Daisy prompted.

"That's what the postman called the mail where the recipient has died or moved without a forwarding address, and there was no return address. Apparently, they're stored in a room somewhere. Considering you are Marianne's daughter, Miss Ashe, the Folgates' mail belongs to you now. Hopefully, something will lead you to an inheritance."

"Thank you," I said. "We'll check at the post office."

He let go of his measuring tape and leapt to his feet. He returned to the photograph album on the counter. "You should have this." He handed me the photo of Marianne and her parents outside their shop. "You'll have more use for it than me."

I thanked him again, attempting a smile even though my heart was thudding and my vision suddenly blurred. Fortunately, Gabe placed my hand on his arm and led me back to the motorcar because I wasn't sure if I could have made it without stumbling.

He opened the Vauxhall's door and assisted me inside. He

rested a hand on the door and leaned down. The concern on his face made my stomach flutter. "That was a lot of information to take in. Do you want to go to the hotel?"

"What time is it?"

He checked his pocket watch. "Just gone five."

"It's too late to go to the post office now. We'll go tomorrow. I want to see if there are any dead letters addressed to my..." I swallowed, "...to my family."

I hardly noticed the direction we took, nor our final destination. I went through the motions at the check-in desk then proceeded to the room I would be sharing with Daisy. Gabe had booked a hotel in a flash part of Ipswich before leaving London, and we'd packed a small bag each knowing we'd most likely stay overnight.

After freshening up, Daisy and I met the men in the ground floor bar. We ordered cocktails and settled into a booth near the back, as far from the band as possible so we could talk. Not that they were playing too loudly yet. The velvet-voiced singer chose sultry tunes suited to the early hour.

As Alex slid onto the seat opposite Daisy, he bumped her knee. She scowled at him and folded her arms over her chest. He pretended not to notice.

He raised his glass in salute. "To Sylvia finding out more about her mother."

Daisy was the only one not to clink her glass to his. "To Sylvia learning her mother's real name."

Alex narrowed his gaze at her.

She turned to me. "You truly had no idea that Alice wasn't her name?"

"None."

"Do you think Ashe is her married name, or do you think that's made up, too?"

"I honestly don't know."

Gabe had been quiet since arriving, but he now leaned forward. "We can check the local registry office for Marianne

Folgate and see if there's a marriage record for her. When she left home, it doesn't mean she left Ipswich altogether. We'll go there after we visit the post office." He studied me as I sipped my cocktail. "This must be overwhelming."

"It is, but I'm relieved to finally have some answers. Although…" I nibbled on my lower lip.

"Go on."

"Finding out that Marianne and Alice are one and the same person doesn't mean I'm not adopted. That's still a possibility."

"Mr. Dowd says you look like Marianne," Daisy pointed out.

"He mentioned a few vague traits, that's all." I fished the photograph he'd given me out of my bag. My mother looked so young, a mere girl of about sixteen or seventeen, but closer to my age now than she was in the later photograph.

It was almost impossible to imagine her as a child. She'd always been middle-aged to me. Her hair had gray through it for as long as I could recall, and her face had always been marred by worry lines. But it was more than her looks. It was her demeanor, too. I couldn't imagine her having the carefree attitude of youth, the fearlessness and sense of adventure. She had been so set in her ways, with rules that governed every aspect of our lives. She never deviated from those rules. Never, and if James or I did, we received a berating followed by moody silence. She had been controlling.

Just like her father, John.

I wondered if she'd ever seen the similarity to the part of him she loathed. I suspected not or she would have tried to change.

I wished I could ask her. I had so many questions springing from the information Mr. Dowd had given us, but no way of knowing the answers. I'd finally found my family, yet I was no better off than before. I still didn't know much.

The overwhelming sense that I was alone returned. I'd first felt it after James died, and again when my mother passed. But I'd not felt such loneliness since making new friends in London, beginning with Daisy.

It was to those friends I now turned. They all looked upon me with sympathy, but none truly understood what it was like to be completely without family. Sometimes I felt as though I were adrift in the ocean without an anchor.

Gabe rested a hand on my arm. His thumb rubbed the bare skin at my wrist. "We won't rest until we have answers, Sylvia."

It was a sweet sentiment and I smiled to thank him and let him think I agreed. But there was a very real chance that answers simply wouldn't be found and no amount of detective work would unearth them.

We finished our drinks then dined in the hotel restaurant. We briefly returned to the bar after dinner, but I didn't stay long before making my excuses. The day had been draining and I didn't feel like dancing, even though the band played jazzy ragtime tunes.

Gabe offered to escort me to my room, while Daisy and Alex decided to stay for a while in the bar. Despite not speaking directly to one another since the picnic, they'd been sneaking surreptitious glances at each other all night. Every time they did, the heat ratcheted up a notch until the iciness between them had almost completely thawed by the time we returned to the bar. When Gabe and I left, Alex was lounging with his elbow resting on a tall bar table, his foot tapping to the music, and Daisy was sipping champagne, hips swaying. They stood very close, yet kept their gazes firmly forward.

"What did you say to him?" I asked Gabe when we were far enough from the band that I didn't have to shout to be heard.

He placed his hand at the small of my back and leaned down a little. "What makes you think I said anything?"

"He broke the ice first by looking at her."

"She *is* wearing a dress that demands attention."

It was true. Her sleek black dress with the scoop neckline showed off her cleavage and narrow waist.

"Yes, but it was the *way* he looked at her. It's not the same as

21

the way *you* look at her, for example. It was an I-forgive-you look."

"I told him what you said about her sensitivity surrounding her lack of education and he decided to give her another chance."

"I'm so pleased. She has a good heart."

We arrived at my room and I unlocked the door. We'd only been given one key per room, so I handed it to Gabe to return to Daisy for later. "Will you keep an eye on them?"

"I think it's best to give them some space."

"You're probably right." I waited, not sure whether to bid him goodnight or talk for longer. If we talked, should I invite him inside? What would we talk about? Was it too forward of me? Did he even want to be alone with me?

In the end, he made the decision for me. He took my hand and rubbed his thumb over my knuckles. He stared at our linked hands for a few heart-stopping moments then, with a sigh, suddenly let go. "Goodnight, Sylvia. See you in the morning." His tone was brisk. He didn't look at me. He turned abruptly and walked off along the corridor.

I bade goodnight to his back.

CHAPTER 3

T he following morning everyone was in an odd mood. While we dressed, I asked Daisy how her evening had been. She said "Fine" and left it at that. No amount of coaxing would get more information from her.

When I got Alex alone, I asked him the same question. His response was identical.

"Fine," he said with bland indifference.

"Did you dance with Daisy?"

"We danced."

That wasn't quite the same as dancing *with* her, but Alex's closed face invited no more questions.

It wasn't until we headed to the post office that I was able to ask Gabe if he knew how their evening went. He had no news, however.

He slowed his pace to put some distance between Alex and Daisy up ahead. "I returned to our room around eleven," he whispered. "Alex didn't come in until after midnight. What about Daisy?"

"I fell asleep and didn't hear her come in." I watched the two of them walking side by side without speaking. "Do they seem friendlier to you?"

"They're not needling each other, so that's a good sign."

It was some time before the postmaster was free to see us, and even longer before he would agree to relinquish the Folgates' mail. It took a telephone call to Alex's father at Scotland Yard and a great deal of handwringing before the fellow gave his authorization. A younger assistant was sent to fetch the mail while we waited in an outer office. He returned fifteen minutes later, covered in dust, with cobwebs in his hair. He handed me a stack of letters tied with string.

I untied the string the moment we sat in the motorcar. There were twenty-two letters in all, but I didn't open any of them. With the Vauxhall's top down, the paper might blow away.

We made one more stop at the Ipswich registry office, but they could find no record of Marianne Folgate marrying. After her birth, there was no record of her at all.

We returned to the Vauxhall and put on our dust coats and goggles for the longer drive back to London. Daisy and I already had scarves in place, covering our hair, but I'd missed a strand. She reached over and tucked it under the scarf.

"Are you all right?" she asked quietly.

I nodded. "You?"

"Me? Yes, of course. I'm always all right." She slid across the seat to her side of the vehicle and turned away. She didn't turn back again until we stopped to refuel and eat pies and cake at a roadside tea shop we'd spotted on our way up to Ipswich the day before. Daisy resumed her position in the motorcar after lunch and stayed like that all the way until we took her home.

Gabe and I watched as Alex carried her overnight bag to the front door, deposited it just inside, then gave her a nod goodbye. She waved at me before closing the door.

"Should we be concerned about those two?" Gabe said.

I blew out a breath. "I honestly have no idea."

* * *

I'D BEEN TOO tired to look through the dead letters after arriving home, so took them to work with me the next day, intending to read them during my lunch break. I settled at the front desk with a book written in Dutch that needed its title and description translated. I'd only just opened a Dutch-to-English dictionary when Professor Nash came down the curved staircase, balancing a tray with coffee cups. He placed it on the desk and handed a cup to me. He took the other and perched on the edge of the desk. Cradling the cup in both hands, he peered at me over the rim of his spectacles. There was a youthful sprightliness about his countenance this morning, something that only ever surfaced when he reminisced about his travels with Oscar Barratt. It made me smile.

"You seem full of beans this morning, Professor."

"I'm on tenterhooks, Sylvia. Tell me what happened in Ipswich."

"But I have to work."

He closed the book in front of me. "Later. I can tell you learned something interesting. It's written all over your face. And you know how much I enjoy hearing interesting things."

I grinned. I couldn't help it. Marianne Folgate and Alice Ashe were one and the same person! Although there were still so many questions, discovering that was a rather large piece of the puzzle that was my family.

I told him everything Mr. Dowd had told us, then concluded with our visit to the post office and registry office. He sat there, riveted to the spot until I finished.

"Well?" he prompted.

"Well, what?"

"Didn't you read the letters last night? Is there anything interesting amongst them?"

"I don't know. I haven't had a proper look."

"Why not?"

I tapped the book cover. "I have work to do. The letters can wait until lunchtime."

"Nonsense. That book has been in the attic for at least fifteen years; it can wait a few more hours."

I fished out the letters from my bag and followed the professor through to the reading nook. He withdrew a letter opener from the portable writing desk and sat beside me on the leather sofa.

He clapped his hands together as I opened the first envelope. "This is so exciting."

"What is?" came the brassy American voice of Gabe's indomitable cousin, Willie. Gabe and Alex followed a few feet behind and greeted us with more courtesy.

Willie wedged herself between the professor and me and took one of the letters off my lap. "I heard about these." She inspected the envelope. "You haven't opened it yet, Sylvia." She picked up the other letters. "You haven't opened any. Why not?"

"I was too tired last night."

Alex snatched the letters from her and placed them on the table beside me, out of her reach. "It looks like she was just about to, so leave her be."

"Too tired, eh?" Willie narrowed her gaze at me then Gabe. "Why? What did you get up to the night before?"

"Nothing," Gabe and I both said.

Alex crossed his arms over his chest and studied the floor near his feet.

Willie turned her gaze onto him. "Alex?"

He shifted his crossed arms higher. "What happened in Ipswich stays in Ipswich."

"That ain't fair. You wouldn't let me come, and now I've gone and missed all the fun."

"It wasn't fun," Alex told her.

"Definitely not," Gabe chimed in. "It was all work, work, work. Isn't that right, Sylvia?"

"All quite dull," I said.

Our united efforts did nothing to wipe the stroppy pout off her face.

"Anyway, you couldn't fit in the Vauxhall," Alex reminded her.

She made a miffed sound through her nose. "That's why we need a new motorcar, a bigger one, to replace the Hudson."

Gabe's father's Hudson Super Six had met a violent end in a crash caused by a thug chasing us through the streets of London. We'd only survived thanks to Gabe's magic slowing down time, giving him a window of opportunity to pull us out before we hit a wall. It had cost him, however. He'd been exhausted afterwards.

"I spoke to a motorcar magician while you were away," Willie went on.

Alex scowled. "Without us?"

"You should have waited," Gabe told her.

"Why? It ain't going to be your motor, it's going to be Matt's. Don't worry. You'll get to choose once I've narrowed down the list. But I reckon we should give Rolls-Royce serious considera-tion on account of them having a motorcar magician, the only one in existence, so they say. It costs extra to have him put a spell on the vehicle you purchase, but I reckon we can use India's name to get a discount. What do you think?"

Gabe gave her an arch look. "I think you need to leave the purchasing of a replacement vehicle up to my father."

Willie sank into the sofa with a loud *humph*.

"Motorcar magician?" I asked. "How can magicians exist for the automobile industry? Motorcars are a relatively new invention."

Professor Nash pushed his spectacles up his nose, ready and more than willing to take on my question. The history of magic was his area of expertise. "You're right, it's a new form of magic. But many industries, and therefore the associated magic, were once new. Watchmaking magic, for instance. Although my travels taught me that a Chinese scientist invented the first mechanical clock more than a thousand years ago, it wasn't until pendulum clocks were invented in the mid-seventeenth century that clock magic came into existence. I happen to know the automobile magician at the Rolls-Royce factory comes from a family of railway magicians, whose predecessors were steel magicians. Steel is an alloy of iron and carbon."

"So iron is actually the base magic for automobile magic," I said, following along. "Just like my paper magic emerged from cotton magic."

"Precisely! It has altered through the generations, of course. Darwin's theory of evolution is a good place to start, but if you want to know more about how evolution relates to magicians, then might I suggest reading—"

"Nope," Willie cut him off. "The only thing worth reading is the Rolls-Royce catalog."

The sound of the front door opening and closing followed by the click of heeled shoes on the floorboards had us all turning in that direction. Lady Stanhope appeared, a newspaper tucked under her arm. Ever since entering our lives a few months ago, the influential wife of a viscount and self-appointed spotter of heretofore undiscovered magicians had become somewhat obsessed with Gabe, convinced he was special.

She made no sign that she heard our collective sigh. She strode up to us as if she were expected and pinned her penetrating gaze on Gabe. "Your butler said I'd find you here, Gabriel."

Professor Nash stood. "Good morning, Lady Stanhope. This is a pleasant surprise."

Willie snorted.

"How can we help you? Do you need a particular book?" Professor Nash indicated the stacks.

"Don't be absurd. I have enough books in my husband's library if I wanted to read one." Lady Stanhope slapped the newspaper with the back of her gloved hand. "Have you seen this? Is it true? I demand to know."

Alex bristled. "By what right do you come in here and demand anything from us?"

I worried that Lady Stanhope would claim her birth and class gave her the right, but she ignored Alex entirely. It wasn't necessarily better.

Gabe didn't say a word as he read the entire article, but it was clear from the way he tensed that it wasn't good news.

"Well?" Lady Stanhope prompted. "Is it true?" She suddenly grasped his forearm and stepped closer. She gazed up at him, unblinking. The change in her was pronounced. One moment she was sermonizing, and the next she was reverent. "Oh, Mr. Glass. You are *very* special indeed."

Willie crowded close to Gabe to read the article. "What does it say?"

"It's an opinion piece about me," he said. "It suggests that I'm a watchmaker magician who can extend the magic of other magicians. The journalist says a rumor has circulated for years that my mother has that power, and speculates that I do too."

I released a breath. It appeared the journalist didn't know the truth of Gabe's magic powers.

"Well?" Lady Stanhope demanded. "*Are* you a magician? *Can* you extend the life of another's magic?"

"It's all bollocks," Alex told her.

"I understand why you wouldn't want the world to know," she went on. "You don't want every magician in the country pestering you to extend their magic. It would be extremely vexing. I can help you, Gabriel. I can protect you from those who'd take advantage of you, like Ivy's family."

Gabe thrust the newspaper back at her. "No, thank you."

"Think about it." She took the newspaper and placed it on the table. "Keep it. And in the future, be more careful about discussing your magic. It's fortunate that was printed in an obscure paper with a small circulation. If *The Times* got wind of it—"

"I am not a magician," Gabe ground out. "Good day, Lady Stanhope."

A muscle in her cheek twitched. "You need me, Gabriel. I can connect you with the right people, *wealthy* people. I can help you succeed."

Willie moved to stand between Gabe and Lady Stanhope. "You better leave, or I'll throw you out and I won't be quiet or discreet about it."

Lady Stanhope's nostrils flared. She spun around and strode away.

Once we heard the front door close, we all breathed a sigh of relief.

Alex picked up the newspaper and read. "This is going to gain attention. You need to be extra vigilant, Gabe. The kidnapper might renew his interest and strike again."

Previous attempts to kidnap Gabe had been thwarted, but until the culprit was uncovered, the danger of it happening again were ever-present.

"The journalist is suggesting I can extend the magic of others." He turned to me. "My mother *can* do that, but it's not widely known, for the reason Lady Stanhope mentioned."

Alex pointed to a paragraph. "It does state she never admitted she could lengthen or strengthen another's magic. The journalist goes on to explain how the rumor began. Apparently one or two magicians found out years ago. Your father stepped in and made sure they never told anyone, and it was largely forgotten. The reporter admits it's all speculation, however. He can't prove anything."

Willie swore under her breath. "Speculation or not, Alex is right. You've got to be careful, Gabe. Just because the kidnapper hasn't tried lately doesn't mean they won't try again. This might renew their interest."

Gabe indicated the article. "This is not why the kidnapper wants me." He glanced in the direction Lady Stanhope had left, but didn't elaborate even though she'd gone. He didn't need to. We all knew what he meant.

The kidnapper wanted to know how he survived so long in the war. They didn't know that it was due to his time-manipulation magic, but they knew there was something special about him.

Alex folded up the newspaper. "Hopefully Jakes won't see this."

Mr. Jakes worked for Military Intelligence. He was Gabe's friend's commanding officer during the war and had asked Francis Stray several questions about Gabe that implied he knew there was a special reason why he survived every battle unscathed. He'd recently come to the Glass Library. Although he'd told the professor he was interested in magic and genetics, his subtle questions about Gabe revealed where his true interest lay.

Willie picked up the newspaper and tore out the article. She threw it into the fireplace and patted her pockets. "Damn it, Gabe, you made me give up smoking!"

Alex withdrew a box of matches from his jacket pocket and bent to set the crumpled paper on fire. "You know this isn't the only copy, right?"

"I do, but it makes me feel better."

Gabe sat beside me and picked up the forgotten stack of letters. He handed them to me. "Let's focus on something else."

We were all more than happy to turn our attention away from Gabe's predicament, although Willie continued to mope, but thankfully did so in silence.

The envelopes were all uniform in size, some yellowing with age or frayed at the corners. There was nothing special about them. None contained paper magic.

I opened the first letter. It was a Bank of England check for the sum of fifty pounds. A handwritten note from one of John Folgate's customers stated the payment was for a trophy made for the Royal Southern Yacht Club.

"It looks like they saved themselves fifty pounds when John Folgate died," the professor said. He winced. "Sorry, that was unfeeling. I do apologize, Sylvia."

I was about to ask why he was apologizing to me, then I

recalled that John Folgate was my grandfather. It still seemed unreal.

I opened the next letter. It was from a toolmaker demanding to be paid. A third letter was from a customer thanking John Folgate for the silver wedding band he'd made for his bride.

Willie yawned. "This ain't as exciting as I thought it'd be."

"What were you hoping for?" Alex asked.

She shrugged. "I'm leaving. Gabe, you be careful when you go out. Alex, protect him."

"Don't go to Rolls-Royce without us," Alex said.

"I ain't going to Rolls-Royce."

"Or Lagonda, or Bentley."

"I'm going to see a friend."

"Who?"

"None of your business." Willie's step as she left had quite the swagger to it.

Alex turned to Gabe. "A lover?"

"Could be," Gabe said as he studied the handwritten address on the next envelope.

"You can open it," I told him. "I don't have to do all of them. I think Willie's right. They're all going to be as dull as these first three."

Gabe cut the envelope with the letter opener and removed the single sheet of folded paper. "This one's a private letter." He started to read only to stop and hand it to me. "It's about Marianne." His grave tone sent a chill down my spine.

I read the letter all the way through then lowered it to my lap. "Oh. That may explain why she left."

"What does it say?" Alex asked.

"It's from a Mr. Bernard Reid," Gabe said. "He's offering three hundred and fifty pounds for Marianne's hand in marriage to his son."

Alex frowned. "Are you sure it's not the other way around? The bride's family pay a dowry if there is one, not the groom's."

"Not when the bride is a rare magician. She was considered a valuable commodity, particularly if the groom had a magician lineage, too." Gabe's grim tone made me wonder if he'd ever been viewed that way by others who suspected he was a magician. It was one thing to be wanted by the Lady Stanhopes of the world. It was quite another to be courted for your potential to sire the next generation of rare magicians.

"Poor Marianne," Alex murmured. "At least we know Bernard Reid wasn't successful in his bid. That letter was never delivered. She left of her own accord."

I passed my hand over the letter, feeling the softness of the paper and the indentations made by the pen against my palm. It didn't contain a paper spell, but it was good quality. "Perhaps this is why she left. She knew her father was going to sell her to the Reids." I tore open the next envelope in the stack. It was another letter from a man named Clyde offering an enormous sum of money to marry Marianne. He stated he was a master engineer.

The next letter was another from Bernard Reid, asking if his previous letter had been received. He offered a further fifty pounds on top of his previous bid for Marianne and reminded John Folgate that he was a successful manufacturer but didn't say what he manufactured.

"That is a considerable sum for 1891," Professor Nash said. "Two offers of marriage from two master craftsmen. They *must* be magicians. I wonder if there were many offers of marriage or if these two were special cases."

"It's not unique." I showed him another letter, this time from a baker. "He states that he heard from a *special* friend that John had been casting around for a *special* husband for Marianne, his very talented and *special* silversmith daughter. Every instance of 'special' is underlined."

"These were written around the time of tensions between the artless and magicians," the professor explained. "They had to be careful not to mention they were magicians, or they could risk being thrown out of their guilds if caught."

Gabe read over my shoulder. "Somehow Folgate put the word out that Marianne was a silver magician and he wanted to marry her to another magician from a strong lineage."

"For a price," Alex bit off.

"She'd just turned eighteen when she left home," I said. "Her father must have thought it was time she married. This way he could make a profit from her." It was a dreadfully cruel thing for a father to do.

"When she got wind of his plan, she ran away," Gabe finished.

"Good for her," Alex said with an emphatic nod. "Your mother must have had a strong character to take control of her own life at such a young age."

"She did," I said. Too strong, sometimes.

I'd continued to read the baker's letter as they talked. He was quite chatty, giving a detailed description of his son, the family's standing within the community, and his plans to expand his business. At the end, he stated he'd pay more for Marianne if he had proof that she could 'perform the skill as claimed, that which the silversmiths of mythology could do.'

I showed the letter to the professor. "What do you think this line means? What could the 'silversmiths of mythology' do?"

The professor's face lit up as he eagerly read the line I pointed to. "Good lord. Folgate must have claimed Marianne could create more silver. No wonder she had a number of offers of marriage. But no sensible person would believe it, surely. And yet…they seem to." He chewed on his lower lip as he read the entire letter.

"*Create* silver?" I echoed. "What do you mean?"

He removed his spectacles altogether, something he did when he was settling into a detailed explanation. "Around the time these letters were written, most magicians only knew one spell. Gabe's mother, India, learned how to combine spells from different disciplines to create new ones. In addition to being a watchmaker magician, she's also a spellcaster, capable of creating entirely new spells, but it's not a skill she honed. After some brief but interesting experiments, she decided not to continue. So, in essence, we are still left largely with magicians who know only one spell. Some know two. Some have teamed up and begun their own experiments in combining their spells, but generally most magicians are satisfied with their one and only spell, the same spell they've always used, that was recited to them by their parents, who learned it from their parents, et cetera." He put his spectacles back on and indicated the full bookshelves. "These texts teach us that spells became lost over the centuries, and each discipline only remembered the most valuable spell for their craft, the spell that made their wares better than their artless competitors'. So, a paper magician's spell ensures their paper won't tear easily, for example; a baker's bread tastes better; a watchmaker's clock kept the most accurate time. A mapmaker magician could find the location of an object using his map. Every product they made or tinkered with was of superior quality anyway, but a spell added something extra, something desirable."

Gabe pointed to the newspaper Lady Stanhope had delivered. "My great-grandfather learned of a spell that could extend the time of his watchmaker magic, or the magic of another magician."

"A spell unique for his discipline, yet highly desirable. In light of that, what would people most want for gold and silver?"

"More," I said.

"Precisely."

"There are no goldsmith magicians left, are there?"

"They're rare, but they do exist. All of their spells have been lost, however. All they can do now is *detect* magic in objects. It was assumed silver magic suffered the same fate."

"Some say the gold and silver replication spells never existed," Gabe added. "That it's just a myth." He pointed to the line in the baker's letter that mentioned the mythological silver magicians. "Either John Folgate knew that spell and told potential suitors that Marianne did, too, or he lied in order to drive up the price of his daughter."

"My guess is he lied," Alex said. "There's no evidence the Folgates were wealthy. If John could create more silver, he wouldn't need to sell off his daughter." We all nodded in agreement. "The question is, did Marianne leave Ipswich only to return to murder her parents a few weeks later?"

I gasped. "She wasn't a murderer!"

Understanding quickly dawned and Alex looked horrified. "I'm sorry, Sylvia. I momentarily forgot Marianne was your mother. If you say she wouldn't harm anyone, then I believe you."

He looked so upset to have caused me distress that I couldn't help but forgive him. "Do you think their deaths weren't accidental?"

"It was just a theory." He put up his hands. "I have a suspicious mind. Sorry."

Gabe had taken a few more of the unopened letters to read. The pile was in date order, with the latest ones at the bottom. "Here's another from Bernard Reid, asking again if John had considered his offer for Marianne. His son is very keen and is anxious to meet her, he writes. It's all he can talk about."

We continued to open more letters. Another five were offers of marriage. The final one in the pile was different. Although it was also from Bernard Reid, it was dated January 1894, well after the others and three years after the Folgates' deaths. The tone was more frantic than business-like, and it didn't ask about his bid to win Marianne's hand in marriage for his son. It pleaded with John Folgate to divulge if he knew where he could find his son. I showed it to Gabe.

"He writes that his son has gone missing," I told the others. "Since he'd often spoken about meeting Marianne over the years, and his continued hope that his marriage proposal wasn't in vain, Bernard Reid wondered if he had, in fact, gone to meet her in Ipswich. Reid acknowledged that his earlier letters to John

Folgate had gone unanswered and that he knew it was likely this one would also suffer the same fate, but he states that he's desperate to find his son and is trying every avenue."

I felt all their gazes on me. They'd reached the same conclusion as me. What if the son of Bernard Reid *had* found Marianne and nine months later, she'd given birth to a child?

I was born in 1894. He could be my father.

CHAPTER 4

The letter from Bernard Reid didn't mention the magic discipline his family performed. It could be anything.

It could be paper.

"We can look through my parents' list of magicians for any Reids," Gabe said. "Even if they're not listed, it doesn't mean they're not magicians. The list is comprehensive but not definitive."

Alex held the envelope to the light coming through the window. "Shame there's no return address."

Gabe showed him the letter. "It's on here, top right."

My heart tripped when I saw the address. Bernard Reid lived in London. We could call on him and ask questions. We could see if there was any family resemblance.

The fact that Reid wasn't one of the London paper magician families on Lady Rycroft's list wasn't lost on me. I knew them by heart. But as Gabe said, the list wasn't definitive. Something else about Bernard Reid's final letter made me think my father could be his son, and it had nothing to do with magic.

But I didn't explore the thought further. I didn't want to.

"We'll call on Bernard Reid tomorrow," I told them. "Now, I

need to do some work. Out, both of you, unless you plan to help me with a translation."

Gabe opened his mouth to speak but Alex got in first. "We'll find something to do for the rest of the day."

"What I was going to say," Gabe said wryly, "was that I want to ask Cyclops if he can look for the Reid case file. Hopefully Bernard Reid's son was found alive and well after this letter was sent. We could stop by Scotland Yard now."

Alex had a better idea. "We'll call on my parents for dinner and ask him then. Mrs. Ling deserves the night off. You should both come too," he said to the professor and me.

"Your mother won't mind the extra guests?" I asked.

"I'll telephone her now and ask, but I'm sure she'll be happy for you to come."

"Then I'd be delighted," I said.

"Not me," Professor Nash said. "I'm going to work on my memoir."

We tried to convince him to join us, but he insisted he wouldn't be good company, and continued to decline. It wasn't the first time he'd refused to go out. Lately, he seemed to have become quite the homebody. I wasn't sure if it was a touch of melancholia or he truly did want to work on his memoir.

* * *

It was almost time to close the library when Daisy arrived, a brown leather satchel slung over her shoulder. She found me on the first floor about to reshelve some books a patron had left on the desk. She took the top one and read the subject code on the spine.

"What are you doing later?" she asked as she slotted the book into the wrong place on the shelf.

I pulled it out and reshelved it while she picked up another from the trolley. "I'm going out," I said.

"Oh? Where?"

"Ummm..."

"It's all right. If you're going to see Alex, it's fine. I don't mind." She stared at the book's spine. "We decided in Ipswich to see less of one another, but that doesn't mean you shouldn't see him. He and Gabe are joined at the hip anyway, so I know you'll see a great deal of him." She talked quickly, something she always did when she was nervous.

"Why did you agree to see less of one another? I thought you two were getting along. The morning we left Ipswich, you were... Well, you weren't at each other's throats."

"That's because we'd come to a decision the night before that all we do is fight, and that's just exhausting. We're not suited, you see, and therefore we need to keep our distance so that we don't give in to certain...desires."

"If you desire one another, then I don't see the problem."

"I told you, we're not suited. *That's* the problem."

I watched her, trying to gauge if she truly believed what she was saying, but she was too busy shelving books in the wrong places. I followed behind her, correcting them. "Are you sure you're not suited?"

"He's from a large, loud family who embrace everyone and are open-minded, worldly and intelligent. I'm from a conservative family who haven't changed so much as a spoon in three hundred years, let alone their stuffy ways."

I grasped her by the shoulders and turned her to face me. "You are not like your family, Daisy. You're kindhearted and fun to be around. You tackle life and don't shy away from a challenge. *You* are not stuffy."

"Alex is intelligent, a thinker," she went on. "He doesn't suffer fools. Unfortunately, I am a fool."

I leveled my gaze with hers. "You are not a fool. You might not be educated, but that doesn't mean you lack intelligence, just book learning. You are bright, curious and energetic. You always lift my mood, even on my darkest days, and you are kindness itself. In fact, I'd say your differences are complementary. You and Alex balance each other."

She thanked me, but it was said mechanically. I hadn't got through to her. I wasn't surprised when she changed the subject.

"Huon Barratt paid me a visit today. He invited us to a party on Friday."

Huon was the nephew of Oscar Barratt, long-time friend and adventuring companion of the professor's who'd not returned to England with him when war broke out, but instead stayed in the Arabian Desert where he suddenly died. The professor always spoke fondly of him, albeit with a heavy dose of melancholia.

He didn't hold Oscar's nephew in the same high regard, however. Huon's recklessness and carousing lifestyle put him at odds with many people of that generation. The kindly professor did allow him some leeway given he'd fought in the war.

"That could be fun," I said. "His last party was marvelous."

"You left early."

"And it was fun until then."

She didn't seem to be in a partying mood, however. Her heavy sighs were a sure sign something was the matter and that she wanted me to ask her about it. So, I did.

"Huon read a few pages of my manuscript when he called on me," she said.

"I thought you weren't letting anyone see it."

"I didn't show it to him. He just read it while I was making the tea."

"I take it he gave you unwelcome feedback."

She tried shoving a book into a spot that was too narrow. I gently took it off her and slotted it into the correct place, a shelf below. "He laughed," she went on.

"Oh dear. I assume you're not writing a comedy."

"It's a romance with adventure."

"Perhaps it's a sign that you should write comedy."

She grunted. "Perhaps it's a sign I shouldn't write at all."

"Are you enjoying it?"

She hugged a book to her chest, frowning. "What do you mean? It's work, just like this is for you. If we were meant to enjoy working, it wouldn't be called work. It would be called something else. A hobby," she added, sounding pleased with herself for coming up with the etymological explanation.

"I think you should at least enjoy part of it, otherwise why do it if you're not guaranteed of being published at the end?"

She chewed the inside of her lip.

"Do you enjoy any part of the process?" I pressed. "Is it something you like to spend a few hours a day doing?"

"Hours? Oh no, I can't sit still for that long all alone in my flat. If I don't speak to anyone after thirty minutes, I go mad."

I continued to shelve books, staying silent to let her think.

She stared at the book in her hands but didn't shelve it. After a moment, she said, "When I told Huon I was struggling to concentrate for any length of time, he told me I should try a different method. He suggested I write the rough draft with pencil. I've been writing my story in a notebook using pen and planned to type it up when I finished, but I've only managed a few pages so far. I think he might have a point. At least pencil can be erased. I've used an awful lot of my notebook after crossing out large passages and starting again."

"Huon suggested pencil? How odd."

"Why odd?"

"He's an ink magician, and there's a great rivalry between ink and graphite magicians. I learned that from a graphite magician when we were investigating the murder of the bookbinder. She knew Huon, as it happens. Their families are long-time rivals. I wonder..."

"Go on."

"Did Huon offer to take you shopping to buy pencils?"

"How did you know?"

I grinned. "The graphite magician I mentioned owns a stationery shop. She's also very pretty."

She smiled slowly. "How intriguing. Shall I ask him to take me shopping for pencils?"

"Yes, but it has to be when I'm not working. I don't want to miss this."

* * *

ALEX'S three sisters greeted me with warm hugs when I arrived at the Bailey house for dinner, then all began speaking at once. It was left to Cyclops, their father, to rescue me by offering me a predinner cocktail. Their mother, Catherine, emerged from the kitchen a few minutes later, her cheeks flushed. She hugged me before accepting a cocktail glass from her husband.

"Nate and I are so pleased you accepted Alex's invitation to dine with us," she said. "Gabe and Alex should be here soon."

Cyclops put his arm around his wife's waist and kissed the top of her head. Their youngest daughter, seventeen-year-old Lulu, thought that was far too much affection for her parents to show one another and made a gagging noise.

Cyclops chuckled and chucked her under the chin. "One day you'll want a man to put his arm around you."

The middle sister, Mae, scoffed. "She has to find someone who'll put up with her first."

Lulu pouted. She idolized Mae and tended to follow where she led, which sometimes annoyed Mae. It resulted in a curious relationship where they were either the best of friends or the worst of enemies. Sometimes they could be both within a ten-minute span. I seemed to be the only one who thought their rapid flip of emotions strange. Perhaps it was because I'd only had one sibling, and a protective older brother at that. James and I rarely fought growing up.

Gabe had been an only child, but I suspected he spent as much time with the Baileys as his own family and was familiar with their dynamics. He treated the girls as sisters, and

43

Catherine and Cyclops as parents. I'd noticed the brotherly comradery between Gabe and Alex the moment I met them.

"Mum," Lulu whined. "Mae's being mean."

"That's enough, girls," Catherine warned. "We have company."

Ella, the eldest daughter, rolled her eyes at her sisters. "There are more important issues to worry about than men. Improved conditions for factory workers. Equal rights for women in the workforce. Allowing women to join the police force." She counted off each point on her fingers. "You should be campaigning for the vote for *all* adult females, not just married ones over thirty-five. And then there's tennis."

Her younger sisters groaned.

"What about tennis?" I asked.

The girls groaned again, louder.

"Well," Ella began. "The female players should be allowed to wear shorter skirts, for starters. The long skirts they have to wear at tournaments are a hindrance. No one can be expected to run fast with a skirt tangled around their legs. And there's the inequality in the prize money between men and women, too."

Alex and Gabe's arrival ended any further discussion about tennis. After greeting them, Catherine finished her cocktail and told us she needed to return to the kitchen. I offered to help and she accepted. When Cyclops began to speak, she gave a half-shake of her head and he closed his mouth.

I followed her into the kitchen and asked for an apron as she put one on over her dress.

She refused. "Thank you for offering, but I'd never ask a guest to help."

"I don't mind."

She lifted the lid on a pot on the stove and stirred the contents. "Everything's under control, anyway." She returned the lid to the pot and glanced down the hallway to the sitting room beyond. "I wanted to get you alone to ask you about your friend Daisy. Nate and I have noticed that Alex mentions her name quite a lot in passing. I was going to ask Gabe, but then I thought you might know more. Female friends tend to confide in one another more than men."

"There's nothing going on between them, unfortunately."

"Unfortunately?"

"I think they'd balance one another quite nicely. Daisy is very bright and lively."

Catherine unwrapped a block of butter and picked up a knife but didn't cut through the butter. She sighed. "Alex used to be lively, too, before the war. He's very serious now. Very gloomy. Your friend Daisy may be just what he needs. So why aren't they together?" She tilted her head to the side and regarded me. "Is Alex being stubborn? He can be too much like his father, sometimes. Nate took so long to act on his feelings for me that I almost had to take it upon myself to seduce him."

I laughed and she smiled back.

"It all worked out in the end, obviously. We had good friends who saw to it that we didn't let our doubts overrule our hearts. Alex and Daisy are equally blessed."

"I'm not entirely sure it's Alex who needs convincing. Daisy believes she's not good enough for him. She thinks she's too silly and stupid."

Catherine huffed a humorless laugh. "Tell her that not everyone sees her as silly. And tell her that she'll feel grown up when the time's right." She smiled a knowing smile. "Now, I know I said I don't need help, but..." She pointed the knife at the butter. "Do you mind?"

* * *

SPENDING time with the Bailey family always generated mixed feelings for me. On the one hand, they were warm and welcoming, a great deal of fun and a source of interesting conversation. On the other, it made me realize what I'd missed growing up. My family was entirely different. We loved one another, but we rarely showed it. We were protective of each other, like the Baileys, but to the point of smothering. We never tossed around silly banter, never teased each other, and certainly never had fun.

At one point during dinner, Gabe leaned closer to me to whisper. "You've gone quiet."

"It can be hard to get a word in. There are eight people in this room and currently three conversations."

He laughed softly. "You have to find the weakest member and start there."

"Who's the weakest?" I thought it might be Lulu, the youngest, but she was holding her own in a conversation with her brother, telling him he was dull because he hadn't seen the latest Douglas Fairbanks picture. She wasn't weak.

"Whoever is not directly involved in one of the conversations is the weakest. Once you've identified your subject, just start talking to them."

I glanced around at the family. As well as Lulu chatting to Alex, Ella was engaged in conversation with her parents about the Wimbledon tournament. Mae, seated opposite Gabe, looked like she was listening, but closer inspection proved she was merely nodding along while twirling hair around her finger.

Gabe winked at me. "Watch." He cleared his throat. "Mae, have *you* seen the latest Fairbanks picture?"

She stopped twirling her hair. "Oh, yes, I saw it the moment it came out. Douglas Fairbanks is corking."

"Are there other pictures that you want to see?"

She resumed the twirling. "Not particularly."

"Plays? Bands?"

"*Dozens* of bands, but I'm not allowed to go to a club on my own and Ella isn't interested and Lulu is too young, and Alex... well, *he* won't take me." The twirling ceased again, and she suddenly sat forward. She lowered her voice. "Are you asking me to step out with you?"

Gabe's eyes widened in alarm. "Ummm..."

"Dearest Gabe, I think of you as a brother." She tossed him a sympathetic look then started twirling her hair around her finger again. "You may still take me to a dance club, of course, but don't be offended if I don't stand next to you. I don't want people to think we're together."

Catherine said something that caught Mae's attention and she turned away from Gabe to speak to her mother.

Gabe slumped back in his chair and expelled a long breath.

I tried very hard not to laugh, but a little snort escaped. "Thank you. That was…educational."

He blinked owlishly at Mae. "It feels like just yesterday I was taking her to the circus and now I'm taking her to a dance club."

"Taking who to a club?" Cyclops asked from the other end of the table.

Catherine shushed him. "Don't be a nosey parker."

Cyclops gave in with a good-natured grunt. "Alex told me you wanted to ask about an old missing person's case. A lad by the name of Reid?" He posed the statement to me, so I answered him.

"Apparently he wanted to marry my mother years ago, then disappeared. His father wondered if he ran away with her. I have Mr. Reid's letter in my bag if you want to read it."

"I remember the case. Not the disappearance, I wasn't at Scotland Yard then, but the outcome. During the war—it would have been 1915—we were informed by his parents to close the case. They'd been notified by the War Office that their son died at the Front. For more than twenty years they'd not known where he was, then to find out he'd died…it would have been devastating. The case was so unusual that it stayed with me."

We adjourned to the sitting room after dinner, and I showed Cyclops Bernard Reid's letter to John Folgate. I also explained that we believed my mother was being sold off to a magician willing to pay for her hand in marriage. Cyclops listened but showed no surprise. Alex must have already informed him what we learned in Ipswich.

He read through the letter. "So Marianne left home in 1891

and never returned, not even when her parents died. She changed her name and moved often, remaining in hiding until her death." He arched his brows at me.

"Yes."

"That implies she wasn't running from her father, John. I doubt she was completely ignorant of their fate all these years. I suspect she was running from someone else."

"Who?"

He glanced at Catherine, chatting to the girls. "One possibility—and the least likely, in my opinion—is the late Lord Coyle," he said quietly.

I gasped. I'd met Hope, the Dowager Lady Coyle, recently. She was Gabe's father's cousin, who'd married a much older man, years ago. The union had produced the current Lord Coyle, although Willie suspected he wasn't Coyle's son but the offspring of Hope's driver. I'd gathered that Coyle had given Gabe's parents a lot of grief, but no one had told me the particulars.

"Bloody hell," Alex muttered.

Gabe didn't think it likely. "Marianne and the man named Cooper rented the Wimbledon house from Coyle. That implies they were on amicable terms."

"Or it could be the reason they left in the middle of the night —to flee without Coyle knowing," Cyclops said. "Coyle liked to manipulate magicians to do his bidding. Sometimes, he merely wanted them to give him an object with a spell in it. Other times, it was more. Marianne could have fled to avoid being forced to do something she didn't want to."

Gabe still wasn't convinced. "If Coyle was the problem, she would have come out of hiding when he died. If your theory that Marianne learned of her parents' deaths holds water, then you also have to assume she knew about Coyle's. He was a prominent figure. It would have been reported in every newspaper in the country."

Cyclops agreed. "That's why I said it was the least likely

possibility. I don't think she was running from Coyle. I think she was afraid of someone else."

"The son of Bernard Reid," I said.

"Possibly, although she left home in 1891, three years *before* he disappeared in '94. It doesn't mean he didn't seek her out, just that her initial reason for running away wasn't to be *with* him. There is reason for concern. The letter from his father to hers raises a few red flags. I see a lot of situations in my work where a man has followed and attacked a woman, and the description Reid gives of his son's obsession with Marianne shows similarities." He pointed to some of the words in the letter. "He's desperate to meet her. Obsessed. Some might read this and say he was in love with her, or the idea of her, but in my experience, obsession is dangerous if it's not reciprocated."

His theory resonated with me as loudly as an alarm clanging in my head. I'd suspected for some time that my mother had been fleeing someone, and now I was quite sure I knew it was a man. Whether it was the Reid lad or another, it was most certainly a man. The key was in my mother's character.

Gabe's fingers brushed my arm. When I looked up at him, his brows arched in question. I mustered up a smile to reassure him.

"You mentioned the Reid lad died in the war," Alex said to his father. "Did you speak to his parents when they came to close the case?"

"No, but the news circulated around the Yard. It also made the newspapers. 'Fallen soldier is man missing for decades', so the headlines read. From what I can recall, the lad disappeared aged nineteen."

"Nineteen?" Gabe frowned. "Are you sure?"

"Yes."

"If he was aged nineteen in 1894 then he was only sixteen when Bernard Reid first wrote to John Folgate offering his son to Marianne in 1891."

"Marrying at sixteen isn't illegal if the parents give consent."

"And then his body turns up in France, several years later?" Alex prompted.

"The War Office notified the Reids and sent his belongings back from the Front. He'd been alive for years and never sought them out. Not a single word to let them know he was all right." Cyclops shook his head. "I can't fathom how a son could do that to his parents."

Alex clasped his shoulder and they exchanged grim smiles.

"He was old to enlist," Gabe said. "He would have been forty in 1915."

Able-bodied men between the ages of eighteen and forty-one had been conscripted, but not until 1916. Many volunteered before then, however.

"So where was he between 1894 and 1915?" Gabe asked.

"No one knew at the time, but maybe his parents have learned something since then. You should call on them, and the War Office, too. His record might reveal something."

"I've been meaning to go there anyway. There's someone in Military Intelligence I need to have a word with. We'll call on the Reids first, though, and find out what we can from them. They live in London."

The girls had grown restless in our absence, and there were only so many times they'd listen to Catherine ordering them to leave us alone. Lulu demanded to know what we were talking about. "Why all the secrecy?"

We rejoined them, but I found it difficult to concentrate on their rapid-fire conversations. I couldn't stop thinking about the missing son of Bernard Reid and whether he was my father. After an hour, Gabe offered to drive me home.

We didn't speak on the journey. It wasn't until we stopped outside my lodging house that he caught my hand before I alighted from the motorcar.

"This must be unsettling for you," he said gently.

"It's overwhelming. There's a lot to take in, and now this Reid fellow, who may be my father, could have been the reason we were always moving from city to city. I know it's something of a leap to assume he is my father, but I can't dismiss the notion. Not yet."

"Try not to think about it until we know for sure." When I didn't respond, his thumb caressed mine. "Sylvia? What is it?"

I withdrew my hand. "Nothing."

He got out and came around to my side to open the door. "You can confide in me. I won't even tell Alex."

I smiled at that. "I know I can trust you. It's just that…telling you would feel like a betrayal of my mother, in a way. She wouldn't want anyone to know our family business. She was very private."

He put out his hand to assist me from the motorcar. "I understand."

"But you do already know much more than she would have liked. In fact, *she* betrayed *me* by not telling me anything about herself, so I suppose I don't owe her that privacy now she's gone."

He walked me to the front door of the lodging house. Mrs. Parry, my landlady, had left the porch light on. She didn't like her girls, as she called her lodgers, going out after dark, but she didn't enforce curfew as long as we told her where we'd be. She approved of Gabe and had been delighted that I was dining with Alex's family.

I fished the key out of my bag but didn't insert it into the lock. I turned to Gabe. "I want to tell you about my mother." We were no longer touching, but I would have liked to hold his hand. He didn't reach for mine, however, so I folded my arms instead. "She was afraid of men. She would always tell me not to speak to them, not to make eye contact or stop to chat to strange men. She taught me to defend myself if I was ever accosted on the street. James, too. We learned how to escape from a larger person's grip from a young age."

"From what I've seen, she taught you well."

"She seemed to have a deep fear that we'd come to harm."

"Was she afraid you'd be hurt or kidnapped? Or both?"

"I don't know, but her fear only extended to men. After hearing about the controlling nature of her father, I suspect that's where her fear stems from. I wanted to tell you that in Ipswich, but..." I shook my head, not sure why I didn't tell him then.

"You weren't ready," he said.

I rubbed my arms. "Perhaps."

He removed his jacket, thinking I was cold, but I wasn't. Even so, I let him drape it around my shoulders. It brought him closer to me. His knuckles caressed the bare skin of my neck. My pulse leapt in response.

"Bernard Reid's letter also made me think about my mother's fear of men. If John Folgate's controlling nature was the initial spark for that fear, then perhaps someone else became the fuel that kept it burning throughout her life. I think you were right about Marianne knowing the Folgates died. She must have learned about it at some point. So her father is not the reason she continued to run."

"Someone else is," he finished. "As Cyclops said, obsession can be dangerous if it's one-sided. Although Marianne disappeared three years before the Reid lad, you think she had reason to fear him?"

"I don't know. All I know is that she was afraid of a man. A man she believed was still alive at the time she passed away last year." I shivered, and this time it was due to a chill that seeped through to my bones.

Gabe opened the door for me. "Go inside and get warm. I'll pick you up tomorrow morning and we'll call on the Reids. Then we'll go to the War Office. Let's see what Mr. Jakes has to say."

"About the Reid lad or about his interest in you?"

"Both."

I removed his jacket and handed it back to him. He draped it over his arm and held my gaze. Time seemed to stand still. Had his magic been triggered and captured me in its time-altering spell? The thought vanished when he suddenly leaned forward to kiss me.

Except that he didn't. He straightened. "Goodnight, Sylvia." He turned away before I responded.

"Goodnight, Gabe." I watched him walk back to the Vauxhall, his jacket hooked by a finger and slung over his shoulder. I thought I heard him muttering to himself, but it might have been the wind.

CHAPTER 5

rs. Reid had died from influenza at the height of the epidemic last year. It was something Mr. Reid and I had in common. When I told him my mother had also died of the flu, he offered no words of sympathy or comfort, however. Perhaps he was thrown off-kilter after Gabe introduced himself as a consultant for Scotland Yard.

Mr. Reid lived in an enormous house overlooking Hampstead Heath. It was designed to resemble a castle, complete with turrets and a gated entry. He told us he lived alone now. His son, Robin, had been their only child. It was difficult to tell whether he was lonely, however. He showed no signs that he needed or wanted company. Indeed, he showed no signs of any emotion at all, and I dismissed my earlier notion that he was discombobulated. There was an emptiness about him, as if the man inside had shrunk away, leaving a mechanical shell. What little hair he had on his head had grown past his collar, and he smelled as though he hadn't washed in some time. He seemed not to care.

There was no butler or footman as befitting such a large house, but the drawing room was neat and clean, so he must have a maid or housekeeper. He did not offer us tea but did invite us to sit. I wondered if he'd lost the will to live when his son went missing, or when he was confirmed dead, or when his wife died.

Gabe explained that, as consultants for Scotland Yard, we were taking a look at old missing persons cases. In this instance, we were looking into Marianne's disappearance from her home in Ipswich. We didn't tell him that she was my mother and that we knew what became of her.

When he merely nodded along as if we were talking about a stranger, I thought perhaps he'd forgotten about Marianne altogether. It was many years since he had corresponded with the Folgates.

"We came across some old letters you sent to John Folgate," I said gently. "About your son marrying his daughter?"

His gaze met mine for the first time. He remembered.

"We thought her disappearance might be linked to your son's, although she disappeared three years earlier."

He glanced at a collection of photographs on a table by the window. They were too far away for me to see the subjects' faces, but I desperately wanted to take a closer look. The face of the man seated opposite me held no resemblance to mine that I could see.

"May I?" I asked.

He nodded.

I picked up one of the photographs, a family portrait with a younger Bernard Reid, aged in his forties and more solid than the thin man in the armchair. His son was a little taller, even though he looked to be only fourteen or fifteen. His hair was dark where mine was light, and I saw no resemblance to me at all.

I handed the photograph to Gabe in case I missed something.

"Can you tell us why you wrote to Mr. Folgate offering to buy his daughter's hand in marriage for your son?" Gabe asked.

Mr. Reid didn't so much as flinch at the accusatory tone. "I heard through a good friend that a man was searching for a suitable groom for his daughter. Arranged marriages between magician families weren't uncommon in those days. It was all done in secrecy, of course, with coded messages and introductions made through trusted sources."

"How did your friend know about the Folgates' search for a husband?"

"I don't recall. My friend was a magician, as am I, but we kept it a secret. The Draper's Guild would have thrown us out if they knew. He and I looked out for one another. I assume he just heard from an acquaintance." Mr. Reid shrugged. "He didn't have a son, only girls, but he thought of Robin when he heard about Folgate's quest."

"Robin was only sixteen," Gabe pointed out.

"Too young, some would say, but he needed a wife, someone to settle him down. And the offer to marry the Folgate girl was too good to let it pass. Folgate wanted a powerful magician to marry his silver magician daughter, you see. He wanted a man from a strong lineage, worthy of a silver magician. They're incredibly rare. She might have been the last of her line, for all I know."

"What's your magic discipline?" I asked.

"Wool. I made a fortune manufacturing undergarments. It'll all go to a distant cousin when I die."

Not paper, or even cotton.

"Going by the unopened letters, you never received a reply from the Folgates," Gabe went on.

"No."

"Did you know they died in 1891?"

"That explains why my letters weren't answered. I thought it was because...never mind. It doesn't matter now."

"It was only a few weeks after their daughter left."

"Did they take their own lives out of grief?" Again, it was asked matter-of-factly, mechanically.

"There was a fire in their flat," was all Gabe said.

"Hmmm."

"What did you do after you didn't hear back from the Folgates?"

"We got on with our lives here in London. I was busy with the factory, and my wife performed charity work. She was very community-minded, always giving of her time."

"And Robin?"

Mr. Reid hesitated. "I tried to involve him more in the factory. If he was going to take over from me one day, he needed to learn all aspects of the business, from the ground up. But he didn't take to the menial tasks on the factory floor. I thought he might prefer office work, but he didn't like that either. He wasn't stupid, he was just...indifferent. He kept to himself in those latter school years. He stopped interacting with others, and just wanted to stay in his room when he came home during the holidays. He wouldn't step foot in the factory." Mr. Reid's shoulders slumped with his deep sigh. "After he graduated from school, he came out of his shell again, but fell in with a bad lot. He stayed out all night, gambling, womanizing... He quickly spent his allowance and his debts mounted. He borrowed heavily from these so-called friends. I don't know where their money came from. They were probably thieves and swindlers. I suspect they befriended him knowing he came from a wealthy family, with a view to fleecing him. I didn't give him money to pay them even when he begged me." His gaze shifted to the table of framed photographs. "That's why, when Robin disappeared, we assumed they'd killed him because he couldn't pay his debts."

"Did you hire a private detective to look for him?" Gabe asked.

"No. As I said, we were convinced he was dead. The police were, too. They said his body would turn up at some point. In hindsight, it shouldn't have been our first conclusion. That would guarantee the money lenders never get their money back. They would have been better off kidnapping him and demanding a ransom to release him. But I wasn't thinking clearly at the time. My wife was distraught. My business was booming, thanks to the heightened demand for magician-made goods. My wife threw herself into her charity work and we just got on with it. No ransom demand arrived, so I assumed we were correct, after all, and he'd been killed."

"And in 1915?" I asked gently. "You must have been shocked to receive notice of his death on the battlefield."

"It was so strange. We didn't know what to feel. We'd grieved for him years earlier. Then to find out he'd been alive the entire time and never contacted us... It was cruel to put his mother through that. I knew he was selfish, but that was hateful." He blinked once, twice, before continuing to stare into space. "There should have been a sense of relief to finally have confirmation of his death, but how can one be relieved knowing he deliberately wanted us to think him dead? As I said, we didn't know what to feel. My wife never fully recovered from the shock. It weakened her, made her susceptible to the influenza."

It had changed Mr. Reid, too, I suspected. The news had robbed him of his spirit and left behind this hollow man.

"Do you have anything of his?" Gabe asked. "Letters, diaries...anything?"

"His room is largely the same. There was no need to clear it out. We didn't need the space and my wife liked to go in there from time to time. The box of Robin's belongings sent by the War Office is in there, too. We looked through it, then put everything back. They didn't seem to belong with Robin's other things. They were owned by a man who..." He swallowed. "...who abandoned his parents without a second thought. A man we no longer knew."

"May we look in his room?" Gabe asked.

"Of course, if you think it will help. But there's no reference to the Folgate girl in there." He stood and led the way upstairs, his shuffling gait making our progress slow. His clothes hung loosely on his frame, obviously having been made for him when he was larger.

He pushed open a door to reveal a bedroom. It comfortably fit a desk and a breakfast table with two chairs by the window, as well as the four-poster bed. The window overlooked the street below and a section of the woodland of Hampstead Heath opposite.

"Your letters to John Folgate say that Robin was very interested in marrying Marianne," Gabe said. "You made him sound eager, desperate almost."

"He was eager, yes."

"And yet there's nothing in here referencing her?"

Mr. Reid shook his head. "He only expressed his wish to make her his wife to us. He never wrote to her. Not that it matters, if she disappeared before my final letter was even received."

"If there was no correspondence between them, and he'd never even met her, he must have only wanted to marry her for her magic."

"Her strong lineage, yes."

"And the theory that silversmith magicians can make more silver?"

"That's just a story, not reality. I never believed it. We wanted her—wanted Robin to marry her—for the strength of her magic. The Folgate line was unbroken, you see. Where magic often skips a generation or two before reappearing, John Folgate claimed to have proof that it never skipped a single member on their family tree, even when the mother was artless. That's a remarkable legacy, Mr. Glass. I'm sure you, as the son of a magician and an artless, understand."

So he did know who Gabe was.

"Robin agreed that she was an excellent choice, just what he needed. He was only sixteen at that point, and although he was already showing some rebelliousness, he hadn't fallen in with *that* crowd yet. He was still somewhat agreeable and believed his mother and I knew what was best."

I suspected I knew why Robin had rebelled, but I wanted to

confirm it before asking. A thorough search of his belongings would give me the proof I needed.

Mr. Reid took up a position by the window, where he stood and stared outside while Gabe and I went through Robin's things. Mr. Reid didn't watch and gave no guidance. He seemed unconcerned.

I looked through the adjoining dressing room while Gabe searched the desk drawers. There were several suits and shirts, and of course underclothes, mostly woolen. They were all very finely made, although only the underclothes held magic. The woolen fibers must have had spells spoken into them.

I checked all the drawers, but found no letters, photographs or personal items. Not even a strand of wool that a wool magician might tease out or twirl around their fingers while performing menial tasks.

I rejoined Gabe in the bedroom. He was sifting through a wooden box carved with a scene that Robin must have faced every day during the war. It depicted a trench with four soldiers either seated on the ground or leaning against the trench wall, cigarettes dangling from their mouths, rifles propped up against the earthen wall.

Gabe showed me the contents of the box. There was a smaller box inside containing tobacco, which was also carved but with a scene of the ocean, complete with whale and octopus. Beside it were woodworking tools.

"Robin was a fine artist," I said to Mr. Reid.

He continued to stare out the window. "Not when he lived here. He never showed an affinity for woodcraft."

"What did he show an affinity for?"

"Nothing. Nothing at all."

Gabe and I exchanged glances and an understanding passed between us. "Was Robin artless, Mr. Reid?"

"Yes. That's why we wanted him to marry a powerful magician from an unbroken lineage. He was our only child and he needed to take over the business from me one day. But without magic, he would just become another manufacturer of woolen undergarments. We hoped marriage to a woman from a powerful, unbroken magician lineage would give him magician sons who could grow up and be what their father could not. Even though their mother's magic would be a different discipline to mine, we hoped the woolen magic would appear in their children. If not, well, silver magic is valuable in itself."

Poor Robin. He'd never been enough, and there was nothing he could do to change it. His artlessness meant he could never be the son his father wanted.

"Anything else in that box?" I asked Gabe.

"Some cigarettes, a small bible, a service medal and official papers. Nothing personal. There's not even a photograph of a girl back home to remind him what he was fighting for."

Gabe had probably kept a picture of Ivy Hobson with him during his service. They'd met in wartime, while he was home in England for a brief respite from the fighting. At the end of his two-week home leave, they were engaged.

I pushed thoughts of Ivy out of my mind. She was the last person I wanted to think about.

We continued to search the desk, and it wasn't long before Gabe found something that made him draw a sharp breath. He showed me the scrap of paper with a torn edge, as if it had been ripped off a larger page. The handwritten message scrawled in capital letters in ink was brief and to the point. My heart thundered at the sight of the familiar name.

I.O.U. THURLOW £200

Thurlow! It was a name I hoped never to see or hear again. I pressed a hand to my chest, but my heart continued its rapid beat.

Gabe showed the piece of paper to Mr. Reid. "Is this Robin's handwriting?"

"No."

"Have you seen it before today?"

"Yes, years ago when my wife and I first looked through this room, searching for clues as to what may have happened to Robin. That's how we knew he got into debt, although we already had our suspicions."

"What do you know about Thurlow?"

"Nothing."

"You said earlier that Robin fell in with a bad lot. Was Thurlow one of them?"

"I don't know. The name means nothing to me. We didn't know any of Robin's so-called friends from that time, just that they weren't a good influence on him. We assumed this Thurlow was one of them given that Robin owed him such a large sum."

"Did you show this to the police when you reported Robin's disappearance in 1894?"

"Yes. They didn't know anyone by the name of Thurlow."

Thurlow would have been young then, too, perhaps only a few years older than Robin. He was probably just beginning his career as a moneylender and crooked bookmaker. The police must have only become aware of him later.

My legs suddenly felt weak. I sat on the chair at the desk and drew in a deep breath in an attempt to calm my jangling nerves. But it was no good. All I could think about was that the lowlife whose thug had driven us off the road and into a wall, almost killing us, had known the man who might be my father.

CHAPTER 6

G abe crouched in front of me, his gaze full of concern. "Mr. Reid, would you mind fetching Miss Ashe a glass of water?"

"I'm all right," I said quickly. To prove it, I stood. Gabe remained close, but didn't touch me. "Mr. Reid, we'd like to speak to your son's friends to see if he mentioned Marianne Folgate to any of them. Not his wayward friends, you understand. The ones from his school days."

Mr. Reid hadn't turned away from the window when Gabe asked him to fetch a glass of water, but he now suddenly whipped around. "Why?"

"Sometimes youths confide more in their friends than their parents."

"He never brought anyone home to meet us."

"Even so, he must have had at least one friend. You can't recall their names?"

"No. My wife would have known, but Robin never mentioned his school chums to me."

"What school did he attend?" Gabe asked.

"Laughton College."

I'd heard of it. It was one of the most prestigious boarding schools for boys in the country. It would have cost a fortune to send Robin there, and he would have only come home for the holidays.

"What about university friends?" I asked.

"He didn't go to university."

"Is that because you wanted him to work in your factory and learn the business?"

Mr. Reid jutted out his chin and turned back to the window.

Gabe and I glanced at each other. Given Mr. Reid had been reasonably forthcoming so far, this sudden caginess was suspicious.

"Thank you for your time," Gabe said. "May we take a photograph of Robin with us? We'll return it when our investigation is complete."

"How will that help you find the Folgate girl?"

"If their disappearances are linked and we find where Robin was living all those years, we might find where Marianne went when she left Ipswich."

Mr. Reid considered this a moment then nodded. He led us along the corridor and asked us to wait while he fetched the photograph. When he opened the door, I saw that it was another bedroom. He retrieved a framed photograph from beside the bed and showed it to us. It was Robin and his parents, seated on a sofa. "This is the last one of him, taken on his nineteenth birthday a few months before he disappeared." Mr. Reid gave it one last look before handing it to me.

"Thank you," I said. "I'll take good care of it."

"I hope you find her, the Folgate girl. The loss of such a powerful and rare magician is a tragedy to the world, not just her family."

Gabe's jaw firmed, but he didn't respond. As much as I wanted to say something, I remained silent, too. It wasn't fair to judge a grieving man when he wasn't in his right mind.

Mr. Reid saw us out and we returned to the motorcar. Once we'd set off, Gabe asked if I was feeling better.

"You looked peaked in there. I was worried."

"I was just shocked to see Thurlow's name. I thought we'd never have to worry about him again."

"So did I," he said, voice grave.

"Do you think he was responsible for Robin's disappearance?"

"Anything's possible."

"Perhaps Marianne didn't leave Ipswich of her own accord in '91. Thurlow may have kidnapped her because she was a valuable magician, especially if he believed the myth that silver magicians could create more silver." I pressed a hand to my stomach as it lurched. "Perhaps she escaped, and he's the one she was running from all these years—that *we've* been running from."

Gabe reached over and squeezed my arm. "We'll get answers soon, I promise. If Thurlow does turn out to be responsible—" He had to suddenly swerve to miss a motorcar that didn't stop at an intersection, and he never finished the sentence.

We drove to the War Office next. Located on the corner of Horse Guards Avenue and Whitehall, it was a commanding building befitting a center of power. It was also arranged in a confusing layout. When we finally found the Directorate of Military Intelligence, we were told we couldn't see Mr. Jakes without an appointment. Gabe had to say he was from Scotland Yard and threaten to contact the police commissioner if access to Jakes was blocked.

The assistant returned a few minutes later with a smiling Mr. Jakes.

He shook my hand first. "What a pleasure to see you again, Miss Ashe. I've been meaning to return to the library." Before I had an opportunity to ask why, he moved on to Gabe. "Finally, we meet, Mr. Glass."

"Finally?" Gabe prompted.

"Your friend, Francis Stray, spoke highly of you. A very smart fellow, Stray. Frighteningly so. But a good man." He smiled again. It would have made his features even more handsome if it weren't so practiced. "Sorry you had difficulty getting to me. Military Intelligence, you know."

I nodded, as if I knew what he meant. I wasn't entirely sure what the department did, except that part of their work involved the coding and decoding of secret messages.

Mr. Jakes led us through to an office larger than my lodgings, with floor to ceiling wood paneling. The faint smell of polish was marred by the more unpleasant odor of cigarette smoke. Ash and butts filled a silver dish placed to one side of the leather-inlaid desk.

Mr. Jakes sat behind the desk and invited us to take seats opposite. "I must say, this is excellent service. Do all your patrons get such special treatment, Miss Ashe?

"Pardon?"

"Professor Nash said he'd notify me if a book on genetic mutations in magicians comes into the library's possession. Is that not why you're here?"

"No. We wanted to ask you about a man who died in the war. We're investigating his disappearance years earlier." I explained what we knew about Robin Reid's missing years and his subsequent enlistment and death in 1915. "We hoped you could access his records for us, so we can learn where he was living when he enlisted." I didn't tell him about the connection to Marianne or me, and he didn't ask the reason for our investigation.

"You could have had Scotland Yard go through the usual channels for that information." He pressed a black button on the edge of the desk. "Of course, you knew that already, Glass."

Gabe sat calmly in the chair, seemingly unconcerned by Jakes's sharp assessment. Jakes *knew* we were here for something else. It wasn't until he pointed it out that I realized it, too. Gabe had wanted to meet Jakes.

The assistant opened the door and Mr. Jakes instructed him to fetch the military records for Robin Reid. When the door closed again, Mr. Jakes offered us cigarettes from a gold case. We declined, but he lit one for himself. He sat back, drawing on the cigarette, and regarded Gabe with cool assessment.

"You've been in the newspapers again," he said.

"They've got nothing of importance to write about now the war is over."

"You think they're making it up?"

"It wouldn't be the first time a journalist got the wrong end of the stick."

"Perhaps on this occasion, but what about previous articles? Weren't there witnesses to your kidnapping?"

"Kidnapping *attempt*, Jakes. I'm still here." Gabe's smile was as charming as ever, but I doubted Mr. Jakes was fooled into thinking Gabe was being friendly. "Tell me, why the interest in me?"

"What makes you think I have any interest in you?"

"You question my friends about me. You asked Francis to introduce us. You made inquiries at the Glass Library about books on genetic mutation. You, Mr. Jakes, believe what's written in the newspapers and think magic kept me alive on the Front. If I were a gambling man, I'd say *you* were behind the kidnapping attempt."

Mr. Jakes chuckled, blowing out cigarette smoke. "Then you'd lose. I admit to being curious about your uncanny ability to survive, and I'd like to know if there is a logical explanation or a supernatural one. But I wouldn't stoop to kidnap. You're also wrong to assume that I believe what I read in the newspapers, Glass. I'm capable of conducting my own investigations."

Both looked composed, but I knew Gabe well enough to notice the tension around his eyes as he held Mr. Jakes's gaze.

"I'd like to study you, Glass."

"No."

"Nothing invasive, I assure you. My men will—"

"I am not, nor will I ever be, your scientific experiment. My answer is no."

"Very well. You know where to find me if you change your

mind." He sifted through some papers on his desk until he found a newspaper cutting. "One other thing. You're acquainted with the Hobson family, of Hobson and Son boots."

"Ivy Hobson was my fiancée until recently. I'm sure you already knew that."

Mr. Jakes handed Gabe the clipping. It was an article about the protests outside the Hobson and Son factory. The protestors were mostly former soldiers who'd lost limbs after getting trench foot during the war. The condition was caused by their feet being damp for a long period of time, something that was difficult to avoid in the war until spell-infused boots were made by the powerful leather magician family who won the government contract to manufacture them. The Hobsons grew richer, the soldiers' feet were kept dry, and the army was very pleased with their investment.

Until it was revealed that a group of soldiers suffered trench foot. They'd all received their boot allocation at the same time and suffered horrific injuries as a result. Like all the soldiers disabled in the line of duty, they'd been given financial support from the government. But it wasn't enough. Many couldn't return to their former occupations, and it was widely assumed the support would end sooner rather than later. There was also the emotional toll. No compensation could relieve that burden.

Mr. Hobson refused to admit that a batch missed their spell and claimed the soldiers wore the boots incorrectly. He'd had the gall to tell the press that Gabe guaranteed the magical quality of the boots. Using the Glass name for his own ends had infuriated Gabe. While I didn't think the betrayal had factored into his decision to end his relationship with Ivy, it had come at a time that made it seem as though it had.

"You made a subsequent statement to the press that no member of your family endorsed the boots," Mr. Jakes said.

"Your point?" Gabe asked.

"Did a batch of boots miss their spell?"

"I wasn't involved in the manufacturing process, something any fool would know."

"I thought one of the Hobson family may have confided in you."

"No. Ivy had nothing to do with the business, and nor did I."

"Yes, but—"

"No, Mr. Jakes," Gabe ground out. "I don't know why a batch failed on the battlefield. Can I make myself any clearer?"

"So you do believe there was a failure, and that the boots in question were worn correctly by the soldiers?"

"Mr. Jakes," Gabe said with a smoothness that must have taken enormous effort to muster. "Pose your questions to someone involved at Hobson and Son. I am not, nor was I ever, involved in the manufacturing process, and no one has confided anything to me." He handed the clipping back to Jakes. "I suggest we move on."

We filled a tense few minutes talking about the weather and other benign topics until the assistant returned with a file. Mr. Jakes opened it and read the first page.

"Reid enlisted in the Royal Army Medical Corps as a stretcher-bearer in November '14. He died in the second battle of Ypres in '15 carrying out his duties." He passed the page to Gabe and read the second piece of paper. "He was an orderly at the time war broke out. That explains why he chose the Medical Corps."

"Which hospital?" Gabe asked.

"Rosebank Gardens, located east of Watford. I've heard of it, although I've never been. It's a clinic for returned soldiers now, but before the war, it was a private hospital." Mr. Jakes handed Gabe the entire file. "Make all the notes you need."

I wrote down the address of the hospital as well as the name of the officer in charge of Robin Reid's subsection. "Do you know where we can find Captain Collier?"

Mr. Jakes accepted the file back from Gabe. "It wouldn't be

ethical for me to give you his personal details. This is, after all, not an official Scotland Yard investigation. Is it?"

Gabe stood, so I gathered he wasn't going to press for an answer.

Mr. Jakes followed us to the door to see us out. "If you change your mind about working with me, Glass, I might be able to help you locate Collier."

Gabe settled his hat on his head. "Thank you for your time, Jakes."

Mr. Jakes hesitated, before smiling that practiced smile of his. "It was a pleasure to meet you. And to see you again, Miss Ashe. Do keep me informed if any books on genetic mutations in magicians come across your desk."

I smiled weakly in response. My nerves were too taut to allow me to be friendly.

Outside, Gabe opened the Vauxhall's door for me and to retrieve the crank handle. Instead of heading to the front of the motorcar to crank the engine, he gripped the top of the door with his spare hand. His thumb tapped a rapid beat against the metal.

"What do you think of Jakes?"

I followed his gaze to the stately facade of the War Office. "I think he'd lie if it got him what he wanted."

Gabe nodded slowly then pushed off from the door to crank the engine. A few minutes later, we set off as fast as the traffic would allow. It was a busy part of London and policemen were stationed at every major intersection to control the flow of vehicles. Most of the vehicles were motorized and I caught Gabe eyeing off some of the motorcars, particularly the larger ones, some of which were driven by uniformed chauffeurs. I hadn't seen his own chauffeur, Dodson, since before the accident. Gabe preferred to drive himself in the Vauxhall Prince Henry.

"It's a shame Jakes wouldn't tell us where to find Reid's commanding officer," I said.

Gabe's lips curved into a sly smile. "We don't need him."

"You know where Captain Collier works now?"

"No, but I think I know someone who can find out."

He drove back to his house at number sixteen Park Street, Mayfair. Bristow the butler informed us that we were just in time for an informal luncheon. Given our arrival doubled the size of those present, he suggested we eat in the dining room.

Gabe agreed, only to frown at the staircase as the sound of raised voices came from above. "Is that Willie and Alex?"

"Yes, sir."

"What are they arguing about?"

"You, sir."

"Me?"

"You departed before either of them was out of bed this morning. They accuse each other of not escorting you to keep you safe from kidnappers. Given the latest report in the newspaper, as shown to you by Lady Stanhope, everyone is concerned there may be another attempt." Bristow's tone was usually bland, so the hint of sternness was as clear as a clanging bell on a still night. He was as concerned as the others, and annoyed that Gabe had left on his own.

Gabe sighed. "I'll speak to them."

Gabe's idea of speaking to them was to greet them amiably, let them rant about his safety, then once it was off their chests, calmly tell them what we'd learned that morning, beginning with our visit to Mr. Reid.

"I'm going to telephone Laughton College after lunch and ask to speak to a teacher who knew Robin Reid well," he said. "I want to find out the names of his friends. Sylvia said something interesting earlier—youths don't confide in their parents. They talk to their friends. If Robin had any plans for Marianne when he was sixteen, a friend is more likely to know than his father."

"His father said he didn't have any school chums," I pointed out.

"His father didn't know him at all. Whether he was too busy or just didn't care, I don't know. But I doubt Robin would have told him anything. I suspect Bernard Reid lost interest in Robin once he realized he was artless and disinclined to learn the business."

"No wonder the son ran away from home," Willie said. "I would, too, if my father was a no-good ass."

Gabe glared at her. "Willie. Language."

She made a scoffing sound and rolled her eyes. "You've heard worse, haven't you, Sylvia?"

"Of course. I've worked with journalists."

Willie looked pleased I'd taken her side. I was befriending her, little by little. We'd started our acquaintance with her loathing me, but once Gabe ended his relationship with Ivy, Willie began to thaw. She still sometimes reminded me in no uncertain terms that Gabe wasn't ready for a relationship, and although I denied having feelings for him, she didn't believe me. When we didn't discuss Gabe, we got along well enough.

Alex hadn't been listening to the exchange. He seemed lost in thought. He now shook his head. "I don't think Robin left home willingly. He may not have got along with his father, but to not inform his mother...it takes a very callous fellow to do that."

"You say that because you got a good mother," Willie pointed out. "You like your family, and they like you. Not everyone's so lucky."

"Even so, we should speak to Thurlow."

"No one will speak to Thurlow," Gabe all but growled.

"Definitely not," I added. "This is an investigation for me into my parents, and I won't have anyone putting their lives at risk because of it."

Alex put up his hands in surrender. "Did you call at the War Office as my father suggested?"

"We've just come from there," Gabe said.

Willie thumped her fist on the chair arm. "You should have woken us up for that!"

Alex crossed his arms over his chest and glared at Gabe. "Agreed."

"Jakes would hardly kidnap me within his own office."

"You don't know that!" Willie jabbed her finger at him. "You walk into the bear's lair, you got to expect it to attack you. Any fool knows that."

"I had Sylvia with me."

Willie snorted. "She doesn't know the spell to turn paper into flying slicers yet, and until she does, she ain't going to save you from the likes of Jakes. Next time, come get me or Alex."

Bristow entered and announced that sandwiches were being served in the dining room. We filed out of the drawing room, one by one. I slowed my pace to speak to Willie.

"It's a pity the Petersons don't know the spell to make paper fly," I said. "It could be useful."

She grabbed my elbow and jerked me to a stop. "That spell's dangerous. It's lucky it disappeared along with the swine who knew it."

She'd often mentioned being attacked by flying paper, but it seemed rather absurd to me. So absurd that I chuckled at the image of her cowering from a paper plane. According to the Petersons, only one paper magician knew the spell and he'd not been seen nor heard from in years. He was the same man who'd attacked Willie.

"It ain't a laughing matter, Sylvia. Magical paper cuts can kill. Slowly."

Over lunch, Gabe told them what we'd learned from Jakes about Robin Reid's military service. When he mentioned Robin dying at Ypres, Willie's chewing slowed. She stared at Gabe, and I realized Gabe must have been at Ypres, too. It may have been one of the battles where stories of his miraculous survival began.

"You drove ambulances there, didn't you?" Gabe asked her.

She shoved a ribbon sandwich into her mouth and shook her head. She chewed a few times and, with her mouth still full, she told us she wasn't in Ypres in 1915. "I was there for the third battle, in '17, but I could find someone who was there in '15 who might remember him."

"How?" Alex asked.

"The network. I got to know a lot of people. They'll remember me on account of me being unforgettable."

Alex nodded sagely.

"We'd like to find Reid's CO, Captain Collier," Gabe told her. "Don't tell anyone why we need to speak to him."

She grabbed a ribbon sandwich in each hand, shoved one into her mouth, and got to her feet. She left the dining room. Ten minutes later, she returned. "He's working at Guy's Hospital."

Gabe suggested we speak to him in the morning. "I want to telephone Reid's old school now, and find out what I can about him. You're welcome to stay for dinner, Sylvia."

I glanced at the clock on the sideboard. "Actually, I need to do something with Daisy."

At the mention of her name, Alex's focus sharpened.

But it was Willie who spoke. "Sounds interesting. Can I come?"

"You don't know where, yet, but I think you're right. It will be interesting. We want to take Huon Barratt to see the graphite magician to buy Daisy some pencils."

"What does she want pencils for?"

"She doesn't, but Huon thinks she should buy some. Given ink magicians don't get along with graphite magicians, there's only one reason he would have made the suggestion."

Willie instantly made the assumption that we had. She chuckled.

"Daisy and I suspect there might be fireworks between them," I went on.

"Then I'm definitely coming. Gabe, can I borrow the motor?"

"I'm coming, too," Alex said, standing.

"The Vauxhall ain't big enough. Me, Sylvia, Daisy and Huon make four. Five won't fit, especially when the fifth is the size of a house."

Alex sucked in his stomach as he strode out of the dining room, muttering about how *some* women liked his size.

Willie gave me a little push in the direction of the door. "Come on, Sylv, let's go. I want to see Barratt make a fool of himself."

Gabe saw us to the front door where he collected a driving scarf to cover my hair from the hall stand and handed it to me. "I never thought I'd say this, but I feel sorry for Barratt."

"He might come out of it well," I said. "Perhaps he'll show Petra Conway the half-decent fellow underneath the conceited one."

"Nope," Willie said. "It's more likely he'll make things worse."

CHAPTER 7

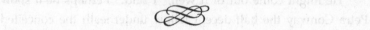

*J*f I couldn't work in a library, I would have liked to work in a stationery shop like the one owned by Petra Conway and her mother. There were enough notebooks, loose paper, planners, and card stock to give the paper magician in me a deep sense of satisfaction. While I was touching the ones laid out on the display tables, Huon was inspecting a bottle of ink. He removed the lid and sniffed the contents. With a derisive snort, he slotted the bottle back into the display. He picked up another.

Petra Conway strode up and snatched it from him. "Is there a problem?"

"The quality of your ink is poor." He pointed to the price label. "I wouldn't pay half that."

"Good, because I wouldn't accept your money."

His grin was smug. "You remember me, Petra."

"I never forget a face, particularly one that belongs to such a thoroughly disagreeable person. You have changed, though, since we last met. It seems you've misplaced your razor, comb, and..." She leaned closer and sniffed. "...soap."

"Be grateful he found shoes," Willie said.

Petra and Huon were too focused on one another to hear her.

76

Huon grunted at Petra's remarks. "You haven't changed. You're still a prim and proper snob with no sense of fun."

"I have fun." She poked him in the chest. "Just never with you. As to being a snob, I have no time for men with the mentality of fifteen-year-olds who think it's amusing to topple a display of pencils that I'd been working all morning to set up."

"I *was* fifteen when I did that. Are you never going to forgive me?"

"Are you ever going to grow up, or are you going to continue to waste your life on gambling, drinking and loose women?"

Considering he was still doing all three, he remained silent.

"I hear you refuse to return to work at your father's factory," she went on.

His lips curved with his smile. "So you talk about me, eh? Nice to know I'm in your thoughts after all this time."

"As much as an insect crosses my path from time to time, so does your name. In both instances, it's annoying but irrelevant."

Petra was running rings around him, and if I weren't mistaken, he was enjoying it. She was very pretty with her sleek dark hair, flashing eyes, and high cheekbones. Her features sharpened when she was annoyed, but softened when she smiled at Willie and me.

"It's a pleasure to see you both again. I read in the newspapers that someone was arrested over the murder of the bookbinder."

"Thanks to your help revealing the letter written in invisible pencil," I said.

"I'm so glad I could assist you. Invisible graphite is an interesting by-product of combining my magic with paper magic that no other writing material can replicate." Her gaze flicked to Huon and back again.

"That's because no ink magician has *tried* to create the spell," he pointed out.

"Firstly, you don't know that for certain. Secondly, what's stopping *you* from trying to create it yourself?"

He folded his arms over his chest. "I've been busy. There's been a war on."

"It ended over a year and half ago. What have you been doing since then, aside from gambling, drinking and womanizing?"

"Those are time-consuming activities."

Petra rolled her eyes and returned to her position behind the counter. "Pens and ink are not our primary sales item."

"Clearly."

She ignored him and spoke to me. "Are you here for other stationery items, Miss Ashe, or do you have some invisible graphite you'd like me to read for another investigation?"

I introduced her to Daisy. "She's a writer and is in need of pencils."

Petra's face brightened. "What sort of pencils? Hard or soft? What thickness? There's a new mechanical pencil which has an improved design, although I'm an artist not a writer, so it might not suit your needs. Do you want your pencil with or without a spell?"

Daisy surveyed the vast array of pencil displays, both on the counter and arranged on the shelves. "I'm not sure..."

Unperturbed by Daisy's uncertainty, Petra pulled out a box from under the counter and lifted the lid. Cushioned on black velvet were two sharpened pencils. She handed one to Daisy. "These have my magic in them. Go on, take one." She watched as Daisy balanced the pencil on her palm. "How does it feel in your hand?"

"Fine."

Petra passed her a notepad containing pencil drawings of flowers, all in different shades of gray. They were beautiful, and very detailed. She flipped to a blank page. "Write something on here to get a feel for it." As Daisy wrote, she added, "I must say, this is very exciting. Writers rarely write in pencil anymore."

"That's because ink's better," Huon said.

"*You* suggested she write in pencil," I pointed out.

Petra stared at him, open-mouthed. Then her jaw firmed, and her gaze narrowed. "Why?"

Huon folded his arms and tucked his hands under his armpits. He shrugged.

"What do you want, Huon?"

"Nothing."

"Have you stolen anything? Show me your hands."

He did. They were empty. "Why would I steal pencils? I simply thought Daisy should try a different writing implement to see if that unlocks her creativity. She was having trouble with her story." He shrugged again. Despite the unkempt hair and stubble on his chin, there was a boyish cheekiness about him in that moment. It was unexpectedly endearing.

Petra noticed it, too, going by the way she dropped the accusation and moved on. The last thing she'd want to admit to herself was how handsome and charming Huon could be. Not for the first time, I suspected he would clean up rather well given the right motivation in the form of a prim and proper dark-haired beauty.

"I can give you a discount on a magic pencil," she told Daisy. "The graphite lasts much longer than one manufactured by an artless."

"Oh, well, in that case, I'll take two."

"You won't need a second one. Not for some time, anyway." Petra winked.

Huon watched her intently as she wrapped up Daisy's purchase and finished the sale. Petra's easy manner was at odds with her frosty reception toward him.

He pointed out as much after we left the shop. "She hasn't changed. She still thinks ink magicians are the lowest of the low."

Willie clapped him on the back. "You sure she thinks that way about all ink magicians? Could just be you."

Daisy agreed. "You don't really give her, or anyone, a reason to think you're anything but a shallow, lazy drunk."

"A fellow can't change his nature for the sake of a few opinions. It wouldn't be honest."

"But is that your true nature?" I asked. "Or are you wallowing in self-pity?"

"Bloody hell, Sylvia, I can't be expected to answer that. I'm not self-aware enough. Give me a few hours and a few drinks, and I'll let you know."

Willie fetched the crank handle from the Vauxhall and shoved it into Huon's chest. "Petra's got you pegged real good, and she doesn't even know about your tattoo yet."

During one of our visits to Huon's house, he was in the middle of throwing a party. Lounging on the sofa with his shirt undone, we'd noticed a new tattoo on his chest depicting the Roman Empire eagle symbol. He'd been too drunk to remember getting it, but wasn't displeased with the result.

He took the crank handle and tucked it under his arm. "Don't tell her about my tattoo." He reached into his pocket for his cigarette case and matches.

"Why not?" Willie asked.

"I want it to be a surprise."

She chuckled. "You devil."

"I don't understand," Daisy said. "A surprise for...? Oooohhh. A surprise for when she sees your naked chest."

He lit the cigarette, took a puff, and smiled at her as he blew out smoke.

She shook her head. "I don't think you stand a chance with her. She clearly doesn't like you."

He merely plugged the cigarette back into his mouth and moved to the front of the motorcar to crank the engine.

I slid into the back seat with Daisy. "Sometimes men and women disguise their interest in each other with bickering. It's a way of getting the other's attention." I watched her for signs that she realized I was referring to her and Alex as well as Huon and Petra.

She leaned over and hugged my arm. "You're so wise, Sylvia, even though you've never had a relationship yourself."

Her observation may have been innocently meant, but it was true. It rather put me back in my place. I was the last person who should comment on anyone's relationship. At this rate, and with so few eligible men nowadays, I was probably going to be a spinster for many years to come.

* * *

DR. COLLIER DIDN'T WANT to be known as Captain Collier anymore. The middle-aged doctor with a slight limp and thinning hair said it was unnecessary now that the war was over. "We should all use our civilian titles again, if we no longer serve. You seem to agree, *Mr.* Glass."

"What makes you think I served?" Gabe asked.

"I've read about you in the newspapers. You were a captain, too."

Gabe sighed. He couldn't escape his notoriety, even in the doctor's office of Guy's Hospital.

"Don't worry," Dr. Collier went on. "I'm not interested in why you survived. You were fortunate, that's the end of it. Any talk of magic is nonsense."

"You don't believe in magic?" I asked.

"Of course I do. I just don't believe that magic helped him get through the war. How could it? It doesn't make sense. No, Miss Ashe. It was luck, pure and simple." He removed a cigarette case from his jacket pocket and offered one to Gabe, then me.

"I gave up when I came home," Gabe said.

"Really? Why?"

Gabe didn't offer an answer and Dr. Collier didn't seem to expect one. He lit his cigarette and sat back with a sigh as he blew out the first puff of smoke. He looked like he'd been eagerly awaiting the cigarette all day. Or perhaps it was the peace and quiet that came with having a few quiet minutes to smoke that he'd been looking forward to. I suspected the hospital was a busy place. Doctors were always in short supply, even more so since the war with some of them not coming back, and many returned soldiers requiring ongoing medical treatment.

"Thank you for seeing us," Gabe began. "We're trying to find out more about this man before he signed up. He was a stretcher-bearer in your subsection."

I showed Dr. Collier the photograph of a young Robin Reid, taken before he left home.

Dr. Collier studied the photograph and shook his head. "He wasn't one of mine."

Gabe slid the photograph across the desk. "Take a closer look. This was taken a long time ago. Reid would have been around forty when you knew him."

"Reid? Do you mean Robin Reid?"

"So you did know him."

Dr. Collier pushed the photograph back. "That's not Reid."

"Are you sure? He was young when this was taken."

"It's not him. Reid's face was squarer, and he had a birthmark here." He tapped his left cheekbone. Ash sprinkled from his cigarette onto the lapel of his white coat. He brushed it off with the back of his hand.

Gabe and I exchanged glances. "What do you remember about him?" Gabe asked.

Dr. Collier blew smoke from the corner of his mouth. "Not much. I didn't really get to know the stretcher-bearers."

"You didn't have a lot in common?" I asked.

"Their job carried a lot of risk, as much as any soldier. They had to run to the front lines to retrieve the injured, often when the battle was still going on around them, and bring back as many as they could to me at the clearing station. Bit hard to keep their heads down while carrying a stretcher. Most didn't last long, so there was no point getting to know them."

"Oh," I said softly.

"Sorry, Miss Ashe. I forget myself sometimes. There's an unwritten rule that we're not supposed to talk about the war, especially to women, but I find I'm not very good at following that particular rule. I've found it's better to talk about it, warts and all. It helps, if that makes sense," he added in a mutter.

"It does."

He offered me a flat smile. "Reid was an unremarkable chap. Liverpool accent. Strong, but they had to be, the stretcher-bearers. He was very tall. That's all I can tell you about him."

The door was opened by Alex who'd insisted on coming to the hospital with us but wanted to remain in the corridor while we questioned the doctor. He stood with two nurses, the senior of whom needed to speak to Dr. Collier urgently. The younger one lingered nearby, her cheeks flushed. Although she appeared to listen to the other nurse telling Dr. Collier he was needed, the coy glances she shot in Alex's direction proved she was there for another reason that had nothing to do with the patients.

I picked up the photograph while Gabe handed the doctor a card with his telephone number. We thanked him before he rushed off. By the time we joined Alex in the corridor, he was alone.

"Who was that?" Gabe asked him.

"A nurse."

"She seemed...friendly."

"She's the one I told you about, the one I met the other night at a club. We danced."

"And?"

"And today's the first time I've seen her since."

"It's fortunate you didn't come into the office with us, or you would have missed her."

Alex responded by lengthening his strides.

I studied the photograph as we crossed the hospital courtyard to the St. Thomas Street gate. "If this is Robin Reid, who was the stretcher-bearer who died at Ypres in '15? Another man who simply happens to have the same name?"

"The War Office wouldn't have sent notification of his death to Bernard and Mrs. Reid," Gabe said. "They got the address from the Robin Reid who enlisted, whose file Jakes showed us. That man must be the stretcher-bearer Dr. Collier remembers."

"So, who was he? And why did he use Robin Reid's identity to enlist?"

Neither Gabe nor Alex had an answer to that, but Gabe did have another point to make. He indicated the photograph. "If this Robin Reid didn't die at Ypres, perhaps he's still alive. If we find him, we might learn what happened to your mother after she ran away from home."

Finding Robin Reid could indeed give us answers. Him potentially still being alive was the most heartening news I'd heard in days.

* * *

GABE'S TELEPHONE call to Laughton College the previous day had been fruitful. Not only had he discovered the name of one of Robin Reid's school chums, but it so happened that the fellow now taught there. We drove to the school campus, located near Slough. It was exactly what I expected from one of the best schools in England. The old Elizabethan manor stood like a grand dame overlooking the broad sweep of lawn where several teenaged boys practiced throwing a rugby ball. Their teacher directed us to the main office, where we inquired after Mr. Rutledge. Given that he was in class, we had to wait for lunch.

Alex had elected to remain in the motorcar, muttering something about never liking school when he was forced to attend, so he wouldn't return now voluntarily.

"Is this the sort of school you went to?" I asked Gabe.

He looked around, taking in the trophy cabinet full of silverware, and the portraits of dour-faced former principals lining the walls. They seemed to glare down at us, judging us for our disregard of the prewar era's rigid standards. "Something like this. I didn't mind it, despite all the rules. I have some good memories and I've kept in touch with some of the friends I made."

"Like Francis Stray?"

"Francis had a harder time of it than me. He probably wouldn't remember his school days as fondly."

Having met Francis, I could imagine that his awkwardness would have made him the butt of the other boys' teasing, whereas Gabe's athleticism and quick wit would have helped him fit in. Without Gabe's friendship, Francis's time at school would have been even harder. It was no wonder he still idolized Gabe.

The clang of the bell signaled the release of pent-up energy as boys spilled out of their classrooms and into the corridors. The dining hall must be located nearby, because their voices grew louder before quietening again. The teachers not assigned to lunchtime duty filed past us in a hurry to enjoy their student-free time. Mr. Rutledge returned a few minutes later, after being told we wished to see him.

The stocky man offered a tentative smile as he shook our hands. "You wished to speak to me about Robin Reid? That's a name I haven't heard in a long while."

"So you know him?" Gabe asked.

"We were at school together years ago." He swept his hand out, indicating the large waiting room. "As you can see, I couldn't leave the place. I've been here so long that Laughton is in my blood now, for good or ill."

I showed Mr. Rutledge the photograph. "Is this Robin?"

"Yes."

"You were friends at school," Gabe said.

"Yes, good friends. We were close. Or so I thought."

"Go on."

"He left school on the last day of our final year and never looked back. He never contacted me, or anyone else as far as I am aware. Not a single letter, even though I wrote to him. He didn't go to university like the rest of us, so perhaps he felt like he no longer had anything in common with us, and that's why he distanced himself."

"What were his plans after school?"

"His parents wanted him to work in the family business. They manufactured woolen undergarments. It was around the time magicians came out from their self-imposed exile and some, like the Reids, had enough business sense to make the most of the boom in luxury magician-made goods."

"So you knew Mr. Bernard Reid was a wool magician?"

"Not then. Robin never mentioned it. Some of us speculated at our first reunion and it was shortly after that when I learned for certain that Mr. Reid was a magician."

"Do you know if Robin inherited his father's magic?"

"I don't, sorry. As I said, he never mentioned magic, even though it was quite a popular topic of conversation in the early nineties. Looking back, it was as if the world changed overnight. Of course, it wasn't that sudden, but we were merely boys then and the years tended to blur together. At our first reunion, after we all speculated whether the Reids were magicians or not, I did begin to assume that Robin was, too."

"Why did you assume?" Gabe asked.

"He used to say he was going to be rich. Richer than anyone could imagine, after he turned eighteen. He was so sure, so... determined, almost obsessed. I supposed his father was going to hand the business over to him, although eighteen does seem too young, and the sort of wealth Robin spoke about was...well, it can only be described as extreme." He shrugged. "Anyway, it was something of a joke between us. We would dream up things we'd spend his money on." He smiled ruefully. "Robin wanted to buy an island off the Scottish coast."

"How old was he when he started talking about becoming wealthy?"

"Goodness, hard to say. It was a long time ago. Fifteen or sixteen, I think."

"When did he stop talking about it?"

"I'm not sure that he did."

The timing fit with Bernard Reid's first letter to John Folgate in 1891. Robin was sixteen when his father put his name forward to marry Marianne. It seemed Robin knew all about it and was keen to go ahead with the union. It also seemed Robin had heard the rumor that silversmith magicians could replicate silver. He wouldn't have talked about becoming extremely wealthy if he was merely marrying Marianne so she could give him magician children. There was no certainty they'd be born magicians, and if they were, their magic wouldn't be useful in a business sense until they were older.

"Did Robin ever mention a silversmith magician named Folgate?" I asked.

Mr. Rutledge shook his head. "As I said, he never mentioned magic at all, not even when referring to his father's success. May I inquire as to why you're asking all these questions? Is Robin in trouble?"

"His father is looking for him," was all Gabe said.

Mr. Rutledge accepted the explanation. He didn't seem to know that Robin went missing in '94 or was thought to have died in the war.

"You've had no contact with Mr. or Mrs. Reid over the years?" I asked.

"None. The letters I wrote to Robin after school ended went unanswered."

"You didn't think that was odd?"

"A little, but..."

"Go on."

"Robin changed in the last couple of years at school. He became withdrawn, shy. Loud noises frightened him. Surprises of any kind made him jump. The only time I saw him exhibit any interest in something was when he talked about becoming rich. Otherwise, he was just a shell of the boy I knew. I suppose that withdrawal extended to not replying to my letters." He paused. "It just occurred to me that I've recently seen a similar change of behavior in another man. He was a student here before the war. He used to be so full of beans, a real character in class, always making jokes and causing disruption. I met him again last year, after he returned from the war. He was suffering from shell shock. I visited him at his parents' home and I couldn't believe the change in him. He was quiet, anxious, not at all like the boy I taught. It was similar with Robin, all those years ago."

His observation somewhat matched Bernard Reid's comment that Robin spent a great deal of time in his room, showing little interest in the factory. Where their accounts differed was in the level of anxiety. Perhaps Bernard Reid never saw the extreme nervousness Robin showed, whereas his school chum did. The other difference in their accounts was in the matter of Robin's friends. Mr. Rutledge had been a friend who'd been shunned the moment school finished. Yet Bernard Reid claimed his son didn't have friends. Until Thurlow came along, that is. It seemed the anxious youth wanted to distance himself from those in his past, while clinging to a new acquaintance. A more dangerous acquaintance.

"Did Robin's character change around the same time as he talked about being rich?" Gabe asked.

"I'd say so, yes, in the final couple of years at school."

"You left school in '93?"

Mr. Rutledge nodded. "I continued to write to Robin for a whole year, then gave up. I wondered if he'd gone traveling, but surely Mr. or Mrs. Reid would have written back and told me. Besides, Robin would have loathed traveling. All that noise and activity."

After we left Mr. Rutledge and returned to the motorcar, Alex told us about a theory he'd formed, where Mrs. Reid had something to do with her son's disappearance but had never told her husband the truth.

"Why would she do that?" Gabe asked.

"Because Bernard Reid was frustrated that his son was artless. Being artless herself, and his mother, she was worried her husband was pressuring Robin, making him feel worthless. She could see how the pressure was getting to Robin, changing him from a confident young man to an anxious one, and she wanted to protect him. So she squirreled him away somewhere and pretended he'd left of his own accord. She took the secret to her grave."

It was a wild theory, but it had merit. Mothers sometimes took extreme measures to protect their children. I knew that all too well. "If we assume he's still alive, where is he now? And why did another man use his name when he enlisted?"

CHAPTER 8

$\mathcal{W}$e drove back to the outskirts of London, to Rosebank Gardens, the hospital where the stretcher-bearer had claimed to be working when he enlisted using Robin Reid's name. The front gate was not only closed, it was also locked, with a guard posted in the booth. He let us through without requiring our names or purpose for our visit. Alex suggested that meant the guard was there to keep people *inside,* not unscheduled visitors out.

It was a lovely sunny day, perfect for driving with the Vauxhall's top down, and equally perfect for sitting in the garden or walking around the manicured lawn. Several patients dressed in loose-fitting clothes either sat and read or wandered about. Some used crutches or wheelchairs, or had visible scars. One man even wore a mask that covered half his face. Others appeared to have no physical injuries at all. Nurses in crisp white uniforms mingled with them, chatting or reading to the patients. All turned suddenly toward us as we drove up the gravel drive. One man fled back into the building, and another started to shout "Stop!" over and over. Two others began to rock back and forth. We apologized for upsetting them, but the kindest thing we could do was enter the building so the patients could no longer see us.

The manor house wasn't as old or as grand as Laughton College, but it was impressive with a blush-pink climbing rose framing the entrance and blue campanula bobbing amongst the white daisies running the length of the facade. Rose beds added color to the vast green lawn, although there seemed to be no pattern to their locations on the estate. The house and garden could have been in the country, so peaceful was it. London felt like a world away.

We followed the sign to the office and spoke to the director's assistant. He was unwilling to inform the director that we wished to see him, until Gabe mentioned we were consultants for Scotland Yard. As discussed in the motorcar, Alex remained in the outer office to question the assistant and any other staff while Gabe and I went through to the director's office.

"This is a fine facility," Gabe began as we sat after introductions. "One that's much needed, in my opinion."

The hands of Dr. McGowan, clasped on the desk in front of him, were smooth, the nails neatly trimmed. He'd taken the same precise care with his mustache, following the curves of his top lip. His gray hair was impressively thick for a man aged in his mid-fifties and slicked back with so much pomade that I doubted it would move even in a gale. "Thank you, Mr. Glass. We do our best for these troubled souls. Did you serve?"

Finally, someone who didn't know Gabe's story! "I did." He nodded at the window that looked out to the lawn. One of the patients was visible as he sat on a chair, the scarred side of his face turned to the sun. "They seem well."

Dr. McGowan turned to follow his gaze before smiling back at Gabe. "They're some of our better patients who are making marvelous progress. They'll likely be released soon."

"There are others?"

"We're currently home to fifty-eight returned soldiers, all of them London-based. Their relatives come to visit when they can, although they're encouraged to make an appointment during visiting hours. Unscheduled visitors can upset some of the patients, as you noticed when you arrived."

"Our apologies. If we'd known, we would have made an appointment."

Dr. McGowan's smile was forgiving.

"You only treat shell-shocked returned soldiers?" Gabe asked.

"Correct."

"And before the war?"

"Our clinic has always been a place of recuperation for the mentally infirm. You say you're searching for a missing man, Mr. Glass. How is he connected to Rosebank Gardens?"

"We're looking for Robin Reid. Is the name familiar to you?"

"I'm afraid not. We have so many patients come and go, and I've worked here for many years. It's impossible to remember them all."

"How long have you worked here?"

He took a moment to calculate. "Thirty years. Goodness, I hadn't realized it was that long."

"Are you certain no one by that name has worked here or been a patient here? This would have been before the war, or in its early stages."

Dr. McGowan shook his head. "I'm afraid it doesn't ring a bell."

I showed him the photograph of Robin, but he shook his head again.

"What about a man with a birthmark on his cheek here." Gabe pointed to his face. "He was a tall, strong fellow with a Liverpudlian accent."

"Oh, yes. I remember him. He was an orderly. Foster was his name. Bill Foster." He frowned. "What does he have to do with your missing Robin Reid?"

"He enlisted as a stretcher-bearer in late '14 using that name."

Dr. McGowan sat back. "Good lord. How extraordinary. Why not his own name?"

"That's what we're trying to discover. He died at Ypres in '15 and Robin Reid's parents were informed of the death. Their son went missing in 1894 and hadn't been heard from since, but they accepted the War Office's notification of his death on the battle-field. However, our investigation has uncovered that the man who died wasn't this man." Gabe pointed to the photograph. "He wasn't Robin Reid. His military papers stated that he worked here as an orderly, and his commanding officer gave us the description we just gave you."

"Of Bill Foster," Dr. McGowan muttered. "Extraordinary."

"Did you know he enlisted?"

"Not for certain, but we all assumed when he didn't show up for work one day. He was very patriotic and wanted to sign up as soon as they asked for volunteers, even though he was a little older than most of the boys who enlisted at that time."

"Was it unusual for him not to confide in anyone?"

"Not particularly. Foster kept to himself. Each to their own, as we say here at Rosebank."

"Was Bill Foster here in the nineties?"

"He started a few years after me, so yes. I started in 1890 and I'd say he arrived in..." Dr. McGowan's gaze drifted to the ceiling as he tried to remember. "...in '93."

"May we look at his employee file, please. Also, can you look for a file for a patient named Robin Reid."

"I am sorry, Mr. Glass, but our files are confidential. Due to the highly sensitive nature of our work here, I cannot share that information without a court order."

Given our investigation was unofficial, we wouldn't be granted one.

"Foster wasn't a patient," Gabe pointed out. "He's also deceased."

"Even so..." Dr. McGowan's thumbs parted before coming together again on the desk.

"Can you at least tell me how old Bill Foster would have been when he left here in '14."

"Let me think. He was relatively young when he started here in '93, so my guess would be late thirties, early forties." He smiled. "Again, I am sorry, but my priority is the well-being of my patients. Many would be horrified if their friends knew they were here, particularly in those days. There's some understanding of mental infirmity now, but back then, there was dreadful stigma attached to anyone who came to a place like Rosebank." He stood and put out his hand. "Thank you for your understanding, Mr. Glass.

Gabe shook it. I put out mine and Dr. McGowan shook it, too, but it was limp. He opened the door to the outer office where Alex was studying a photograph on the wall. We thanked the doctor and left.

"Any luck with the assistant?" Gabe asked Alex.

"No. He kept telling me he had no authority to answer questions about patients or staff."

Alex slid into the driver's seat and Gabe cranked the engine. "How did you fare with the director?" Alex asked once we were all seated.

We waited until we were driving away from Rosebank Gardens before telling Alex the name of the man impersonating Robin Reid. I scribbled notes on my notepad as Gabe spoke.

"We know Bill Foster worked there many years as an orderly, beginning in 1893. He would have been about Reid's age."

"A year before Robin went missing," Alex said. "You think he was a patient here and that's how they met?"

"I do. For some reason, Foster used Reid's name, age and address on the enlistment form when he joined the army." Gabe turned to me in the back seat. "Robin's old school friend said he became nervous, so it's conceivable that he was being treated for anxiety here. Remembering that Robin was a similar age to him, Foster took his identity many years later."

It made sense, except for the dates. "Mr. Rutledge said

Robin's character changed in 1890 or '91 which is years *before* Foster began working at Rosebank. They couldn't have met."

Alex agreed. "Rutledge couldn't have been mistaken about the date by that much. He said Robin changed in the couple of years before they finished school, and they both left in '93."

"Also wouldn't his father have mentioned his son's anxiety was being treated at the hospital?" I asked.

"Maybe not, because of the stigma surrounding his so-called mental infirmity," Gabe said darkly.

Alex changed gears, a deep frown scoring his forehead. "Is that what Dr. McGowan called shell shock?"

"Yes. As if the men are weak and all they need is exercise to build them up to the way they were before."

Both Alex and Gabe had more experience with shell shock than me. Gabe's friend, Stanley Greville, even suffered from it, although he wasn't as bad as some men.

Alex was also thinking about Stanley. "That reminds me. I was looking at the photographs on the walls while I waited. There were five, all taken a year apart beginning in 1915. Stanley was in one of them."

Gabe showed no surprise. "I didn't realize he was at Rosebank, but I did know he spent some time in a facility for treatment."

"Could we ask him if he has any insights into the place?"

Gabe thought about it then shook his head. "Stanley doesn't like discussing the months immediately after he demobbed."

"We don't have to ask anything personal, just some general questions. If he shows signs of distress, we'll stop."

Gabe's thumb tapped his thigh, over and over, before he seemed to become aware of it and stopping. He checked the time on his pocket watch. "It's only seven past four, so all right. We'll call on him before he starts work."

"He found work?" Alex asked.

"He stacks shelves in a pharmacy. Evenings are quieter,

which he prefers. Shame he didn't return to his studies, but at least it gets him out of the house and gives him an income."

"Can we not call on him at *eight* minutes past four?" I teased.

He flashed a grin at me over his shoulder. "Sorry. I know it's an annoying habit."

"Not at all. I find it interesting."

Gabe arched his brows at Alex. "Do you hear that? Interesting. Not annoying."

Alex kept his gaze on the road ahead as he navigated the narrower London roads with their heavier traffic. "She hasn't known you very long. Give it a few months more and she'll be rolling her eyes along with the rest of us when you get pedantic about the time."

Gabe turned to face the front and *humphed*. "My mother's known me a long time and she doesn't find it annoying."

* * *

WE SHOULD HAVE STOPPED to telephone Stanley Greville and ask if we could call on him. Like the patients at Rosebank Gardens, he didn't like surprise visits. At least we weren't strangers, however, and after his initial hesitation upon seeing us on his doorstep, he widened the door and invited us inside. He rushed around his small flat, picking up books and organizing loose notes into stacks. He closed a journal he'd been reading and dusted cigarette ash off one of the armchairs positioned by the grate.

"Please, Sylvia, have a seat."

I would have declined, since there weren't enough chairs for everyone, but he seemed so earnest for me to be comfortable. I said no to tea, however, even though I was parched. He only had a small kettle on a portable stove and two cups that I could see, both in need of washing along with the pile of plates and a bowl.

Gabe picked up the journal Stanley had set aside on the desk and flipped to a page with the corner turned down, marking his position. "Blood as a carrier for disease? Interesting."

"It's all related." Stanley picked up a tin of cigarettes and offered one to Gabe.

He declined. "Glad to see you're taking an interest." At Stanley's frown, he held up the journal. "Juan and I have been worried about you." Juan Martinez was another friend from the regiment Gabe and Stanley had served with. "You missed our last two gatherings and you haven't returned telephone calls."

"I've been busy with work, reading." Stanley indicated the journal. "I'll be at the next one. Tuesday?"

Gabe nodded. He returned the journal to the desk and sat on the edge. "We have some questions about the hospital you spent some time in after the war."

Stanley lit his cigarette with a shaking hand.

Alex glanced at Gabe. "You don't have to tell us anything if you don't want to."

"Or if you'd rather speak to Gabe alone, Alex and I can leave," I added.

Stanley drew deeply on the cigarette and blew out the smoke away from us. His hand still shook, but he tried to hide it by brushing his cheek and chin, then plugging the cigarette back into his mouth again. It was hard for me to imagine the man he'd once been, before these nervous habits took over, and without the sallow skin and bloodshot eyes. It was obvious he slept poorly and worried constantly. Perhaps he ought to check himself back into Rosebank.

"You don't have to leave," he said. "There's not much to say about that place. The nurses are nice, and some of the doctors. Others consider us to be...weak of mind."

"We just came from there," Gabe said. "Alex saw you in one of the photographs."

Stanley's gaze slid to Alex then back to the cigarette, wedged between his fingers so firmly it was getting squashed. "I was a patient for about six months after coming home. I still go once a month, as an outpatient."

"You must find the treatment helps if you keep going back."

"Some of it is helpful. As I said, the nurses are nice. I like talking to them, that's why I still visit. They listen, although I can see they don't really understand. At least they pretend to."

"The doctors didn't?"

"They had their theories and never deviated from their treatments, even ones that didn't work."

"Ones they've used for a long time?"

Stanley shrugged. "Why do you want to know all this anyway? Are you investigating a magical crime? Or a book one?" He nodded at me.

"We're looking for a man who disappeared years ago. He's connected to Sylvia's mother, and we hope finding him will help us find out more about Sylvia's family."

He blew smoke into the air. "Sounds intriguing."

Gabe told him about Robin Reid's disappearance and the orderly taking his identity when he enlisted.

Stanley stared at Gabe, smoke billowing from his nostrils. "He signed up before conscription? Idiot."

"Do either of those names mean anything to you?" Gabe asked.

Stanley shook his head. "Before my time there."

"True, but we wondered if you'd heard of them."

He shook his head again.

I showed him Robin Reid's photograph but there was no recognition in his eyes.

"If he was a patient there, then he had a psychological problem. That's the term they use nowadays. Even before the war, Rosebank only took in those who weren't altogether in their right mind." He tapped his forehead with the fingers that held his cigarette. "It's a smaller version of Bedlam, for people with money, or it used to be, so I heard, before the military took it over and threw the former patients out. I don't think there were many left by then anyway, so the war probably saved the clinic from closing its doors forever. Did you ask the director if he knew either man? He's been there for years and might remember."

"He remembered Foster but not Reid," Gabe said. "He wouldn't give us any personal information about Foster and refused to check if Reid was a former patient."

"I'm not surprised. McGowan wants the patients to feel safe. He'd tell us that no one will know we were there unless we wanted them to know. It was comforting, in a way. It was another form of shutting out the world. I needed that, in the beginning. Others still do." He folded one arm over his chest and placed the cigarette to his lips before removing it again without inhaling. "How badly do you want to see those records?"

Gabe and Alex exchanged glances. "Badly," Alex said at the same time that Gabe said, "It depends."

Stanley placed his cigarette on a tin plate then joined Gabe at the desk. "I saw the records office once. It's located on the first floor, in the western end of the building." He withdrew a piece of paper and pencil from the top drawer.

Gabe, Alex and I crowded close as Stanley sketched a crude map of the house at Rosebank Gardens, complete with stairs, sleeping quarters, nurses' stations, and an X to mark the storeroom where the files were kept.

"It'll be locked," he warned. "I'm not sure who'll have keys."

"Don't worry about keys," Alex said with a sardonic tilt of his lips.

Gabe clapped Alex on the shoulder and squeezed, hard. Alex winced. "Thank you, Stanley," Gabe said. "We won't be breaking in. That would be illegal."

Stanley looked disappointed.

We thanked him and filed out of his flat. He saw Gabe take the sketch and tuck it into his pocket, but if anyone asked, he could claim we never mentioned breaking into the filing room at Rosebank Gardens, and it wouldn't be a lie.

* * *

WILLIE REFUSED to listen when I told everyone after dinner that I didn't want them to break into the hospital. She dismissed me with a click of her tongue and a roll of her eyes and continued to give orders to Gabe and Alex with the officiousness of a military general.

"I'm serious," I said, more firmly. "This is *my* investigation into *my* family, and I refuse to put anyone in danger because of it."

She rolled her eyes again. "No one will be in danger. The patients will all be asleep."

"They might have staff on night duty. We could be arrested if we're found breaking and entering."

"Why do you think I stay friends with Cyclops? It ain't for his charm. It's so he can get us out of sticky situations."

Gabe cleared his throat. "May I point out that you're the only one here who has been arrested. No one else has needed him to get them out of sticky situations."

Alex smirked. "Except for that one summer when we decided to swim in the Serpentine in the middle of the night."

"Is it illegal to swim in the Serpentine?" I asked.

Alex opened his mouth, but Gabe cut him off. "Getting back to the break-in. Willie, it's Sylvia's decision and we will abide by it."

She smiled ever-so-sweetly at him, turned to me, and said, "Gabe was arrested for public drunkenness and nudity, not swimming."

Gabe glared at her.

I pressed my lips together to smother my smile, and tried to focus on the task at hand, not on a youthful Gabe cavorting naked in the lake at Hyde Park. "There will be no breaking into the hospital. Not when we haven't explored all other options."

"Like what?" Willie asked.

"Like questioning Bernard Reid again. Based on Mr.

Rutledge's evidence of Robin's behavioral change, it's likely Robin underwent some sort of treatment that changed him around 1891. We should ask him about that, as well as why he never responded to Mr. Rutledge's letters. Also, does he know anyone named Bill Foster?"

My string of questions built quite a case for my refusal to break into the hospital, one Willie couldn't argue with. So, she pouted instead.

I'd thought about it all the way through Mrs. Ling's multi-course meal and, in the end, I couldn't justify it. The only time I'd broken the law was when Willie and I entered Lady Stanhope's house one night and stole a book. It had been a terrifying experience. Immediately afterwards, I'd felt exhilarated, and more alive than ever. It wasn't until later that I thought through the consequences, and how awful it would have been to be caught.

Willie acquiesced regarding breaking into the hospital, but brought up another, equally contentious issue. "We should speak to Thurlow."

At least this time, I didn't have to be the negative one. Gabe gave an emphatic shake of his head. "Definitely not. He tried to kill us after the card game."

"You tried to cheat. I'd want to kill you too if you tried to cheat me."

For once, Alex was on her side. "We can't dismiss Robin's connection to Thurlow at the time of his disappearance as inconsequential. We know Thurlow is unscrupulous. We know Robin owed him money. Put the two facts together and it spells danger."

"If Robin owed money to Thurlow, why didn't Thurlow try to get it from the Reids when Robin couldn't pay? There's no ransom demand, no contact at all. Bernard Reid wouldn't have held that information back from us when he brought up Thurlow's name."

"Perhaps Thurlow went too far when he roughed Robin up

in an attempt to get his money back, and Robin died, so no ransom demand was sent. It wouldn't be the first time."

It was a sobering thought, and only made Gabe reiterate his reluctance to question Thurlow. "He's too dangerous, particularly now that he knows us, and doesn't trust us. We wouldn't even be able to get close to him."

"True. It could only work if we sent someone he doesn't know. Someone with experience in dealing with people like him, and is cool under pressure."

The door to the drawing room opened and Murray entered, carrying a tray with a cup of tea for me. I'd asked for one after dinner finished as I didn't feel like a brandy. The others had refrained from pouring themselves drinks out of politeness while I waited.

Murray's arrival had Gabe and Alex exchanging knowing glances, although I couldn't tell whether they decided the policeman-turned-footman should be sent to question Thurlow or not. Willie hadn't noticed, nor had she considered Murray for the task. She was deep in thought when she asked him to pour her a bourbon.

The glare he gave her suggested she could have poured it herself, since the drinks trolley was in the room. He poured it anyway and bowed as he handed it to her. "Your bourbon, my lady."

She frowned at him a moment before rolling her eyes. "All right, there ain't no need to call me that. Your snide tone made your point well enough."

Bristow entered and stood to one side near the door. "Are you in to see Lady Stanhope, sir?"

Alex and Gabe sighed.

Willie pulled a face. "What does she want?"

"Nothing from you, Lady Farnsworth," Lady Stanhope quipped as she swept into the drawing room. "Good evening, everyone. You there, I'd like a brandy."

Murray stiffened and didn't move. Bristow poured the

brandy instead and handed it to Lady Stanhope, who'd seated herself on the sofa between Gabe and me.

She took a large sip, draining half the glass. "Now, Gabriel," she began, lowering the glass to her lap. "I have called on the newspaper that printed that article claiming you're hiding your magic."

"I didn't ask you to do that." Gabe's tone was far milder than the one I would have employed in his place.

"That's what I told the journalist when he accused you of sending me. I decided not to tell you my plan to call on him, so you wouldn't feel obliged to stop me. I was determined to get to the root of his information, and I knew you'd be reluctant to confront him over it. Besides, it looks better if the one confronting him has no personal attachment to you."

She lifted her glass in salute, apparently to congratulate herself, and finished her brandy. She held the empty glass out and Murray stepped forward. Instead of refilling it, he placed the glass on the drinks trolley and stood there, hands behind his back. "I'd like another," she demanded.

Murray didn't move and Bristow had left.

Alex sat forward. "Did the journalist tell you where his information came from?"

Willie made a scoffing sound. "No journalist worth his salt is going to divulge that."

Lady Stanhope's smile was wicked. "*I* made him divulge it. You'll never guess who his source was."

"Who?"

"Mrs. Hobson."

CHAPTER 9

"$\mathcal{W}$hy would Ivy's mother tell a journalist that I can extend another magician's magic?" Gabe asked.

Lady Stanhope patted his arm. "Revenge, dear boy."

"She's not that petty."

"It's not petty to want revenge on the man who ended his engagement to her daughter *and* refused to help the family business when they needed him most. Gabriel, you seem to think those are inconsequential things, but for a woman like Mrs. Hobson, they are significant. She's a grasping social climber who's never satisfied standing on her own rung. She always has to reach for the next one."

Considering Lady Stanhope had once courted Mrs. Hobson's friendship in an effort to get closer to Gabe through Ivy, her assessment was just as much a criticism of herself. Not that she realized that.

"Mrs. Hobson wanted Ivy to marry a man who'll inherit a title, but she's pretty enough and rich enough that she could have had her pick of poor members of the peerage. But *you*, Gabriel, are the son of the most powerful and respected magician in England. Those two facts are an addictive combination for someone like her. You could not only help improve the family's social standing, marriage to you would also shore up the business if the issue with the boots blows up. You ruined her plans on two fronts. It was quite a blow. Hence her need for revenge."

Gabe looked a little bamboozled. "You make it sound like she hates me."

She patted his arm again. "I know it's something new for you, but it happens to us all at some point."

"Some more than others," Willie muttered.

"We cannot be adored by everyone forever. So, what will you do now?"

"Nothing," Gabe said.

"Don't be naive. You *must* do something. People like her can't be allowed to tattle to journalists every time they want revenge on someone they don't like. People like us will never be able to get away with anything again."

Gabe blew out an exasperated breath, but somehow managed a placating tone. "The article was printed in a small newspaper. It'll soon be forgotten."

"When word got out that your mother could extend the magic of other magicians, was it soon forgotten, Gabriel?" She addressed her question to Gabe, but looked at Willie.

Willie sank into the chair. "It took a while."

"Don't worry about me," Gabe said. "Mrs. Hobson's opinion is irrelevant."

Lady Stanhope didn't look convinced. "I've invited her to meet us at eleven in the morning at my house."

"I'm not having a meeting with her. It'll only agitate her more."

"Nonsense. She must know that you're very cross with her. Make her tell the journalist she was mistaken. Then we'll demand a retraction from the newspaper." She stood and he stood, too. She brushed his lapel and smiled gently. "Think about it, Gabriel. If you don't nip this in the bud, it will spread.

I'm only trying to protect you, dear boy, while your parents are away."

"I don't need protecting. I won't be there tomorrow."

She walked off, wagging a gloved finger in the air. "Don't make a hasty decision. She will be at my place tomorrow at eleven, whether you are there or not."

Murray saw her out. Once she was gone, Gabe poured himself another drink.

Alex asked for one, too. "She's exhausting."

"Amen," Gabe muttered.

I picked up my teacup and watched Willie over the rim as I sipped. Of the three of them, only she was old enough to know whether Gabe's mother suffered when other magicians became aware that she could extend their magic. She sat silent and sullen in the armchair.

* * *

I SPENT the following morning in one of my favorite places—the library's attic, accessed from Professor Nash's flat. Surrounded by dusty books written in mysterious languages—some so ancient that it was possible no one alive could read them—I forgot all about Gabe's troubles and my family's history. The small circle of light cast by the gas lamp hanging from the beam above my head concentrated my focus on the book on my lap to the exclusion of all else.

The professor's voice startled me. "Sylvia? Do you mind manning the library while I go out?"

I peered through the trapdoor in the attic floor. "Not at all. I'll be down directly." I returned the book to the trunk I'd found it in and closed the lid. With the lamp in one hand, I descended the ladder then extinguished it. "Is it lunchtime already?"

"It is. You don't mind, do you? I don't have to go. I could stay and work on my memoir."

"Professor, it's my job to look after the library, too." I took his arm and steered him toward the door. "You go to your lunch. You'll enjoy it when you get there."

The professor rarely went out, so I didn't want anything to get in the way of his luncheon with his old university friends. For a man who'd traveled the world, this need to stay home in the library baffled me. I didn't want him to change his mind before he left.

I was about to close the door behind him when one of the last people I wanted to see entered Crooked Lane. She did not acknowledge the professor as she passed him, but strode directly up to me, still standing in the doorway trying to think of a polite excuse to escape.

It turned out that politeness wouldn't have made a difference. Mrs. Hobson was determined, and furious.

"Where is he?"

"Who?"

"Don't be coy with me. Gabriel. Where is he? His butler told me he was here when I called there."

"He isn't here."

She pushed past me and entered the library. She searched the entire ground floor but decided against looking for Gabe on the next floor.

"He must be on his way. I'll wait." She sat on the armchair in the reading nook, her back stiff, both hands clasped on the large black and white leather bag perched on her lap. She wore a black straw summer hat with a broad brim, with a matching white ribbon around the crown and fluffy white feathers on the side. Her striking black-and-white-striped outfit matched. She always wore elegant, fashionable clothing, but her makeup was new. While younger women wore lipstick nowadays, particularly at night, most women of Mrs. Hobson's age considered the trend gauche and refused to apply even a little color.

"I'll let him know you were here," I said, hopeful.

"I'll wait," she said again.

I returned to the front desk. Not that I had to stay there to work, but I didn't want to be near her. Unfortunately, she followed me a few minutes later. It would seem she had to tell somebody what was on her mind, and without Gabe, I would do.

"That horrid little cousin of his ambushed me today."

She could only mean Willie. "Literally or figuratively?" I wouldn't put it past Willie to tackle someone in the street, even Mrs. Hobson. *Especially* Mrs. Hobson.

She must have thought I was joking because she continued as if I hadn't spoken. "Lady Stanhope invited us to her place for elevenses. She seemed to be expecting someone to join us, but I never thought it would be that *woman*. Lady Stanhope claimed she shouldn't be there, and tried to get rid of her, but the cousin was like a rabid animal. Shouting and carrying on like a hoyden. She was rude and vulgar, and I am *most* upset. Most upset indeed. Gabriel needs to know. He needs to be told to rein her in."

"I don't think it would make a difference."

The front door burst open, and Ivy rushed inside, out of breath. She sighed with relief when she saw her mother. "You told me you wouldn't come here."

Mrs. Hobson's jaw hardened so much it could cut glass. "He needs to know, Ivy."

"His cousin won't moderate her behavior. She's simply cross because she believes you told a journalist that Gabe is a magician who can extend magic. She's just being protective of him. Once she understands it wasn't you, she'll calm down. We'll explain to Gabe and he'll explain to Willie."

Mrs. Hobson's nostrils flared. "I'll wait for him through there."

"Actually," I said before she could disappear into the library, "Lady Stanhope told us that the journalist claimed you were his source, Mrs. Hobson."

Ivy's eyes widened. "Mother!"

Mrs. Hobson jutted her chin forward in obstinate defiance.

"Is that true?" Ivy demanded.

"Gabriel got what he deserved after the dreadful way he treated you, and our family."

"Mother!"

Mrs. Hobson decided she'd rather not face Gabe's wrath now that she'd been exposed as the source. She jerked open the front door and strode down the lane. I resumed my seat at the desk, expecting Ivy to follow her.

Ivy approached the desk, her teeth nibbling her lower lip. "I'm so sorry, Sylvia. This has nothing to do with you, and it's not fair you had to witness that. I'll telephone Gabe later and apologize for my mother's interference. She had no right to speak to a journalist about him."

"Thank you."

She still didn't leave, however, even though I made a show of shuffling papers. "She's usually so composed, but ever since my father's illness, she hasn't been the same. She's worried about him, of course, and about the business, too. It made me realize how important my father is, how much he takes on."

"I'm sorry he's ill. I didn't know."

"He's better now. You grew up without a father, didn't you? That must have been incredibly hard for your mother, and for you too, of course. I can't imagine how she coped."

"She was very capable." My response was tart, but there was something about her comments that set me on edge. While they were kind on the surface, there was an underlying condescension in her tone. Perhaps she'd decided I was at least partly to blame for Gabe ending their engagement after all, despite his denial.

"Where were you raised again?" she asked.

"I lived in Birmingham before coming to London."

"That's right, you did tell me, but I forgot. You don't have a Birmingham accent."

"I've lived in lots of different places, none long enough to pick up a particular accent."

"What an interesting life you've led. What other places have you lived in?"

"Here and there. Ivy, if you don't mind, I have a lot of work to do."

Her smile was cheerful and friendly, but I no longer believed it to be genuine. "Of course. I'd better go after my mother anyway, or she'll drive off without me."

I blinked at the empty space after she left. What a strange conversation. She'd been so angry with her mother, then talking about her father's ill health had brought on quite a change.

I settled into my work but was interrupted again fifteen minutes later with the arrival of Willie.

"Is Gabe here?" she asked.

"No. Do you know who was here, though, looking for him?"

She must have guessed from my tone that it wasn't a friendly visitor. "Who?"

"Mrs. Hobson and Ivy."

She groaned. "They complain about me?"

"Vehemently."

"You going to tell Gabe?"

"No, because *you're* going to tell him you went to Lady Stanhope's and confronted her. If you don't, Mrs. Hobson will, so I wouldn't delay if I were you."

She shrugged. "Fine. I'll tell him when I see him." She leaned against the desk and picked up a pencil. She studied it then tucked it into the nest of hair piled up on her head. "I don't regret it. She shouldn't be allowed to get away with speaking to the press. It ain't right."

I held up my hands in surrender. "You won't get an argument from me."

"Good." She picked up another pencil and tucked that into her hair, too. "You and me are getting on better now that you realize I'm always right."

The door opened and Daisy entered, wheeling her bicycle. She stopped upon seeing Willie. "Is Alex here?"

"Hello, Daisy," I said.

"Sorry. Hello, Sylvia. Hello, Willie." She leaned her bicycle against the wall near the door. "So, is he here?"

"No," I said.

"Why?" Willie asked. "Do you want him to be here, or not want him to be here? I can never tell with you two."

Daisy joined us at the desk, eyeing the two pencils sticking out of Willie's hair. "You ought to buy a handbag to carry around your things. I saw one recently with similar fringing to that old jacket you sometimes wear. I would have bought it for you, but I'm a little low on funds."

"I don't need a bag. You going to answer my question or you going to keep avoiding it?"

Daisy sighed. "I want to avoid him, I think. Last night, I saw him at the Buttonhole, but he didn't see me. He was with a pretty woman. They danced together all night and couldn't take their eyes off each other."

"If you're jealous, you should tell him," Willie said with the authority of someone who knew from personal experience. "Men like it when women get jealous."

Daisy lifted a shoulder in a nonchalant shrug. "I'll only come off looking like a fool. Anyway, I can't compete with her. I found out she's a nurse. She tended to wounded soldiers in France." She sighed dreamily. "It's so romantic."

"There ain't nothing romantic about war. It was muddy, chaotic, bloody and frightening."

Daisy sighed again.

"I thought you and Alex agreed to see other people, because you decided you weren't suited," I said. "After Ipswich."

Willie picked up another pencil and pointed it at Daisy. "You think you ain't suited? Why not?"

The door opened again and this time Gabe and Alex entered, putting a stop to the conversation.

"Did I miss a meeting?" Gabe asked.

Willie glanced at me. I encouraged her with a nod, and she

gave in with a determined set to her jaw. "Gabe, come with me into the reading nook. I've got to tell you something."

I grabbed the pencil from her before she tucked it into her hair with the others, then watched her lead Gabriel through to the library.

Alex wasn't in the least curious about their exchange. He was too busy trying to look disinterested in finding Daisy there. I wasn't fooled, however. I'd seen his expression brighten upon seeing her.

With Alex and Daisy avoiding one another, awkwardness quickly descended. Neither of them would break it, so it was up to me. "Did you enjoy yourself last night, Alex?"

Daisy shook her head at me, warning me not to tell him she saw him.

"I hear you were at the Buttonhole," I went on.

His gaze shifted to the entrance through which Gabe and Willie had gone. He must have assumed she'd told us. "It was fine."

"Did you dance much?"

"A little."

"Meet anyone interesting?"

"Not really."

That was promising. Surely if he liked the nurse a lot, he would have answered differently. I tried to signal to Daisy with my eyes that it was a good sign, but she was rearranging the stack of books on the desk and looking more invested in them than the tall, handsome man beside her.

Gabe and Willie returned. Gabe looked a little cross, while Willie looked sheepish.

She sidled up to me, pulled the pencils out of her hair and returned them to the holder on the desk. She cleared her throat but said nothing.

"Sylvia, Willie has something to say to you," Gabe said.

Willie toyed with the pencils in the holder. "It's my fault Mrs. Hobson came here."

"And…" Gabe prompted.

"And I'm sorry," she quietly muttered to the ceiling.

"Again, and with a little more sincerity this time."

"I'm sorry Mrs. Hobson is such a bi—"

"Apology accepted," I said quickly. "And thank you."

"I need a drink. Does the prof have anything in his flat?"

"I can make tea," I said, standing.

Daisy grabbed her bicycle handles and excused herself. "I have to go. My novel won't write itself."

"How is it coming along?" Alex asked, ever so politely.

"Slowly." She smiled at him.

He smiled back and opened the door for her, then watched her ride off down the lane.

I headed upstairs to make the tea while the others followed only as far as the first floor reading nook, the larger of the two reading areas with plenty of natural light streaming through the enormous arched window. Gabe offered to help me, but I declined.

I returned a few minutes later carrying a tray, to find him waiting in one of the aisles, shelving books. It was a task I'd meant to get to that morning, but had put off in favor of the more interesting work in the attic. I poured the tea and passed around the cups before sitting beside him on the sofa.

"I telephoned Bernard Reid this morning," he told me as he accepted a teacup. "I asked him if Robin had ever been to a hospital called Rosebank Gardens. He said he hadn't then hung up before I could ask anything else."

I sipped my tea thoughtfully. There was only one direction this was leading, and we all knew it. But the final decision was mine to make and I couldn't bring myself to make it.

"He was lying," Willie told me bluntly.

"Yes, I realize that."

"If we want him to tell the truth, we need to present him with proof we know Robin was there. To do that, we have to see the hospital records."

I looked to Gabe, but he was no help. He seemed as calm as could be, not a hint of his thoughts in his eyes as he sipped his tea. I looked to Alex. Like Willie, he was easy to read.

Alex set his teacup down with a decisive *clink* in the saucer. "We have a large period of time unaccounted for prior to 1914, when Foster enlisted in November. Somewhere in those years, Foster learned about Robin. They may not necessarily have met, but he at least knew *of* him. That may or may not have been from Rosebank Gardens. We're merely speculating that Robin was there in '91, before Foster even started working there. At the moment, that's our only possible link between them, so looking at the hospital records is the next logical step to take. That's if you want to keep pursuing Robin Reid at all."

I did want to pursue him. I knew that with certainty. The dead letters had fallen into my lap for a reason, and I felt compelled to know why. They were my only link to Marianne's life before she became my mother; before she became Alice Ashe. I still held some hope that Robin had fathered me before he was reported missing, and that he might also be alive and living a happy life somewhere, oblivious to the fact he had a daughter. Admittedly, that hope faded with every new discovery our investigation brought to light, but while it was still a possibility, I wanted to pursue all avenues.

"Very well. We'll break in tonight. I'm coming with you." This last point I made to Gabe.

He hesitated then gave the smallest nod.

Willie let out a cowboy's *whoop*. "This'll be fun!"

"Since Sylvia will be inside with me, you can keep watch outside," Gabe told her.

"Why me? What about Alex?"

"I'll drive the motor for a fast getaway," Alex said.

"Why can't I drive?"

"Last time you drove, we all nearly died."

Willie *humphed*. "That was Thurlow's thug, not me." She slumped in the chair and crossed her arms, glaring daggers at me as if it was all my fault that she wasn't given one of the fun tasks.

I sipped my tea but it tasted sour in my mouth, so I set it down. I suddenly felt a little ill. When we'd broken into Lady Stanhope's house, there were only a few servants to worry about stumbling upon us. This time, there was an entire hospital filled with staff and patients. Lady Stanhope wouldn't have pressed charges if she discovered us, but I had no doubt Dr. McGowan would.

It wasn't going to be fun. It was going to be nerve-racking.

* * *

ALEX PARKED the motorcar around the bend from the hospital and wished us good luck. Willie led the way to the front gate, only to stop and signal to go no further. She pointed to the booth. Moonlight shone on the sleeping guard, his chest rising and falling with his steady breaths. She put a finger to her lips then made a forward moving gesture.

The gate's padlock gave her no trouble. Once it was unlocked, she lifted the latch and opened the gate just wide enough for us to slip through. Fortunately, it didn't squeak.

We tiptoed past the guard then walked on the grass instead of the gravel drive. A few moments later, Willie was once more using her lock-picking skills, this time on the front door.

While she worked, Gabe lit the small lantern we'd brought with us, and we used the light to inspect Stanley's diagram of the layout. Even though we'd memorized it beforehand, one final look couldn't hurt.

Once inside, we wordlessly approached the main staircase. A distant shout sent my heart lurching into my throat, and a responding cry from another patient almost made me turn and flee. Gabe's hand on the small of my back was reassuringly firm.

"Nightmares," he whispered.

Up ahead, Willie stood on a creaking step. She paused, but

Gabe kept moving. He quickened his pace and Willie and I fell in behind him. He was right to continue on. The distant shouts and cries coming from somewhere to our right would probably have blocked out any sound we made. Even so, I held my breath every time one of us stood on a groaning floorboard. The old building seemed to be riddled with them.

We counted the closed doors along the corridor until we reached the third one. According to Stanley, the filing room should be behind it. Gabe tried the handle. The door wasn't locked. He didn't enter, however. He stood in the doorway, his frame blocking our view. Willie nudged him aside to peer past him and I peered past her.

It was a bathing room with six porcelain baths lined up in two rows. Even though the lighting was dim, I could still make out the ring of grime on the closest ones. Taps sprouting from the floor near each bath added to the strangeness of the room. The lack of privacy and the whitewashed walls gave the space a clinical feel, but I supposed that was to be expected in a hospital.

Gabe looked grim as he turned away.

We failed to find the filing cabinets behind the next door, too. That room was smaller with only one bed, currently vacant. Beside it on a stand was a contraption with levers and switches on the front panel and a slender length of metal hooked onto the side and connected to the contraption by a wire. Several small circular discs were also attached to it with wires, but it was the leather straps bolted to the bed that sent a chill through me. They were restraints to hold a patient down.

"Electroshock therapy," Willie whispered as we exited the room.

I'd heard about such treatments used in asylums, but never wondered how the patient received the therapy. The cold room with its wired device and bonds must be a frightening place for men already suffering anxiety. I failed to see how it would cure someone like Stanley of his fears.

Stanley had misplaced the filing room by only two doors.

Unlike the treatment rooms, it was locked. Gabe handed me the lamp and wordlessly ordered Willie to watch the corridor while he crouched and used her tools to pick the lock.

The hinges creaked as the door swung open. Gabe quickly grabbed it and slipped inside. I followed, leaving Willie to stand guard.

There were only three filing cabinets, each containing three drawers. I expected more for a hospital that had been operating for decades. I held the lamp close to read the typed labels on the drawers. Two were for staff, the rest for patients, arranged alphabetically.

I placed the lamp on top of one of the cabinets and searched through the drawer containing the patients whose name began with an R, while Gabe looked for Bill Foster's records.

I had no success, but Gabe found Foster's file. He pointed to an address where Foster lived at the time of his employment at Rosebank. He gestured to the filing cabinet I'd been searching through, but I shook my head. I indicated he should flip through the records to see if I'd missed it, while I looked through the other drawers. It could have been misfiled.

I didn't find Robin Reid's records, but I did see two other names I recognized. I expected to see Stanley Greville, but the other was a shock. I checked the date he was admitted—1913, a year before war broke out.

I glanced at Gabe, but had no opportunity to speak.

Willie poked her head around the door. "Hide! Now!"

The room was small, and with the filing cabinets pushed up against the wall, there was no place to hide. Gabe gave me a little shove toward the open door, indicating I should slip behind it. I grabbed his hand to take him with me, but he resisted.

It was too late anyway.

"You there!" came a gravelly male voice from the corridor. "What are you doing?"

CHAPTER 10

"I'm just standing here." From her indignant tone, Willie seemed to think the guard had no right to question her presence in the hospital in the middle of the night.

"Step away from the door and put your hands on your head!" he barked.

She grumbled and swore but must have complied because the next moment, the guard's head popped around the door. He raised his lamp, but upon seeing that we posed no threat, he lowered it again.

"Outside. Both of you. Stand with your friend."

"Does Dr. McGowan live on the premises?" Gabe asked as he moved past him to the corridor.

"Why?"

"Can you fetch him, please. Once we explain, he'll let us go.

The guard snorted. "Unlikely." He pushed Gabe in the shoulder. "Keep walking. Take the stairs, single file."

"If you'd be so good as to let my friends leave," Gabe went on. "I forced them to come here. They're innocent."

The guard snorted again. "You, in the front. Keep your hands where I can see them."

Willie put her hands in the air. "Gabe. It doesn't have to be this way."

Gabe didn't respond.

"Use your—"

"Willie," he warned.

She sighed. "By the time the local constabulary telephone Cyclops, it'll be morning. I hate spending the night in holding cells."

Holding cells? We were truly going to be arrested? It suddenly hit me that this was real and very serious. What if Cyclops couldn't help this time? What if we'd overstepped beyond the reach of his authority? My heart dropped like a stone. I'd never been in trouble with the police before.

Gabe moved closer to me. "It'll be all right."

We continued down the stairs to the front reception area where the guard pointed to the desk. "Over there. Now!"

Gabe's hands closed into fists at his sides and he drew himself up to his full height. Gabe towered over him, but the guard had a strong build and fearless attitude. If neither man backed down, the unspoken threats in their glares might be carried out.

Thankfully the tension broke when a matronly nurse emerged from one of the wards. Her gasp echoed in the eerie silence. "Mr. Buckley, what is this? Who are these people?"

"Intruders." The guard pointed to the telephone on the desk. "Call the police."

She studied Gabe and me with a quick, assessing gaze that halted when it reached Willie. Her brows shot up before angling into a frown. She made the telephone call at the desk then bustled off, but not before sneaking another glance at Willie.

The guard ordered us to stand in a line, facing forward while we waited. Dr. McGowan arrived before the police, the nurse at his heels. She must have fetched him.

He wore trousers and a shirt, but no tie or jacket. His shirt was buttoned incorrectly and his hair was messy. He may have just woken and dressed hastily, but he didn't look tired. He looked furious. "What is the meaning of this?"

Willie answered before either Gabe or I had the chance. "If you'd let them see your files when they asked, we wouldn't have to sneak."

Dr. McGowan bristled as he regarded her from head to toe, as the nurse had done. But where her final look at Willie held curiosity, his was full of contempt. "Who are you?"

Willie clamped her hands on her hips, much to the displeasure of the guard who ordered her not to move. She ignored him and jutted her chin at the doctor. "My name's Willie and I got links with Scotland Yard, too. They won't like being called here for no good reason."

"You broke in. That's a good reason."

"The door wasn't locked."

"It was!" the guard bit back.

The doctor turned to Gabe. "If you're working for the police then you wouldn't need to break in. You'd get proper authority."

"Let Miss Ashe go," Gabe said. "She was coerced."

I wanted to point out that if he and Willie were in trouble, then I must own up to my involvement, too. But my tongue felt thick and my mouth dry. I couldn't speak.

Dr. McGowan scrubbed a hand over his face. "The police can sort this out."

"Let. Her. Go." The ominous growl in Gabe's voice had Dr. McGowan swallowing hard.

"Control yourself, Glass. Here at Rosebank, such displays of unbridled passion are not welcome. We treat patients who show signs of anger in the same way we treat other unsocial behaviors."

Gabe's fists tightened at his sides. "You think this is anger?"

Before anyone saw what Gabe's anger really looked like, I enclosed one of his fists in both my hands. I don't know why I did it. It was an instinctive move, one that I probably wouldn't have done if I'd thought it through. But I just wanted to defuse the tension, to draw Gabe away from a powder-keg situation before it exploded. Usually, I would run from a man who displayed signs of anger, but I couldn't desert Gabe when I might be of help.

The nurse was the only one who looked relieved. The guard looked as though he'd been spoiling for a fight, and Dr. McGowan merely seemed annoyed.

"Buckley, make sure they don't wheedle their way out of it," he snapped.

"Sir."

The doctor stalked off.

Gabe called after him. "Where are Reid's records?"

Dr. McGowan stopped. He stroked his hair, suddenly conscious of his state of dress. "The hospital is used only by the military now. The prewar files were moved."

"Did you destroy them?"

The doctor's jaw firmed, then he strode away.

The nurse hurried after him. "Doctor, may we discuss Mr. Jeffries' treatment now?"

"Can it wait until the morning?" he growled.

"It's urgent."

I didn't hear the doctor's response as they left the room. I turned to Gabe to see if he was all right, but he seemed fine. Willie, however, fumed and glared coldly at the guard until the police arrived.

* * *

DESPITE WILLIE'S PROTESTS, the local constabulary did not notify Scotland Yard immediately upon our arrival at their station. Nor did they listen to Gabe's plea and release me. They locked us in the holding cells and waited until the morning to notify Cyclops. It was a very long night, not least because I was stuck with Willie. Gabe was somewhere to our right. We could speak to one another if we raised our voices, but not see each other.

Cyclops arrived the following morning, keys in hand, the duty sergeant behind him. I'd never been happier to see someone.

The sergeant scratched his head. "You sure you know them, sir?"

"I know them," Cyclops said.

"Even her?"

Cyclops hesitated.

Willie pointed to the night soil bucket. "If you don't let me go, I'll throw that at you."

"Want me to arrest her for threatening a police officer, sir?"

Cyclops sighed. "As tempting as that is, we should do as she says. Trust me, it's simpler that way." He unlocked the door of their cell and then handed the keys to the sergeant. "Release Mr. Glass."

While the sergeant unlocked Gabe's cell door, Cyclops led us along the corridor. "Are you all right, Sylvia? Were you harmed?"

"I'm fine. Thank you for coming to our aid. I don't know what we would do without you."

He jerked his thumb at Willie. "She might be in serious trouble, given her arrest record, but you probably would have been released with just a warning."

I couldn't tell from his tone whether he was annoyed, amused or indifferent, so I offered an apology anyway. "We are sorry to be a bother."

"No, we ain't," Willie said.

"Well, I am. It is my fault, after all. If it wasn't for wanting to learn more about my mother, we wouldn't have needed to break into Rosebank Gardens."

Cyclops gave my shoulder a gentle pat. "I understand why you went to such lengths. Knowing one's family is important."

Gabe joined us in the processing room. He looked as dapper as always, although his hair was a little ruffled and stubble shadowed his jaw. It lent him a roguishness that was thoroughly appealing. He grasped my arms and dipped his head to peer at me levelly. "Are you all right?"

"I'm fine, thank you. You?"

"Don't worry about me."

"But I do."

He blinked, his fingers springing apart and letting me go. He straightened and turned away to sign the document the sergeant presented to him.

Willie cleared her throat. "I'm fine, too. Thanks for asking."

"You're used to this," Gabe said without looking up as he signed. "Sylvia isn't."

"It's all right for you. You were kept in the men's cell. I've seen it before. It's got a longer bench. Our bench wasn't big enough for two. You were also on your own. I had to put up with Sylvia."

"What did I say or do?" I asked.

"Nothing. That's the whole problem. You sulked in silence. I tried to get you to talk, but you just wanted to mope with your ears covered."

"I was trying to block out your endless chatter. You also snore."

"I do not!"

Outside, Alex leaned against the Vauxhall, arms and ankles crossed. His gaze quickly assessed the three of us, then he clapped Gabe on the shoulder.

"Were you seen?" Gabe asked him.

"The police drove right past me. I thought it best not to interfere and left."

"Why didn't you contact your father straight away?" Willie said.

"I did."

Cyclops opened the rear door for me. "These things take time, Willie. I can't just march into another station in the middle of the night and demand the release of three detainees. I had to wait for the station chief to come in."

She grunted at him. "I hope you enjoyed a nice sleep in a comfortable bed with your pretty wife beside you while we were treated like animals."

Cyclops merely sighed and assisted me into the motorcar with a flat smile.

Alex opened the front passenger door and reached inside for the crank handle. "You must be getting old, Willie. You never used to complain this much about the holding cells."

Cyclops gave a good-humored grunt. "You only say that because you were too young the last time she was arrested to remember much about it. Believe me, she complained loudly with the kind of language that makes sailors blush."

Willie punched Alex in the arm. "I ain't old!" She slipped into the front passenger seat then slid across to the driver's seat while Alex cranked the engine. Once it was going, she moved back to the passenger side, which meant Gabe had to share the back seat with me.

Before he joined me, he shook Cyclops's hand. They shared a few quiet words before Cyclops headed to his own vehicle.

Alex pulled away from the curb. "I'll take Sylvia home first."

"I should inform Professor Nash that I'll be late," I said.

"It's Saturday," Gabe said with a crooked smile.

It was a relief to see he was back to his usual cheerful self. After the confrontation with Dr. McGowan, I worried his anger might simmer overnight as he stewed in the cells, but it would seem he wasn't the stewing type.

His fury had taken me by surprise last night, given that we weren't harmed. It was as if McGowan's talk of the returned soldiers' displays of unsocial behavior cracked Gabe's shell. The crack was small but enough for the rage boiling inside to seep out.

* * *

MRS. PARRY DIDN'T BELIEVE me when I claimed I'd fallen asleep at Daisy's. When she greeted me with hands on hips in the hallway, she'd seen Gabe's motorcar drive away, so it was not a surprise when my excuse for not coming home last night was met with pinched lips and a disapproving glare.

"Because you didn't telephone me and my heart can't take the worry, you'll be assigned to the dishes for the entire week."

I doubted I would have got off so lightly if she'd known I spent the night in a police holding cell.

"Oh, and Sylvia? Next time you're at Mr. Glass's house, ask Mrs. Ling what she thinks of my treacle. I sent her the recipe and I'm simply dying to know if she made it."

I smiled. "I will, Mrs. Parry."

* * *

I SLEPT SOUNDLY for a few hours and woke up in time for dinner. Afterwards, I telephoned Daisy and we met at her house before going out dancing. I considered asking her if she wanted Alex to join us, but I couldn't think of a way to make it sound like I wasn't using Alex as an excuse to invite Gabe.

We ended up at the Buttonhole. Daisy spent much of the night scanning the faces of the crowd, only to deny she was looking for Alex when I asked. We were in the middle of dancing the foxtrot when she spotted Willie by the bar. When the dance ended, we made our excuses to our partners, and joined her.

Willie, however, wanted nothing to do with us. "Go away and find someone else to pester. Ain't no one going to come up to me with you two buzzing around like flies."

Daisy ordered two gin fizzes from the barman, then watched his quick, fluid movements as he made a great show of pouring the contents into a cocktail shaker.

"If you don't leave, I'll tell Alex you were flirting with the barman," Willie told her.

Daisy spun around. "I'm not flirting. Why do you want to get rid of us, anyway?"

"I told you, no woman's going to approach me with you two around. She'll think I already have my hands full."

Daisy's lips made an O. "You want to attract *women*. I forget, sometimes, considering you were married twice."

"What's that got to do with it?"

Daisy searched the club then discreetly nodded at a brunette at the other end of the bar. She wore a loose pair of pants with a shimmery gold waistcoat, and her black hair was slicked back off her face. She was striking rather than pretty, and there was a boldness in the way she surveyed the room that was alluring.

"What about her?" Daisy asked.

Willie craned her neck to see, but just as she spotted her, the woman looked directly at us, as if she sensed she was being scrutinized. Her ruby-red lips curved with her smile.

Willie turned away, swearing. "Now she thinks I'm desperate."

"Aren't you?"

Willie accepted the cocktails from the barman and handed one to Daisy and the other to me. "Go away."

The rest of our night was a rather dull affair. Willie and the brunette were our only entertainment as they chatted and flirted in a corner booth. When they left, we left, too.

* * *

MRS. PARRY WAS all smiles for Gabe when he collected me on Sunday morning. Whereas I'd been subjected to a lecture before going out the night before, Gabe was given four shortbread biscuits wrapped in paper and tied with string to take with him today in case he was too busy to stop for tea later.

"Do I get any?" I asked hopefully.

She crossed her arms over her chest. "No, Sylvia, you do not. Now don't be home late. The dishes won't do themselves."

"I'll have her home by dinnertime," Gabe said.

She smiled and patted his arm. "Thank you, Mr. Glass. You're a good man."

He opened the front door and I slipped past him. "She thinks I was with you on Friday night, yet she gives *you* gifts while I get more chores. It's not fair."

"It's not my fault she likes me."

"It is your fault. You could switch off your charm once in a while and allow me to be the favorite."

He grinned as he opened the Vauxhall's door. "I might be Mrs. Parry's favorite, but you're Mrs. Ling's, so we'll call it even."

"I thought *I* was Mrs. Ling's favorite," Alex said from the driver's seat.

Willie handed Gabe the crank handle. "You're all wrong. I'm her favorite."

She spoke with such certainty that no one disagreed. She also sported a small smile that she wore all the way to Mr. Reid's house. It didn't even waver as we slowed for an elderly couple crossing the road outside St. Mary's Church.

"You're in a good mood," I said. "Any particular reason?"

"Nope."

"So it has nothing to do with the striking brunette you met at the Buttonhole last night?"

She placed her hand to her hat as Alex sped up. "It's just a nice day, is all."

"You certainly looked like you were enjoying yourself when we left."

"Who did you go with?" Alex asked me, oh so casually.

"Daisy."

"And Barratt?"

"No. It's a pity you didn't go, Alex. Daisy and I were in need of good dancing partners."

Willie snorted. "Then you wouldn't want these two elephants anywhere near."

Alex faced forward, concentrating on the road. Gabe leaned closer to me and whispered. "Let me know when she's going to the Buttonhole again. I'll make sure he goes, too."

* * *

MR. REID ANSWERED the door himself. From the grouchy look he gave Gabe and me, I suspected he wished he could close it in our faces. That would make him look guilty of something, however. I wasn't yet sure what he was guilty of, but hopefully we'd know more after this meeting.

The grouchiness was a remarkable change from the shell of a man we'd first met a few days prior. Our inquiries had awakened something within him, something that had lain dormant, probably for a long time.

"I thought you were my housekeeper." He checked his pocket watch before snapping the case closed again. "She'll still be at church."

"We have a few questions for you," Gabe said. "Shall we talk in the drawing room?"

"I suppose, although there'll be no tea."

"That's quite all right," I said. "We won't be long. We just need to clarify some points."

Mr. Reid led the way to the drawing room and indicated we should sit on the sofa. He eased himself into a chair and pointed to the photographs on the table near the window. "Have you finished with the one you borrowed?"

"We need it a little longer," Gabe said. "Mr. Reid, when I mentioned Rosebank Gardens over the telephone the other day, you refused to discuss it."

"I don't know what you're talking about. I know nothing about Rosebank Gardens. If that's all you have to ask, then you can leave. I can't help you."

"The thing is, we believe Robin was there in 1891 or thereabouts."

"Who told you that?"

"Robin's old school friend mentioned that he changed at about that time, going from a confident young man to an anxious one. We know Rosebank Gardens was a private asylum at the time."

"Don't use that word! *Asylum*," Mr. Reid sneered.

"So, Robin did go there?"

Mr. Reid gripped the chair arm, digging his fingers into the leather.

"Was Robin a patient at Rosebank Gardens?" Gabe gently pressed.

"We know he wasn't mad," I added. "Not when he was admitted, anyway."

Mr. Reid smashed his fist on the chair arm.

"Why was he there?" Gabe asked.

"We did nothing wrong!"

I jumped at his vehement reply.

"No, of course not," Gabe said. "You're his parents. You loved him. You did what you thought was best. But the hospital changed him, didn't it? It took a bright young man and destroyed his confidence."

Mr. Reid's face distorted as he battled to control his emotions and suppress demons he'd carried with him for years. But that's the thing about demons. They can lie dormant for a long time, and we think we've beaten them into submission, but they wake up eventually.

"Mental infirmity, they called it," he bit off.

"Who's they?" Gabe asked.

"The doctors at Rosebank, that so-called hospital. But they couldn't cure him of anything. He came out worse than he went in. He was a normal boy when we left him there and they sent back a broken, pathetic, *useless* child." He smashed his fist on the chair arm again, harder. "My son was *not* mentally infirm when he entered that place, but he was when he came out of it."

He closed his other hand into a fist, but didn't bring it down on the chair arm. He pressed it to his mouth and closed his eyes. A small sob escaped, and he squeezed his eyes shut even tighter.

Gabe gave him a moment before speaking again. "Help us understand. If Robin was a fine young man when he was admitted, what ailment did he have? Why did he need to go to Rosebank in the first place?"

"Don't you know?" Where before Mr. Reid's sneers had been directed at the hospital, he directed this one squarely at Gabe. "I read in the newspapers that you claim to be artless, Glass. If that's true, then you know the pressure of being the artless child, and the only child at that, of a strong magician. You know your parents will go to whatever lengths they can to bring out the dormant magician within you, and you know that you'll do anything to please them, to avoid seeing the disappointment in their eyes when you fail yet again to perform the magic wielded by generations of your ancestors."

Mr. Reid's insult seemed to have no effect on Gabe. He pressed on with his next question. "You took him to Rosebank Gardens in 1891 because he was artless?"

"Yes. We did."

CHAPTER 11

Gabe's ability to remain unaffected by Mr. Reid's admission amazed me. He forged on with his questions, his tone even and without judgment. "You thought the doctors at Rosebank could make Robin into a magician?"

"Not *make* him into a magician, simply draw it out of him. It was a different time. Magic was flourishing again after so many years in the shadows. It wasn't very well understood, however, not by the medical profession or even by those of us born into magician families. The doctors at Rosebank Gardens claimed their therapies would stimulate magic that lay dormant within the artless patient; patients with at least one magician parent. The doctors at Rosebank specialized in such treatments, so they told us. We trusted them." He sniffed. "But the therapies didn't work. The so-called experts didn't know what they were doing. I don't know what they did to him in there, but Robin came home a different person."

"When did Robin go to Rosebank?" Gabe asked.

"The summer of '91. He was sixteen."

"Before or after you wrote to John Folgate the first time?"

Mr. Reid stared down at his hands in his lap. "After."

"You hoped to make him a more attractive prospect to Marianne."

Mr. Reid nodded. "Folgate wouldn't want his daughter marrying an artless, no matter how strong *my* magic was."

"How long was Robin there?"

"Five weeks, perhaps six."

"You didn't send him back later?"

Mr. Reid's head snapped up. "No! Not after we saw what it did to him the first time. We did not send him back, Mr. Glass, I assure you. Not then and not in '94 when he disappeared. Robin's stint in the hospital had nothing to do with his disappearance. It couldn't. There were three years in between. That's why I didn't mention it. It's irrelevant."

"Does the name Bill Foster mean anything to you?"

"No. Is he the fellow who took Robin's name when he enlisted?"

"We believe so. He was an orderly at Rosebank Gardens from 1893."

"Then he couldn't have met Robin there and wasn't involved in his disappearance." He pushed himself to his feet. "If you don't mind, I'm very busy."

We both rose, but I had another question. "Were there other artless children of magician families there at the same time as your son?"

"Yes, many. Drawing the magic out of the artless was supposedly Rosebank's specialty, although I believe they received fewer and fewer patients as time passed. Word must have got out that they were charlatans. If it wasn't for the war and the shell-shocked soldiers, Rosebank probably would have closed."

Whenever there is new technology or a world-changing event, the unscrupulous look for a way to turn it to their advantage. Rosebank Gardens was no different. Reintroducing the world to magicians after centuries of hiding brought about much good, but exposed the bad, too. It was an unexpected dark side of Gabe's mother's legacy.

Hearing about Rosebank's former specialty reminded me of something I'd forgotten to tell Gabe.

Mr. Reid led the way from the drawing room. "You're wasting your time looking for a link between Robin's disappearance and Rosebank. Too much time passed. It has something to do with the people he associated with after he left school. Thugs and thieves, the lot of them. They took advantage of Robin, and when he failed to do something for them, whatever that may have been, they...they did away with him."

I thanked Mr. Reid and told him we'd do our best to find out what happened to Robin and Marianne. I tried to put myself in his shoes and feel some empathy toward him. He'd lost his son, after all. But I could not. He'd wanted Robin to be different, to be something other than what he was born to be. Robin would always have struggled to thrive while he lived and worked with his father. Perhaps he knew that and simply walked out of his parents' house in '94 so he could live his own life, away from his father's shadow and free from his judgment. I truly hoped we would find him happy and well.

Gabe thanked Mr. Reid, too, but offered no words of comfort. Indeed, he had something quite different to tell him. "By the way, you're wrong. Not about me being artless, but about my parents. They've never been disappointed in me. They didn't wish I was a magician. They simply wanted me to be me, no more and no less."

He offered me his arm and together we trotted down the steps. Neither of us looked back to see what effect Gabe's words had on Mr. Reid. Neither of us cared enough.

* * *

"WE SHOULD SPEAK TO THURLOW," Willie said from the front passenger seat after we recounted the meeting for her and Alex's benefit. "I reckon Reid's right and Thurlow's got something to do with Robin's disappearance. The timing with the hospital ain't right, but Robin's association with Thurlow is."

"The hospital is still the only link between Robin and Foster," Gabe pointed out. "And we can be fairly certain Foster was aware of Robin's disappearance, otherwise he wouldn't have used his name in 1914 when he enlisted."

Willie faced forward again, satisfied her suggestion wasn't flatly dismissed.

Alex had been quiet ever since we'd finished the account of our meeting with Mr. Reid. I'd assumed he was concentrating on driving, but when he finally spoke, it was clear he'd been thinking about Bernard Reid's answers, after all. "To think, the doctors actually believed they could cure Robin of his artlessness, as if it were a disease. I know magic was new back then, and medicine has come a long way in the years since, but it's still despicable."

"Not just the doctors," Gabe said. "Reid suggested a lot of people thought the artless children of magicians could be treated to draw out their magic. They filled the hospital beds in the early nineties."

Most but not all. "That reminds me," I said. "In the commotion of our arrest the other night, I forgot to tell you about a patient file I saw in the hospital's records room."

Willie spun around like a spinning top in the front seat at the whiff of gossip. "Who?"

"Bertie Hobson. He was there in 1913."

"Ivy's brother?" She frowned. "But he *is* a magician. Why would he need to be admitted to a hospital for the artless?" She considered it a moment. "Do you think he *was* artless, and the treatments worked for him?"

Gabe set her straight. "It's more likely he's not a magician, and never has been." He fell silent, turning away to stare at the passing buildings.

"His parents must have admitted him," Alex said. "They want him to take over the family business one day, and it needs a magician's magic to continue the superior work to make luxury boots."

Willie agreed. "They don't want to admit he's artless. It could ruin them if word gets out that the son in Hobson and Son ain't a magician." She shook her head. "No wonder Bertie's got no personality. The hospital robbed him of it."

"That's not true," Alex chided her. "Anyway, I don't blame the hospital entirely. His parents must take a lot of the responsibility, since they would have been the ones to admit him. He would have been a child in 1913."

The world had known by then that artless and magicians were born that way and there was no cure for either. People must have been desperate or foolish to think of one or both as conditions that could be cured, and I knew the Hobsons weren't the latter. I was willing to admit that they must have been ignorant of the hospital's results, however, because I refused to believe they were so cruel as to admit their son to Rosebank knowing he could be permanently damaged.

* * *

WE'D ALREADY DECIDED to visit Bill Foster's last known place of residence, as noted on his employee file at Rosebank Gardens. Although he'd used the Reids' address when he enlisted under Robin's name, we were confident he'd actually lived at the Nutall Lane address, at least at some point, if not in 1914 before enlisting.

Nutall Lane was located on the bus route that passed the hospital, making it an easy commute to work for Bill Foster. The facade of the modest two-up two-down terraced house was dark from decades of soot settling on the bricks, but pretty blue-and-white checked curtains flapped in the upstairs windows, opened to let in some air. The middle-aged woman who answered our knock wore an apron that matched the curtains, and a curious expression that took in Gabe and me, as well as Alex and Willie seated in the Vauxhall parked at the curb.

She wiped the back of her hand across her shiny brow and touched her hair, although it was neatly pinned off her face. She gave us a friendly if somewhat apologetic smile. "If you're with one of the veterans' or war widows' charities, I should warn you that folk around here haven't got much to give. I'll see what I can spare for you, though." She opened the door wider, inviting us in.

Gabe removed his hat and we stepped inside. "We're not with a charity. My name is Gabriel Glass and this is my friend, Miss Ashe." He put out his hand and she shook it.

"Mrs. O'Brien."

"Have you lived here long, Mrs. O'Brien?"

"Oh yes, years. I moved in as a young newlywed in the eighties, and stayed on after my husband passed shortly after. We had only a few short years together, but they were good years. Anyway, I always say the only way I'll leave here is if they carry me out in a wooden box." She chuckled. "Why do you ask?"

"We're looking for a young man who disappeared years ago. He was linked to Bill Foster who we believe used to live here."

She shook her head and shrugged. "The name isn't familiar."

"Are you sure? He gave this address to his employer, the hospital known as Rosebank Gardens."

"It doesn't ring any bells. Sorry, Mr. Glass. I wish I could help. Is that all?"

Gabe pointed his hat up the staircase. "Do you take in lodgers?"

"I do."

"Could Bill Foster have been one of your lodgers several years ago?"

"As I said, the name doesn't sound familiar. If you wouldn't mind, I have to make the tea for my current lodger. He doesn't like it to be late."

"This would have been a number of years back. Please, Mrs. O'Brien, it's important."

"I'm sure it is, but if I can't remember then I can't remember. Perhaps there was a fellow here by that name at one time, but lodgers come and go, Mr. Glass, and I'm dreadful with names."

"He had a birthmark on his cheek," I said. "And a Liverpudlian accent."

She shook her head. "Sorry."

We left and returned to the motorcar. Gabe cranked the engine then slipped into the back seat beside me.

"Well?" Alex asked.

"No luck. She can't recall Bill Foster."

Willie clapped her hands together and rubbed them. "Talking to Thurlow is the only option we have left. We have to do it, Gabe."

Gabe said nothing. He turned to look behind him at the house. I turned too, following his gaze. One of the upstairs curtains fluttered more than the other. It could have been the breeze, but I was quite sure I saw Mrs. O'Brien's face there before it disappeared.

* * *

THANKS TO ITS NAME, people often thought members of the Glass family worked at the Glass Library or, at the very least, frequented it often. As it happened, Gabe *was* there frequently, particularly when we worked together on an investigation. It was no surprise when he showed up on Monday morning, Alex and Willie in tow, as usual. The ruddy-cheeked fellow with ink-stained hands who arrived a few minutes later also seemed unsurprised to find Gabe there.

The professor showed him through to the reading nook where the fellow greeted Willie with an enthusiastic shake of her hand. "Nice to see you again." He looked around at the rows of bookshelves in awe. "My, so many books! I can't remember the

last time I picked up one, let alone read it through to the end."
He chuckled. "Is this your cousin?"

Willie took the man's presence in her stride. "Mr. Felton, this
is Gabe Glass. Gabe, Mr. Felton works for Rolls-Royce."

"Chief engineer," Mr. Felton said as he vigorously shook
Gabe's hand. The stains must be from oil, not ink.

Gabe arched his brows. "You came here looking for me?"

"Willie said I might find you at this place if you weren't at
home. She told me to come around at any time. Bit of a book-
worm, are you?"

"Are you trying to sell me a new motor, Mr. Felton? Because
if Willie told you I wanted a Rolls—"

"No, no! She told me you haven't made up your mind yet,
and advised me to speak to you in person to...come to an
arrangement." He beamed.

Gabe responded with a tight smile that he turned on Willie.
"Did she?"

Willie clapped him on the shoulder. "The latest Rolls-Royce is
a great motor, Gabe. Let Mr. Felton tell you why they're the best.
He came all the way here to speak to you in person, so it'd be
polite to listen. He told me he could sweeten the pot if you do."
In case Gabe didn't understand that she was referring to getting
a discount, she nudged him in the ribs with her elbow and
winked.

"I told you, I'm not ready to make a purchase."

"You will be, when you listen to my offer," Mr. Felton said,
still smiling. He was a lightbulb without an off switch, always
beaming.

Alex cleared his throat and introduced himself. "Just one
question. Why are *you* here, and not a salesman?"

"Felton's the fellow I spoke to at Rolls," Willie answered for
him. "The salesman didn't understand the mechanics. My questions were too complicated for him. So he introduced me to Mr.
Felton."

"Willie has a fine mind for mechanics," Mr. Felton said.

"She's a unique woman, in my experience. Usually they can't grasp the concepts, but she asked some pertinent questions. Then she said she'd bring you in to speak to me, Mr. Glass, but mentioned how busy you were, so I suggested I come to you instead." He stretched his arms out. "And here I am, in your marvelous library."

"It's not my library," Gabe said, somewhat automatically. "Very well, Felton, since you've come all this way. Go ahead. Tell me what makes the latest Rolls-Royce so good."

"Magic." He jerked his thumb at his chest. "Mine. I'm sure I don't have to explain it to folk like yourselves." He went on to explain anyway. "It works the same as watchmaker magic. The magic isn't in the individual parts that make up the watch, it's in the art of putting them together. Your mother, Mr. Glass, the extraordinary Lady Rycroft, makes perfectly working watches that are superior in form and function. I make perfectly working motor vehicles that are superior to our artless competitors." His smile finally faded. "For a period of time, at least."

His magic didn't last long. *Now* I understood why he was here.

Gabe understood, too. "You think I can make your magic last longer?" he asked.

"I want to offer you a free car, Mr. Glass." Mr. Felton's pause was punctuated by an expectant look and a hopeful smile. "Well? What do you say to that?"

"I'm afraid you've wasted your time. I can't extend anyone's magic."

Mr. Felton's smile didn't waver. "You can! It said so in the paper."

"You can't believe everything you read. I'm artless."

Mr. Felton chuckled. "Of course, you are." He winked. "So, do we have a deal, Mr. Glass?"

Gabe sighed.

Willie stood by her cousin, arms crossed over her chest. She looked thunderous. "You told me you'd give him a discount, but you never said you wanted something in return. If I knew, I wouldn't have told you to come."

"You thought I'd give away a free motorcar and get nothing in exchange?"

Willie lowered her arms to her sides. "Not free," she muttered. "Just...cheaper."

Mr. Felton pulled out a notepad and pencil from his jacket pocket. "You drive a hard bargain, sir. You force me to dig deep, but as head engineer, I can make you this offer." He scribbled on the notepad then tore the paper off and held it out to Gabe. "Take this to the sales office and ask for George Fortescue. He has the authority to honor it."

Gabe shook his head without looking at the paper. "I think it's time you left."

Mr. Felton flapped the paper in Gabe's face.

Willie snatched it and gasped. "*Two* free vehicles?" She sighed heavily. "Damn it."

Mr. Felton's frown deepened. "You'll truly refuse my offer? My word, you are a principled fellow."

"It has nothing to do with principles," Gabe said. "Now, if you don't mind..." He indicated the exit.

Mr. Felton didn't move. He simply stared at Gabe, as if trying to decide if he was truly artless or not.

It wasn't until Alex stepped forward and ordered Mr. Felton to leave that he finally departed. Alex followed him to make sure.

Once they were out of sight, Willie threw herself onto the sofa with a huff. "*Two* free Rolls-Royces! They're mighty fine vehicles, Gabe. Mighty fine."

"Sorry to disappoint you."

"You ain't a disappointment. It ain't your fault. Now, *India* would have disappointed me because she would've turned him down and she *can* extend magic. That would've been a waste."

"If only she was here," Gabe said wryly.

"Yes," Willie said on yet another sigh. "Damn that Hobson woman and her pet journalist. This is *their* fault."

Alex returned to the reading nook with Francis Stray. As always with Francis, greetings were perfunctorily polite, as if he wanted to expend the minimum amount of effort required to say the socially acceptable words that he considered somewhat pointless.

"It's good to see you," Gabe said. "What brings you here?"

"Someone has been asking about me."

Alex and Willie exchanged worried glances. Francis still worked for Military Intelligence and his commander during the war was Mr. Jakes. Mr. Jakes was also our suspect in Gabe's attempted kidnappings. What if his failures had led him to try something else, like targeting someone he thought weak and friendless? Although I wasn't sure how targeting Francis would achieve his aim of understanding Gabe's so-called luck.

"Who's asking after you?" Gabe asked.

"A man. He went to my old faculty at university and made inquiries."

"What sort of inquiries?"

"He described my appearance and character. My former colleagues knew instantly that he was referring to me. Apparently I am distinctive, although I have always thought I look quite ordinary."

There was certainly something distinctive about Francis. Distinctive yet oddly endearing. Outwardly, he was rather bland. He had no distinguishing features and he showed little emotion, making his thoughts difficult to read. He wore his hair short and neat, and his tie and hat were never askew. But once I had got to know him a little better, I realized he wasn't like most men. He was awkward, yes, but child-like, too. He was curious about the world and yet he often hesitated before responding, as if he needed to think about his words first or observe further to avoid making a social faux pas. I imagine it would be easy for a stranger to describe him to a friend without mentioning a name, and that friend would instantly know who he meant.

"He wanted to know if I attended that university or ever worked there, and if they knew where to find me now."

"How did the man know which university you attended?"

"I suppose he went to all the leading education centers in the country. He was looking for one of the brightest mathematical minds in England, if not *the* brightest, so naturally if he was looking for me, he'd try Cambridge and Oxford first."

"Did he say he was looking for a specific mathematician?"

"Yes. One with a prodigious memory, capable of memorizing cards in a deck if shown them."

Gabe sat back, his gaze connecting with mine. "Thurlow."

Willie swore softly. Alex rubbed a hand over the back of his neck.

"I believe it must be him," Francis said. "The description my friend gave did not match Mr. Thurlow, but he seems to have numerous henchmen working for him, so I assume it was one of those. I am unable to think of anyone else who would be interested in my proficiency with card counting, and the timing, coming so recently after that incident at the Degraves Hotel, also points to Thurlow."

I almost wished it was Jakes, or at least someone after Gabe. Thurlow was unpredictable and dangerous. He also wasn't looking for Francis to get to Gabe. He was looking for Francis to use his card-counting skill for himself. Where Gabe was capable of fighting off kidnappers, Francis was vulnerable.

Gabe lowered his head. "This is my fault. I should never have brought you along that night."

"It's true you introduced me to Thurlow, however you could not have known this would happen. I don't blame you."

Gabe's thumb tapped against his thigh. "You must move in with us at Park Street."

"Why?"

"You live alone, don't you?"

"Yes, but Thurlow doesn't know where. My former colleague told him nothing about me. He did not even admit to knowing me."

That was something, at least.

"Even so, I'd feel better if you move in with us."

Francis blinked at Gabe. "That would mean learning your household routine."

"You don't need to follow it. My household is very informal."

Francis didn't look convinced. Indeed, he looked more and more panicked as he considered the move. "You have staff. I would need to get to know them, and they me."

"My staff can also help protect you from Thurlow. Plus, all your needs will be taken care of. They'll cook for you and do your laundry."

"I like the way my laundrywoman does it."

"You can instruct Mrs. Bristow. She'll do it the same way."

Francis continued to blink rapidly. "I will need to learn the most efficient way to get to work."

Gabe's thumb-tapping intensified. "It's best if you take a short holiday from work until Thurlow's interest in you wanes."

The faster Gabe tapped his thumb, the more agitated Francis became. "But I won't have all of my belongings. They won't fit into one room."

I signaled to Gabe to remain silent and looked pointedly at his thumb. He tucked it beneath his fingers.

I sidled closer to Francis on the sofa, but didn't touch him. "I know moving to a new house is overwhelming. There's so much to do, and new things to learn. It can be very unsettling. I used to move a lot, right up until before the war. Not only did I have to learn a new street, but an entirely new city, too."

"You moved from city to city?" He stared at me, horrified. "You would have to get to know new neighbors, new teachers, and school chums. Not to mention learn new bus routes, and where all the important amenities are."

"Like the public library," I added.

"And museums. My word, Sylvia, that sounds truly horrid. I really shouldn't complain about moving in with a friend I know well, who lives not far away."

"You're just voicing how you feel, and there's nothing wrong with that. It will be difficult for you, at first, just like it was difficult for me when I moved cities." I leaned in, conspiratorial. "Do you want to know how I managed?"

"How?"

"Every time we moved, I set myself a task to accomplish each day. Just one. It might be learning the names of the surrounding streets. Or finding which bus I needed to catch to go to the library. It could be meeting a new neighbor, or making a new friend at school. Just one. All those little achievements added up, and by the end of the first week, I'd done seven things. The following week, I'd achieved fourteen. If I thought of them as a list of fourteen things, it was overwhelming. But achieving just one new thing was manageable."

"I see. Well... I can do one thing a day. I'll meet a new member of Gabe's staff on the first day."

"You already know Bristow and Murray," Gabe pointed out.

"So I do! Well then, I can meet the others in due course. First, I'll need to find out how to get to work. I can't take a holiday at the moment."

"I can drive you," Willie said. "That way you won't have to learn the bus route."

"Oh! All right. That would be nice. I do like Gabe's motorcar. Then if I don't need to do that, or learn new staff immediately, I will spend the first day arranging my room just so. Which way does it face? And how large is it?"

Gabe relaxed into the armchair. "It overlooks the rear courtyard. I can show it to you now, if you like. That way you'll know which things to collect from your flat."

"All right. Shall we go?"

"No time like the present." Gabe got to his feet and indicated

Francis should walk ahead of him. Once his back was turned, he mouthed "Thank you" to me.

I smiled, although I felt somewhat raw after speaking about my unsettled childhood with such candor. What must Gabe think of me having a fear of moving to a new house when he'd fought in the war? He'd experienced *real* danger and must have known fear like I couldn't imagine. Yet he'd not looked at me oddly, nor did he seem to find it necessary to treat me gingerly as he did Francis. Indeed, he *thanked* me for doing something he could not—calm an anxious man.

I realized I was staring at him when Willie's words snapped me back to the unpleasant reason for Francis's visit.

"You know what this means?"

Alex grunted. "I do. It means we're going to speak to Thurlow."

CHAPTER 12

That afternoon, Gabe, Willie and Alex went to the races. Since we didn't know where Thurlow lived, they hoped to find him at one of the tracks he regularly frequented.

Meanwhile, I had a visit from Huon Barratt. He was dressed as though he'd come directly from a sporting event, in a light-colored suit, striped shirt and straw boater, but closer inspection made me wonder if he'd been up all night. His eyes were blood-shot, his skin sallow, and his tie loose. The top button of his shirt was missing altogether. He threw himself onto the sofa in the first-floor reading nook, stretched out his legs, and yawned loudly.

Professor Nash had escorted him upstairs, although Huon knew the way. I suspected the professor was concerned Huon might not make it and either fall down the stairs or decide to take a nap on them. When Huon closed his eyes, the professor cast me a look of appeal, as if to ask what we should do.

I gestured that we should let him sleep.

An hour later, Huon woke up. He blinked sleepily as he looked around. "Good lord. How did I get here?"

I set aside the book I'd been trying to translate using a dictionary. "You don't remember?"

Huon pressed a finger and thumb into his eyelids. "Er, no? Wait, yes I do! I was at the cricket, then afterwards I went to a party. I can't recall where, but I do know they were fascinated by my ink magic."

"Oh?"

He fluttered his fingers in the air. "Making ink float is a simple trick to amuse simple minds. And drunks."

"I've always rather liked that trick." The professor's voice came from the mezzanine level above us where he'd been reading in the armchair by the window.

Huon glanced around, searching for the professor, his hands on the chair arms, ready to push himself up at any moment. It wasn't until I pointed up that he relaxed. "There you are, Prof. Thought I was hearing things again. The old ears haven't been the same since the war. All those bombs. Deafening. What were you saying?"

"Making ink float…it's very elegant."

"I suppose. And it does come in handy in a combat situation. I can fling it at my enemy's face and temporarily blind them."

"You did that in the war?" I asked.

"No. The enemy was too far away. I've used it in pubs to end brawls, which I seem to get into from time to time. Some say it's cheating, but I'm no great fighter and a fellow must use whatever weapons he possesses, don't you agree, Sylvia?"

"I think you should avoid fighting at all costs."

"I try. The problem is, trouble seems to find me. It's not my fault."

I tilted my head to the side and arched my brows.

"I suppose it is my fault *sometimes*," he muttered. "Let's get to business, shall we?"

"Business?" I glanced up at the professor, but he merely shrugged.

"Didn't I mention it when I arrived?" Huon asked.

"You didn't utter a word. You simply fell asleep in the chair."

"Did I?" He picked up his hat, which had fallen to the floor, and placed it on the lampshade. "Then let me rectify the situation. Take a seat and I'll tell you my proposal. But first, a drink! I'm parched."

"I'll make tea," the professor said.

Huon's face fell. "I was hoping for something a little stronger."

"Yes, of course. Coffee, it is."

Huon sighed. "Coffee is probably best. Business matters should be discussed sober."

"*Are* you sober?" I asked.

"I believe I may be almost, very nearly, half-way sober. That's close enough, in my book." He watched the professor descend the staircase from the mezzanine and disappear into the stacks. "Listen carefully and don't interrupt until I'm finished."

"Shouldn't we wait for the professor?"

He frowned. "Why?"

"Isn't your business proposal related to the library?"

"It's magic in nature. Specifically, it's your magic I need, Sylvia. I want to combine our magics and create invisible ink." He beamed at me, his eyes bright, although that might have been a result of the alcohol or whatever else he'd consumed the night before.

"You mean like Petra Conway's invisible graphite?"

"*Better*, because it's ink."

"I'm afraid I can't help you, Huon. I don't know any paper spells yet."

He blinked back at me. "Why not?"

"I haven't got around to asking the paper magicians I know." At Huon's confused expression, I added, "I have no need of a paper spell. I don't manufacture it."

His face didn't change. "Don't you want to meet others? They could be your family."

"Actually, we're currently investigating my mother's connection to a man who wanted to marry her. He could be my father. He went missing years ago, but we hope our investigation into his disappearance will give me some answers about my family."

"Seems a complicated way when you have a list of paper magician names to call on already."

I studied the book on the desk without really seeing the text. "You're putting it off," he said.

I turned the pages of the translation dictionary. "I'm simply following one lead at a time. Following a second thread would be confusing and overwhelming."

He came up behind me and picked up the book before slamming it closed. "You're afraid of what you'll uncover."

"And you're drunk."

"Quite possibly. I've been told I'm extremely insightful when I'm blotto." He returned the book to the desk and tapped the cover. "If you don't want to meet any other paper magicians yet, why not look up paper spells in the library? There must be a book on paper magic somewhere amongst all these words."

"The spell to make paper stronger is listed in a few."

"There you are then! We can begin."

"But I haven't learned the correct pronunciations of the words. If I get it wrong, I might cause mischief." I'd hate to send paper flying around the library, cutting people with its sharp edges instead of making it stronger.

"Mischief is my favorite kind of trouble. Ah, here's the professor with coffee. Prof, can you convince Sylvia to learn the paper-strengthening spell? I want to create invisible writing with my ink."

Professor Nash set the tray on the table and straightened. He adjusted his spectacles and peered at Huon. "Is this so you can compete with Petra Conway?"

"There will be no competition, because I will win. Ink is superior to graphite. Everyone knows that. Even her, I suspect." He picked up the coffee cup and waved it as he made a point, yet somehow didn't spill any. "I simply want to make invisible ink so I can make money. I'm a little short of ready at the moment, and a sideline like that could prove lucrative. I'd set up a little enterprise at my house and sell my services to anyone who wishes to write a secret letter or have one read to them. Imagine the husbands and wives who'll want to send their lovers little notes. I'll make a fortune, and my father will stop pestering me to return home and learn the ink-making business."

"So this has nothing to do with Petra?" I asked.

"Of course not. I've not spent a moment thinking about her since I last saw her." He sipped his coffee thoughtfully. "She's missing a trick by not advertising invisible graphite in her shop. She should have pamphlets on the counter. I was bored one evening so I drafted something, although I wasn't entirely happy with the wording. Not that it matters. I'm not giving it to her."

The professor and I shared a smile. It would seem Huon had spent more time thinking about Petra Conway than he was willing to admit.

* * *

THE FOLLOWING MORNING, I awoke early and headed directly to the library without waiting for breakfast. Gabe hadn't contacted me to tell me how they fared with Thurlow, and not knowing tied my stomach into knots. I needed to be near books or, more specifically, paper to soothe my nerves.

But not even the library gave me comfort. Professor Nash tried to reassure me that Gabe's silence meant he hadn't been able to find Thurlow at the races. He insisted I have a cup of coffee if I couldn't eat, but once that was consumed, I threw myself into work to distract myself.

It wasn't long before the professor was proved right, but it wasn't Gabe who confirmed that he hadn't been able to find Thurlow. It was the weaselly criminal himself.

Flanked by two burly guards, he sauntered into the library and stood in the foyer as if it were his local pub and he owned it.

I sprang to my feet, knocking the book I'd been reading off the front desk.

Thurlow bared crooked, crowded teeth with his slick smile. "No need to fret, Miss Ashe. Please, be seated."

I picked up the book from the floor and sat.

"Is Mr. Glass here?"

"Who?" I managed to keep my voice steady and my gaze direct, even though I felt quite scattered. Gabe had introduced himself to Thurlow using Willie's maiden name of Johnson. At no point had he given his real name. So how had Thurlow come to know it?

"He came looking for me yesterday, but I was unavailable," he went on. "Someone recognized him as Gabriel Glass, along with his distinctive-looking friends. I realized he was speaking about the fellow I knew as Johnson. My associate suggested I might find him here." He turned around on the spot, arms out to encompass the entire library. "This belongs to his family?"

"It's a public library. It belongs to everyone."

"How generous."

Thurlow perched on the edge of my desk and picked up the book I'd been studying. "This is gibberish."

"It's in Dutch."

The professor arrived in the foyer through the marble columns. "I heard a thud. Are you— Oh. I do apologize, I didn't realize we had company." He smiled and held out his hand.

Thurlow hesitated before shaking it. "Is Glass in?"

"No, but he'll probably be in shortly. May I help you?"

Thurlow stepped around him and entered the main section of the library. His men followed behind, silent and menacing with their scars and scowls.

The professor watched them go. "Well, he's rather a frosty fellow."

"That man is the reason Gabe's motorcar crashed."

The professor's jaw dropped.

"It's best if we leave him alone in there. I'll telephone Gabe."

According to Bristow, Gabe was already on his way to the library. He arrived five minutes later with Alex and Willie. Gabe's cheerful greeting quickly changed when I mentioned the name of our visitor.

With his hands bunched into fists at his sides, he strode through to the library, Alex and Willie on his heels. The professor and I followed.

Thurlow didn't rise from the chair in the reading nook. He simply crossed one leg over the other and steepled his fingers. "Ah, you've arrived. Please, take a seat."

Gabe stormed up to him, causing Thurlow's men to step forward, their thick features settled into warning scowls. Gabe ignored them. "If you want to speak to me, you come and see me. Don't come here."

"How can I when I don't know where you live? This was the only place I could find that was associated with you." Thurlow indicated the library with a sweep of his hand. "Anyway, *you* wanted to speak to *me*, Glass. Or is it Johnson? I'm confused."

Willie stabbed her finger in Thurlow's direction. "Stop playing games. You ran us off the road!"

Thurlow put his hands in the air. "That wasn't me."

She stabbed her finger at one guard then the other. "It was one of your fat-brained, turd-faced morons, acting under your instructions."

One of the guards cracked his knuckles.

Willie pulled back her jacket to reveal the gun tucked into her waistband.

The second guard matched her move to reveal his own gun.

Beside me, the professor gasped. "Oh my."

Thurlow flicked fluff off his trouser leg with the back of his hand. "My men saw how upset I was after Glass cheated at cards and decided to get revenge on my behalf. I never instructed them. Anyway, since then, my girl disappeared and I suspect one of you had something to do with that." His gaze settled on me, as piercing as a shard of ice. "Shall we call it even?"

"Leave Sylvia out of this," Gabe growled. "Your problem is with me, and me alone."

"I have no problem with you, Glass. As I said, we're even. Now, you wanted to speak to me. Why?"

"Two things. First of all, leave my friend Francis alone. You know I instructed him to cheat. He's innocent."

"Oh, I know. You shouldn't jump to conclusions about folk, Glass. I don't want to get revenge through him. I simply wanted to offer him employment."

"He's not interested."

"Forgive me for not taking your word for it. I'll ask him personally. It's a very good opportunity for someone on a professor's salary."

It was a relief that he still thought Francis worked at the university and didn't know he was now employed by Military Intelligence.

"Francis won't be interested in your kind of opportunity, Thurlow."

Thurlow merely shrugged. "And the second thing?"

"We're investigating the disappearance of an acquaintance of yours from the nineties, named Robin Reid."

Thurlow shook his head. "I don't know him."

"You did."

"That may be true, but the nineties were a long time ago. I can't be expected to remember every associate I once had."

"You loaned him money. I'm sure a man in your type of business remembers everyone he's ever dealt with."

"You expect me to rack my brain for you? In exchange for… what? An evening with Miss Ashe?"

Professor Nash gasped again.

Gabe stilled. "Step outside," he snarled.

Thurlow chuckled. "Good show, Glass. I'm sure she's impressed. But I won't fight you. Everyone will just get in the way and there are too many weapons. We don't want to attract attention over a little harmless fun." He bowed his head to me.

"My apologies for any offense, Miss Ashe, but you are quite pretty. I simply couldn't help myself. There, Glass. Am I forgiven?"

"I'll let it go this once," Gabe said. "But not a second time."

Thurlow's lips stretched with his twisted smile. "Isn't he so very masculine, Miss Ashe. No wonder women find him appealing. Some men, too, I'm sure. Now, is that all, Glass? May I leave without fearing that creature will accost me?" He nodded at Willie.

She sneered back.

"Did Robin Reid owe you money?" Gabe pressed. "In an attempt to get it back, did you rough him up too much and accidentally kill him?"

Thurlow waggled his finger at Gabe. "How quickly you jump to conclusions. It's a bad habit of yours."

Alex grunted. "It's not a big jump to make."

Thurlow regarded Alex for the first time. "The giant speaks."

Alex crossed his arms over his chest.

"If you ever want to make good money, come and work for me. I can always find a use for a strong, capable fellow like you."

"I don't do the dirty work of men like you."

"So you do his instead for much less?" Thurlow nodded at Gabe. "You're a fool."

"And yet I'm free to do as I please. I can reject work if I don't like what it entails." Alex met the gaze of one thug then the other. "Can either of you say that?"

The larger of the two cracked his knuckles again. Neither seemed fazed about doing the unsavory tasks their employer assigned them.

Thurlow chuckled. "What a rousing speech." He steepled his fingers again. "Back to the case of the missing fellow. You accused me of killing him. Does that mean you know he's dead?"

"If you're not going to help, why do you care?" Gabe asked.

"You've piqued my curiosity. Well?"

Gabe paused a moment before deciding there was no harm in telling him. "Another man named Foster enlisted using Robin Reid's name. We assume he did that because he knew Robin was dead and wouldn't be needing it, in a manner of speaking."

"What an intriguing mystery you have on your hands. If I were you, I'd follow up with Foster."

"He died in the war."

"But he may have left clues as to *why* he took Robin's name. The thing is, just now, you said you *assume* he used Robin's name because he knew Robin was already dead. I put it to you that your assumption is correct. And there's only one reason someone uses someone else's name. They're trying to hide their own identity from the authorities."

Willie scoffed. "We know that. We ain't stupid."

Thurlow parted his fingers before steepling them again. "So, if Foster is a criminal, you need to think like a criminal to learn more about him." He got to his feet and buttoned up his jacket. "I give you that information free of charge."

"You're all heart," Willie sneered.

Thurlow strode past her, only to stop and turn around. "Tell your mathematician friend about my offer. Let him make up his own mind. He can find me at the track."

"Leave Francis alone," Gabe growled. "Do not follow him. Do not try to speak to him. He's innocent."

Thurlow merely smiled that slick smile of his again and walked off.

Gabe swore under his breath.

What Thurlow said about criminal minds made sense, not just in our search for Foster, but also regarding Francis. I went to follow him, but Gabe caught my hand.

"Don't go near him," he whispered.

"Trust me, Gabe."

His lips settled into a thin line, then he let go. He followed me to the foyer where Thurlow was about to leave.

"Mr. Thurlow," I called after him. "Wait. You're right about thinking like a criminal. It might help us find Foster. But we *are* capable of thinking that way because we have imaginations. Francis cannot. When Gabe says Francis is innocent, he means he has a naive nature. He's honest to his core and thinking about doing something dishonest makes him anxious. It's not a choice; it's a quirk of his nature that he's entirely incapable of thinking dishonestly."

"Your point, Miss Ashe?"

"You can deny it all you want, but we know your enterprise skirts the law. Someone like Francis would not only be of no use to you because of his natural innocence, he might inadvertently give away your secrets to others. The police, for example. Ordering him or frightening him into silence won't work. That will only increase his anxiety and make him incapable of functioning at his full capacity. And what would be the use of him to you then? If you have a position to fill that requires a sharp mathematical mind, I suggest you look for someone else. Francis would not be the right man for you."

Thurlow regarded me with a curious frown for several heart-stopping moments. Then he took my hand and kissed it. Gabe advanced until Thurlow moved back, hands in the air.

"You should take a leaf out of Miss Ashe's book, Glass. Sometimes reason works better than threats to achieve your ends." He bowed to me. "Until we meet again, dear lady."

"We won't be meeting again," I told him firmly.

He simply smiled and left.

Willie and Alex decided to escort Thurlow and his men to the end of the lane. Once they were gone, my heart began to race. I pressed a hand to the desk to steady myself. I thought I was being discreet, but Gabe noticed. He pulled the chair out and suggested I sit.

"Professor, some tea for Sylvia, please."

"Yes, of course. And something to eat. She missed breakfast."

Gabe crouched before me. "Why didn't you eat breakfast?"

I watched the professor leave because looking at Gabe

suddenly seemed like a very risky thing to do. Those warm eyes of his had a way of making me lose myself and all sense of propriety. They made me want to kiss him. "I was worried when you didn't tell me how you went yesterday at the racetrack." It sounded so foolish, like I was a silly girl fretting over nothing. "I overreacted. I should have known everything was all right when I didn't hear."

He clasped my hand in his, tucking his fingers under mine. "I would have worried, too, if the positions were reversed. Thurlow is not someone to be taken lightly. I should have telephoned, I'm sorry."

I squeezed his fingers and finally leveled my gaze with his. His eyes flared, as if he were taken aback by something. Perhaps he suddenly felt hot, too, and his heart beat out a wild, erratic rhythm like mine.

"Sylvia." My name was a mere whisper, caressing my lips. He leaned in, just a little, not even an inch, and lowered his gaze to my mouth.

Kiss me.

CHAPTER 13

K iss me.
   I may have only said it in my head, but it was as if Gabe heard it…and did the exact opposite.

He stood suddenly and dragged his hand through his hair. "I, ah, that was… I shouldn't have."

I didn't need to ask why. He was still reeling from his long engagement to Ivy. He was still trying to find himself, and learn about the man he'd become since the war. He didn't want an entanglement to complicate things.

I knew all of that, but I said nothing. We didn't get the opportunity to talk anyway, because Willie and Alex returned, although I suspected neither of us would have welcomed conversation. A lifetime of avoiding difficult discussions was a hard habit for me to break. In Gabe's case, I suspected he simply felt too raw.

Willie slammed the door shut, making my taut nerves jump. "That pigswill reckons he's so clever and so superior, but he wouldn't have lasted a day in Broken Creek when Grandpa Johnson was alive. He'd be running scared, tail between his legs, begging for protection."

Alex rolled his eyes. "Are we about to get another 'American history according to Willie' lesson? Because if we are, can it wait until I'm not here?"

"I should clip you over the ear for being disrespectful."

"You would if you could reach, you mean."

"Any more sass from you and I'll tell every girl you ever talked to that you're in love with her and want to settle down."

That shut Alex up.

Willie turned to me and clapped me on the shoulder. "Real quick thinking telling Thurlow that Francis would make a hopeless criminal. It ain't a lie either, that's what makes it so smart. Why didn't you mention it, Gabe? You usually think of ways to divert someone's attention when it ain't wanted."

Gabe dragged his hand through his hair again, messing it up even more. I found it rather endearing considering he was usually so polished. "I wasn't as coolheaded as Sylvia in the moment. Thurlow had me riled. He seems to know how to get to me."

"Then stop letting him get to you." She spotted the professor coming down the stairs carrying a tray laden with cups, a teapot and a plate of toast. She rubbed her hands together. "A second breakfast! You're a good man, Prof. One of my favorite men, in fact. I put you ahead of Alex, for sure."

Alex gave her a withering look.

The professor blinked at the tray in his hands. "Oh dear. Now I feel terrible. This is for Sylvia. She missed breakfast and I'm worried she might faint."

Willie pouted.

"I can't eat it all," I told her. "Have a slice of toast."

She grabbed one and took a large bite quickly, as if she were afraid I'd change my mind. She still had a mouthful of toast when she thanked me. "You're also above Alex on my list of favorite people."

"What happens if I fall off your list altogether?" Alex asked.

"Ask your parents. They fell off it about seventeen years ago."

"What happened seventeen years ago?"

"Lulu was born and they said they weren't having any more children."

"So?"

"So they had four children and didn't name a single one after me. And Willie could be a girl or boy's name. I didn't care which."

As we headed back into the reading nook for tea and toast, Alex drew alongside Gabe. "Did you know she kept a list of her favorite people?"

"Sorry? I wasn't really listening. My mind was elsewhere."

Alex smirked. "I noticed you were in the middle of something when we returned." He glanced over his shoulder and, seeing me close enough to hear, swallowed heavily.

"I was thinking about Thurlow's comment," Gabe said. "We should think like criminals in order to find out more about Foster."

"It was sound advice, although I hate admitting it. Have you thought of a way to follow it?"

"I think I know what to do next."

Willie, walking in front of them, had been listening, too. "Does it involve me using my Colt?"

"No."

"Burglary? Blackmail? Arson? Kidnap?"

"None of those."

She grunted. "Back in Broken Creek..."

Alex groaned as she rattled off another story from her youth.

* * *

GABE SPENT the afternoon at the library's front desk placing telephone calls to Liverpool and waiting for responses. One of the distinguishing features that Bill Foster's old army captain, Dr. Collier, had pointed out was his accent, and Dr. McGowan at Rosebank Gardens had also known who we meant when we mentioned Foster's accent. He must have spent a significant amount of time in Liverpool.

According to that city's General Registry Office, there were four men named William or Bill Foster who were born there and were the right age to be our Bill Foster. There was a chance that our man was born elsewhere and moved to Liverpool at a young age, so Gabe then followed up with the electoral office. The person on the other end didn't question Gabe when he said he worked for Scotland Yard, and was eager to assist. He even opened his telephone directory and rattled off numbers corresponding to the relevant Fosters. Two didn't have telephones.

Gabe put calls in to each number and repeated his same question: "Has a man named Bill Foster with a birthmark on his left cheek ever lived at this address?"

Each time, the answer was no.

"They could be lying," I said when Gabe joined me in the upstairs reading nook. I'd moved the book I was trying to translate to the desk there, enjoying the peace and quiet after Alex and Willie left. Neither had been interested in waiting once they realized how long Gabe could be.

"That's possible, although I sensed they were telling the truth."

"If the Bill Foster we're searching for isn't from Liverpool, did he put on a false accent?"

"He would have needed to keep it up constantly, for years." Gabe shook his head. "I think it's more likely that he *is* from Liverpool, but changed his name when he left. If he's running away, it makes sense."

It did make sense, particularly when he'd had no qualms using Robin Reid's name when he needed it. "So we're not looking for Bill Foster, after all." I sighed. "We'll never find him without the correct name."

"Not necessarily. As Thurlow suggested, if he was running away, there's a good chance it was because he was wanted by the police. I'll telephone the Liverpool constabulary now. But first, I should warn Cyclops that I might need to mention him. No police department will give out important information without checking I am who I say I am."

It was almost an hour before he reappeared again. "After going around in circles for a while, one of the Liverpool detectives agreed to search through their archives for reports of persons matching Foster's description who went missing around 1893."

"That's good news."

"The bad news is, it will take him a day or two."

"There's no urgency."

He blew out an exasperated breath. "I need something to do in the meantime. Can I help out around the library?" He picked up the book I was attempting to translate. "Dutch?"

"Yes."

He returned the book to the desk. "I can't speak Dutch. Do you have anything in French? I could translate it reasonably accurately, although you'd need someone to check it over when I'm finished. I know a little Latin, although it's quite rusty and mostly limited to legal terms."

"You studied law?"

"I took some classes at university, but don't ask me to defend you in court if you're ever arrested."

I laughed. "I'm afraid there isn't much for you to do here." I could have put him to work on a French translation, but I suspected he needed to do something that required physical activity, not sitting at a desk. "Why not go for a drive? Or take the train to Brighton and stay overnight. I'm sure Alex wouldn't mind a short jaunt to the seaside. Not Willie, though. I can't imagine her being separated from her gun long enough to go for a swim."

He chuckled. "Willie at the seaside would be a painful experience for the rest of us. You and Daisy could come. It might even be the beginning of something between Daisy and Alex."

"It didn't work out so well in Ipswich. Besides, I shouldn't go."

He rubbed a hand over his jaw, avoiding my gaze. "Right. Of course. We really shouldn't. It's too…soon."

Were we talking about the same thing? "I have to work. I've taken enough time off for this investigation already."

"Oh. Uh…yes. I suppose you're right." He cleared his throat and stood. "I'll find something to do while we wait for the Liverpool police to respond." He offered me an awkward smile and a little wave. "Well, goodbye for now."

"Goodbye, Gabe."

He got as far as the staircase and suddenly turned around, catching me staring at him. I hastily gathered up the Dutch book and pretended to study it.

"Join us for dinner tonight. You and the professor." He paused. "Francis would like to see you."

"I wouldn't want to disappoint him when he's feeling somewhat vulnerable. Thank you, I accept and I'll check with the professor to see if he's free. But are you sure Mrs. Ling won't object? It's rather short notice."

"She loves cooking for guests, but I'll see that she has everything she needs in time." He twirled his hat with his fingers then flipped it onto his head, looking smug when it landed perfectly.

"Very flash," I said, grinning and shaking my head.

His good mood was infectious, and I missed his presence the moment he disappeared from sight. I threw myself into work for the remainder of the day. Like Gabe, I needed a distraction. I wondered if he needed a distraction for the same reason as I did.

* * *

GABE WAS STILL in a buoyant mood when Professor Nash and I arrived for dinner. We joined Gabe, Francis, Alex and Willie in the drawing room for cocktails, and I asked Francis how he'd settled in.

He listed a series of tasks he'd completed so far, from putting his clothing in the wardrobe to learning the route to work. He was determined that Willie shouldn't drive him every day.

"It may not be for long," he said. "Gabe told me that Thurlow merely wants to employ me, not kill me. He says you explained to Thurlow that I have no interest in working for a criminal, which is true. Thank you for that, Sylvia. Anyway, Gabe suggested I stay here until he's absolutely sure Thurlow will leave me alone."

"Is that all right?" I asked, watching him closely.

"I believe it will be. I enjoy the company, although it can be tiring constantly having conversations with different people and learning the new routines. Sometimes there is no routine, apparently. The butler tells me mealtimes vary depending on what everyone is doing."

"And you prefer to have your meals at the same time every day?"

"How did you know?"

I smiled. "It was a guess."

Despite his anxiety, Francis seemed to enjoy himself at dinner. He particularly liked Mrs. Ling's food, which he'd tasted before when dining with Gabe. He contributed to conversations that ranged across a variety of topics. He got along particularly well with Professor Nash. After dessert, we adjourned back to the drawing room for a glass of port before leaving. Francis wanted to hear the professor's stories about traveling to exotic lands and the professor was more than happy to regale him.

"You really must write these down," Francis urged him. "I would very much like to read about the places you went to. They sound fascinating, and I know I'd never get to see them in person."

"You might," the professor said. "I thought I'd never travel either, but Oscar was the perfect companion for me. He took care of all the little difficulties that crop up when overseas." He laughed softly. "Even when he got the translations wrong, he managed to extricate us from some sticky situations."

Francis's eyes widened. "Were there many sticky situations?"

"Several. They became a regular occurrence." The professor pushed his glasses up his nose. "I can't begin to tell you how many times we almost missed a connecting train, or got lost, or lost our luggage. And then there were the times we nearly died. But we almost always managed to bring home something to add to the library's collection, and we had adventures along the way, too. Not that I saw them as adventures at the time. It was only after each journey was complete that I could reminisce fondly about it."

"You simply must write them down, Nash. I love a good adventure story."

"I have been working on my memoir, as it happens. I might see if a publisher is interested."

Gabe came up beside me and offered to top up my glass. I declined. I'd had enough wine over dinner already, and another port would send me to sleep.

He sat on a chair nearby. "I thought of something to do tomorrow. We should call at Bill Foster's address again, but this time I don't want to speak to the landlady. I want to question the neighbors."

"You think she lied to us?"

"Perhaps. I can't put my finger on what it was, except to say that her answers seemed too smooth and practiced."

I didn't know why she'd lie, given that Bill Foster was dead, but it was as good an idea as any. "What happened to the seaside?"

"Why take a holiday with Alex when I can investigate?"

Had he cut himself off? Had he been about to say, 'investigate with you?' It was something I would ponder for the rest of the evening.

* * *

GABE COLLECTED me from the library in the middle of the morning and escorted me along Crooked Lane to the Vauxhall Prince Henry, parked near the lane's entrance. I greeted Alex as I slid onto the backseat. "No Willie today?"

"She went out last night after you left and hasn't come home yet. She probably fell asleep in someone's bed." We both watched Gabe as he cranked the engine. Once the motor rumbled to life, Alex turned to me with a grin. "Unless she got arrested again."

"If she isn't doing any breaking and entering for our investigation, what would she get arrested for?"

"Drunkenness, disorderly conduct, affray, murder, prostitution—"

"Prostitution!"

"That one was a mistake and the police let her go."

"And the murder?"

"Of one of her husbands. It was downgraded to manslaughter, then dismissed altogether."

Good heavens.

When we arrived at Bill Foster's address we sat in the motorcar outside the row of featureless terraces, trying to catch glimpses through the windows of Mrs. O'Brien. The only person we saw, however, was a man. That didn't mean she wasn't near the back of the house, in the kitchen, perhaps.

Gabe and I were about to knock on the doors of the neighbors' houses when Mrs. O'Brien's door opened and she stepped out, basket over her arm. She didn't see us, and went on her way up the street, her short but determined steps taking her quickly around the bend and out of sight.

"Forget the neighbors," Gabe said as he got out of the motorcar. "I have a better idea."

Alex joined us and knocked on Mrs. O'Brien's door. Beside me, Gabe removed a notepad and pencil from his jacket pocket. "Play along," he said.

A middle-aged man wearing a neatly pressed pinstripe suit,

his gray hair parted perfectly down the middle, greeted us genially enough but didn't invite us inside. "If this is about a charitable donation, I've already given to the Red Cross this week."

"This isn't about a donation." Gabe introduced us using false names. "We're conducting research into the changing nature of dwellings and their occupants for the local council. Since the war ended, there has been a great deal of movement amongst the population. Young folk no longer live at home, others move in together, that sort of thing. We are conducting a study of the changes over the years, and this address was randomly selected."

"How intriguing. Come in, come in."

He led the way to a small parlor with just enough seats for all of us. It was furnished in a turn-of-century style, with thick-legged chairs and too many side tables, all of which were covered in knickknacks. Mrs. O'Brien seemed to have a liking for little creatures carved from wood.

"How can I help?" the lodger asked Gabe.

"Have you lived here long, Mr....?"

"Tovey. I've boarded here a number of years. It'll be thirteen this winter, I believe."

That was far longer than we'd expected. We'd assumed Mrs. O'Brien's current lodger had moved in after Bill Foster vacated the room when he joined the army in November 1914, six years ago. But if Mr. Tovey had been here thirteen years, did that mean Foster was no longer living here at the time he enlisted? It also probably meant Mrs. O'Brien hadn't lied, after all, and really couldn't remember her former lodger if he had stopped leasing the room that long ago.

"I never left," Mr. Tovey went on. "There was no need. They were good to me when I moved in, and Mrs. O'Brien has remained an excellent landlady, even after she lost her husband in the war."

Gabe frowned. "Our records say Mr. O'Brien died well before

the war. It was our understanding they hadn't been married long before she became a widow."

Mr. Tovey leaned forward and lowered his voice. "The man I'm referring to wasn't actually her husband. He was her former lodger. He'd boarded here a while before moving into her room. They then re-leased the spare room to me."

"And you say he enlisted and died in the war?"

"I assume he died, although she never received a letter, unlike other war widows. His letters stopped suddenly, just like that." He clicked his fingers. "I suspect she knew he wouldn't be coming home, however. She was terribly upset for a long time, the poor thing. They were very much in love. He was a good man. Kind, to me and to her."

"What did he look like?" Gabe asked.

"About my age, but fit as a fiddle." He sucked in his stomach. "Tall, rather ordinary to look at. He had a birthmark on his face."

"Was he a local man?"

"I don't think so. He had a strong accent. Something northern." He frowned. "I'm sorry, how is this relevant to your study?"

"It's giving us a fuller picture of the dwelling and its occupants from before the war for a baseline."

"I see."

We heard the front door open, and my heart somersaulted. The only person who'd open it would be the landlady.

"I forgot my purse," she called out.

"In here, Mrs. O," Mr. Tovey called back. "We have visitors."

It was too late to escape through a back door. Alex muttered something under his breath, perhaps cursing himself for not waiting outside to keep watch.

I steeled myself and tried to think of a logical excuse for our lies. But my mind went blank. We'd have to admit everything. She might notify the police. At the very least, she'd continue to deny ever knowing Bill Foster.

Unless we could convince her there was no point anymore.

Mrs. O'Brien peered around the door. She gasped. "You were here before! Mr. Glass, isn't it? And Miss Ashe?"

Mr. Tovey shook his head. "No, you've got it wrong, Mrs. O. They're with the council."

"They are not. They were poking around here before, asking questions about someone I'd never heard of. A man named Bill Foster." She pointed at Mr. Tovey. "If they ask you about that name, you've never heard it. *Have you?*" The glare she gave him spoke the threat she couldn't voice.

Mr. Tovey's eyes widened. He stared at her a moment then quickly shook his head. "No," he squeaked. "That's not a name that's familiar to me. I know lots of Bills and Williams, but no Bill Fosters."

"Yes, you do," Gabe said mildly. "He was the lodger before you." He turned to Mrs. O'Brien. "You lied to us the other day. Bill Foster did live here for many years. He was your husband in every way except in the eyes of the law. Why did you lie, Mrs. O'Brien? What are you hiding?"

She thrust her chin forward and her nose in the air. "I am *not* lying."

"He's dead. You no longer have to protect him. Please, tell us about the man you knew as Bill Foster."

She sniffed. "If you think I knew him, prove it."

Gabe pressed his lips together and blew out an exasperated breath. He was frustrated beyond measure.

I, however, had realized something. "I can prove it," I said. "I can prove you knew him and that he cared for you."

169

CHAPTER 14

The small wooden bird felt warm from the sun. Now that I was up close, I could see how beautifully it was carved. The smooth head, cocked to the side as if listening for predators, invited stroking. The detail on the feathered back and wings was so fine, it must have been carved by a master craftsman. If a wood magician made the bird and the other creatures on display, it would only take a moving spell to give them the appearance of life.

I balanced the bird on my palm. "The man we know as Bill Foster made this, didn't he?"

Mrs. O'Brien snatched it up and returned it to the side table, carefully positioning it just so amongst the other animals. "I don't know what you mean."

Her lodger, Mr. Tovey, sat silently, studying his fingernails. He wouldn't want to speak out of turn and risk offending his landlady.

"Bill Foster carved a beautiful box when he was on the battlefield," I said. "We saw it, and it was lovely."

Her head snapped up. "Where? Where did you see it?" Her hunger for information about her lover overrode her caution. She was desperate for knowledge of him, even if it confirmed her worst fears.

"It was given to Mr. and Mrs. Reid by the War Office, along with Bill's other belongings. They were told they were their son's things, but of course they weren't. No one knew the man who enlisted as Robin Reid was in fact Bill Foster. Not even Robin's parents. The carved box meant nothing to them, it was just a box. But it would have been a treasured keepsake for Bill's loved one because they would have known he'd made it with his own hands while he waited in the trenches."

Mrs. O'Brien withdrew a handkerchief from her sleeve and dabbed at the corner of her eye. Then suddenly, as if she could no longer hold it in, she began to sob.

I put my arm around her and steered her to a chair. I held her as she cried the tears she'd not dared to shed while she waited for Bill to come home. She'd never received official word of his death, so she'd lived in hope, like so many war widows whose husbands were listed as missing. Without proof, she could tell herself he was recovering in a hospital somewhere, unable to write to her, but the carved box sent to the Reid family was the proof that he'd died in battle.

Her reaction was also the proof Gabe and I needed that she not only knew Bill Foster, but also knew he'd enlisted under a different name.

When her tears subsided, she finally admitted that Bill Foster had been her lodger when he moved to London in 1893. "We fell in love. I'd been a widow only a year, but I knew immediately that Bill was special. He was the kindest man you'd ever hope to meet. A true gentle giant. That's why he signed up as a stretcher-bearer. He didn't want to fight. He didn't want to kill anyone. He just wanted to help the injured boys; help them get home. He wasn't a young man when he enlisted, but he was strong and with his experience as an orderly, he felt it was his duty. That's the sort of man he was. Loyal, capable, kindhearted." She pressed the handkerchief to her eyes again as fresh tears welled.

"Do you know why he moved to London?" I asked. Gabe

seemed to be leaving the questioning to me. Perhaps he thought a woman's touch was required now.

Mrs. O'Brien drew in a deep, shuddery breath. "He wanted a change."

"From his life in Liverpool? What happened there? What prompted his move?"

"I told you. He wanted a change."

I glanced at Gabe, hoping he'd weigh in, but he remained silent.

"Was he in trouble with the Liverpool police?" I pressed.

"He wouldn't hurt a fly, my Bill. People would be afraid of him because of his size, but once they got to know him, they saw how sweet he could be. He was a gentle man and I won't hear another word said against him."

She was getting angry, so I decided to change tactic. "Why did you never marry? Was it because Bill Foster wasn't his real name, so legally you couldn't?"

She teased the damp handkerchief between her fingers, but her lips were set in a firm line.

"Was he running away? Is that why he had to change his name?"

"It's time you left. I have to do the shopping."

Gabe hitched his trouser legs and crouched before her. "He's gone, Mrs. O'Brien. Telling the truth now can't hurt him."

She sniffed and jutted her chin at the door. "Mr. Tovey, if you wouldn't mind seeing these people out."

Mr. Tovey kept Gabe and Alex in his sights as he skirted around us, keeping his distance. He hurriedly opened the front door and then slammed it closed behind us.

"Why won't she talk?" Alex asked as he trotted down the front steps. "She can't get Foster into trouble now."

"Perhaps she still has hope that he's alive," I said.

"Or she's worried about tarnishing his memory," Gabe added. "If he's wanted for a crime in Liverpool, the police may retroactively attribute guilt to him. If it made the newspapers, it might upset family he left behind."

Alex retrieved the crank handle from the motorcar. "Did you notice she kept making the same point, over and over, that he was gentle and kind? It makes me more confident than ever that he's wanted for a crime, and a violent one at that."

"If that's true, then the Liverpool police should be able to help us."

"We just have to wait," I said.

I expected Gabe to sigh in frustration and start tapping his thumb impatiently on the steering wheel, but when Alex slipped into the passenger seat after cranking the engine, Gabe had a determined look about him. Instead of heading south to take me back to the library, he drove west, in the direction of Rosebank Gardens.

"I want to return to the hospital," he said. "According to Bernard Reid, Robin's stint there changed him. Dr. McGowan may not remember Robin, but he would remember the treatments meted out to the artless patients."

"He won't admit anything that will harm his reputation or that of the hospital," Alex said. "But I agree. It's worth trying. We haven't got any other leads."

"Have you two forgotten what happened the last time we were there?" I asked. "We won't be allowed through the front gate, let alone be able to speak to Dr. McGowan."

Gabe flashed a grin. "Leave that to me."

* * *

THE GUARD at the gate posed no problem once Gabe passed him a few pound notes. Patients on the lawn stared blankly into the distance, not even heeding our presence. There was none of the distress of last time, no shouting or wailing. The nurses and orderlies, however, took more interest but didn't approach. Only one man did—Stanley Greville. He smoked a cigarette with an orderly near one of the rose beds. When he spotted us, Stanley spoke to the orderly then crossed the lawn to greet us.

"What are you doing here?" Gabe asked, extending his hand.

Stanley shook it and nodded at Alex and me. "Visiting a friend I met when I was a patient. What are you doing here? I heard a rumor you're no longer welcome." He looked back at his friend, still standing by the roses, watching us.

"We're not very popular with management," Gabe conceded with a crooked smile. "But we need to speak to McGowan again. It remains to be seen whether he'll talk to us, however. Are you coming in?"

Stanley's gaze flicked to the entrance and away again. "I'd rather not." The fingers that placed the cigarette between his lips trembled. "I should go."

"Can I ask you something about your time here?"

"Such as?"

"I want to know more about the treatments and cures they used." Gabe cast subtle looks at Alex then me, and we both moved away, but not before we heard Stanley apologize then refuse.

Gabe joined us and we entered the hospital.

The nurse on duty at the front desk hadn't been warned about us and smiled warmly. She asked an orderly who was passing by to take us up to Dr. McGowan's office. We waited a few minutes until he was ready to see us, then marched inside and closed the door before he had a chance to call for the orderly to return and escort us off the premises.

"We just have a few more questions," Gabe told him. "If you don't answer, you'll look guilty."

Dr. McGowan stood and buttoned up his white coat. "I have nothing to hide, but I take offence to being railroaded. I'm also still furious that you broke in here the other night. We have vulnerable men in our care, Glass. Their mental state is delicate. Your presence in the middle of the night could have caused a major setback."

"We weren't going near the wards. If anything, the commotion you caused when you threw us out was more detrimental to the patients than us quietly looking through the records. Just like it will be if you throw us out now, in front of all the patients currently enjoying the sunshine outside. If I were you, I wouldn't want to draw attention and upset anyone."

Dr. McGowan's nostrils flared. "State your piece then leave. I'm busy." To drive home the point, he picked up a clipboard and tucked it under his arm.

"You told us that you remember the orderly named Bill Foster."

"And?"

"That wasn't his real name."

Dr. McGowan blinked. "That's news to me, but what does it matter now if he lied when he applied for work?"

"He was running away, hiding from someone. He changed his name to Bill Foster, then changed it again to Robin Reid when he enlisted. He chose Robin's name because Bill Foster wasn't real, and he needed a name that was. He needed the name to be associated with a real address and a real date of birth, all of which he knew from Robin Reid's hospital admission records."

"I didn't employ him, Mr. Glass. I wasn't involved in administration back then and the people who were are no longer here. So, what is your point?"

"My point is, Bill Foster knew Robin's name was available when he enlisted in 1914. As in, Robin was dead. Considering the Reids and the police all assumed he was simply missing, the question is, how did Bill Foster know otherwise?"

"I don't know and I don't care. Is that all?"

"Bernard Reid informed us that his son was sent here to be cured of his artlessness. This hospital claimed it could turn the artless children of magician parents into magicians."

"That's absurd. No doctor can *create* a magician."

"Everyone knows that now, but in the nineties, magic was

175

still very much an unknown art. It's feasible that doctors thought they could *cure* the artless if magic was in their bloodline."

Dr. McGowan's jaw worked but he otherwise didn't move. He stared back at Gabe, defiant.

"Patients were subjected to treatments that left them worse off than when they were admitted. The treatments didn't work. All it did was destroy their spirit. When they left here, they were mere shadows of their former selves. They've been likened to the shell-shocked patients you have in your care now, in fact."

"You don't know what you're talking about."

"The so-called cures must have been horrific, perhaps even dangerous. Do you still employ those cures in the treatments of your current patients?"

Alex and I both stared at Gabe.

Dr. McGowan emerged from behind the desk and charged past Gabe, only to be blocked by Alex. "Move aside."

Alex settled his feet apart and crossed his arms.

Dr. McGowan turned back to Gabe, his chest rising and falling with his seething breaths. "You want to hear the truth, Glass? The truth is that parents did admit their children back then, and adults admitted themselves, too. They wanted to become magicians. They were desperate to draw the magic out. The medical profession thought it lay dormant with those artless whose parents were magicians. We know now that magic doesn't work that way, but everyone was still learning back then. We doctors don't always get it right. We're not miracle workers. We're just trying to help. There was nothing wrong with what we did."

"There is if patients were harmed and you didn't stop."

"We used treatments that were common practice at the time in other mental institutions."

"And now?"

Dr. McGowan stiffened. "As you can see, we no longer treat the artless children of magicians. We only treat returned soldiers.

Soldiers who were fine before the war and have come back damaged. Their problems are different."

"Do you still use those treatments?" Gabe pressed.

"We use the same methods as other institutions, Mr. Glass. Now, tell your man to move. I have work to do."

"Will you look up Robin Reid's records for us?"

Dr. McGowan's only answer was to glare at Alex. Alex stepped aside and Dr. McGowan marched out. "Do I need to summon the orderlies and have you thrown out in front of everyone?"

We made it easy for him and left. We walked along the corridor behind a nurse hurrying away. I recognized her as the same one who'd been there the night we were caught in the records room. Had she been listening at the office door?

Outside, the orderly who Stanley had been talking to was no longer on the lawn. The patients who were still there sat on chairs, staring into the distance. They did not play checkers with the nurses and didn't read or chat to one another. They didn't cry out at the sound of the engine. In fact, they didn't look around at all. Perhaps these men were in a worse way than the patients we'd seen the other day.

Alex had another theory. "Do you think they've been given something to keep them calm?"

Neither Gabe nor I had an answer, but both theories were troubling.

* * *

THE YOUNG MAN loitering at the entrance to Crooked Lane stopped inspecting his fingernails and straightened upon our arrival. "Are you Gabriel Glass?"

Alex spoke up before Gabe could answer. "Who's asking?"

"Leonard Flagg from *The Weekly Mail*." He removed a notebook and pencil from his jacket pocket. "Mr. Glass, what do you have to say about—?"

Alex grabbed his lapels and forced him out of the way.

"Oi!" The journalist batted Alex's arm until he let go. "I could have you arrested for assault!"

"Likewise."

"But I didn't assault anyone."

"Who would be believed? Me, a former police officer with a decorated military career or you, a gutter-dwelling weasel?"

"I'll have you know that I served, too."

Alex indicated that I should enter Crooked Lane ahead of him,

Gabe didn't follow us. He addressed Flagg. "Why are you here?"

Leonard Flagg adjusted his tie, but instead of fixing it, he made it worse. "Everyone knows the Glass Library belongs to your family and I thought I'd find you here."

Gabe merely sighed at the common mistake instead of correcting it. "And why do you want to speak to me?"

Leonard Flagg eyed Gabe carefully, as if he suspected he was being led into a trap. "I want to know what your response is to the latest reports that you can extend the magic of other magicians."

"The journalist who wrote the story you're referring to was given false information."

"By whom?"

"It doesn't matter. The point is, I'm artless." The lie came out smoothly, perhaps because he'd has so much practice. "I have no magical ability whatsoever. Don't you think I would have taken advantage if I could?" Gabe laughed softly. "I assure you, I'd like the benefits these magician manufacturers are offering me in exchange for extending their magic, but unfortunately I can't do it. I know this is a good story, which is why the journalist printed it without checking his facts, but it's simply not true." He stepped through to Crooked Lane and together we walked to the library.

Leonard Flagg dogged our steps. "Are you saying someone deliberately fed false information to the press?"

Alex suddenly stopped and turned on the journalist. "It's time you left." He settled his feet apart and nodded at the lane's exit. "Understood?"

Leonard Flagg swallowed heavily. "Another time, perhaps."

Movement at the end of the lane caught Alex's attention. "You have a visitor, Gabe."

Stanley Greville remained at a distance, one arm crossed over his stomach as if he had an ache. It was a common stance of his, however, and I knew it didn't mean he felt unwell. He stepped forward, only to step back again when the journalist looked his way.

"Your friend looks sick," Flagg said.

"Didn't I just tell you to leave?" Alex snapped.

Flagg returned the notebook and pencil to his jacket pocket and pulled out a business card. "If you ever want to give me a quote, you can find me here."

"He already gave you a quote."

The journalist handed the card to Gabe. "If you want the rumors to end, you should give your version of the story. I'll print the truth."

"I'm artless. You can print that." Gabe signaled to Stanley that he should join us in the library.

Stanley walked toward us, his head bowed.

Inside the library, Alex peered through the window and watched Leonard Flagg walk away. "That bloody Hobson woman. She started this fresh wave of interest with her ridiculous theory."

"It's not entirely ridiculous given my mother was once rumored to be able to extend the magic of others." Gabe nodded a greeting to Professor Nash as he came down the stairs.

"I thought I heard voices," the professor said. "Mr. Greville, what a pleasant surprise. Can I get you some tea? I was just about to make a pot."

Stanley politely refused and the professor returned upstairs. Gabe invited Stanley through to the reading nook, but he insisted he couldn't stay.

"I wanted to speak to you about the hospital, Gabe."

"Is this regarding your visit to Rosebank Gardens this morning?"

Stanley brushed his cheek with trembling fingers and nodded. "Mind if I smoke?"

"I'm sorry," I said, "but this is a smoke-free library. Professor Nash believes it might damage the texts, some of which are old and very delicate."

He put away the tin of cigarettes he'd retrieved from his jacket pocket. "I wanted to explain why I was at Rosebank."

"You told us you were calling on an old friend," Alex said. "Is that not true?"

Stanley's fingers fluttered over his cheek again as if brushing off a crumb. "I had another reason for going. I wasn't sure I wanted to mention it at first, but I think you should know. It might help your investigation." Another flick of fingers over his cheek. The nervous habit was worse than usual. "When I was a patient there, I saw some...things. Things that the doctors did to the other patients in an attempt to cure them. They didn't subject me to these cures," he added quickly. "They reserved them for the men suffering the worst cases of shell shock, the ones who couldn't get out of bed or speak a single coherent word. Those are the men they subjected to their so-called cures."

"What precisely did you see?" Gabe asked.

"Ice-cold baths in the middle of winter." He folded his arms over himself and shivered. "Electric shock therapies where they'd wire the men up to a machine and blast electricity through their bodies."

"The therapies didn't work?" Gabe asked.

Stanley passed a hand over his face. "It only made the patients worse. But that didn't stop the doctors. They kept trying and trying, every day subjecting those poor souls to another horrific treatment. You know I was studying medicine, Gabe. I was taught that an experiment should be abandoned if there's no evidence of success. From what I could see, not a single former soldier was cured after one session, let alone multiple sessions."

"Did any die?"

"Not that I am aware." He removed the tin of cigarettes from his pocket but didn't open it. "McGowan should be stopped. You should look into his background and see if he's a proper medical professional."

"You think he's a fraud?"

Stanley shrugged one shoulder. "It's worth checking. The General Medical Council will know." He shuffled toward the door, opening the cigarette case as he went. "That's all. I should go."

Alex held the door open for him. "I don't understand why you needed to visit the hospital before telling us this."

Gabe narrowed his gaze at his friend, but didn't tell him not to pry.

Stanley glanced at Gabe before addressing Alex. "The orderly you saw me speaking to was one of the ones who encouraged me to leave the hospital a few months ago. He didn't think my condition was as bad as the other patients there, and he suggested I would cope better on the outside than in a hospital where the men were severely damaged. He's a friend, of sorts, and I trust him. I wanted his thoughts about McGowan before I spoke to you. I worried I might be causing trouble by telling you all this. He assured me I wasn't imagining it, said he also dislikes McGowan's therapies and believes they do nothing to cure the patients. It was he who suggested McGowan doesn't know what he's doing." He glanced at Gabe again. "Should I not have spoken to him?"

"It's all right," Gabe assured him. "You did the right thing."

Stanley removed a cigarette from the tin and placed it between his lips.

Alex lit it for him and opened the door wider, then closed it after Stanley left. He pocketed his matchbox. "I know what you're going to say, Gabe, but I had to ask. There seemed no reason for him to call at the hospital before coming here."

"That's true, but it's Stanley. What would his ulterior motive be?"

Alex held his hands up in surrender. "It was simply my police instincts wanting a reason for everything people do."

"So, what do you think about his claims?" I asked. "Should Dr. McGowan be trusted?"

"Definitely not," Alex said. "He shouldn't be in charge of men like Greville. His so-called therapies could set them back, not make them better. They need peace and quiet, not shocks."

Gabe agreed, but had misgivings. "McGowan insists he's doing nothing wrong, that his therapies are the same that are used by other medical institutions to treat shell-shocked patients."

"So he says. We don't know what other hospitals do. We can't take his word for it, particularly in light of Stanley's suspicions."

"All right," Gabe said. "We'll look into McGowan further."

Gabe and Alex left to call at the office of the General Medical Council and search through their register of doctors. I offered to join them, but was glad when they declined my assistance. I felt guilty for not working.

I found Professor Nash seated in the library's smallest reading nook, located on the mezzanine level on the first floor. It wasn't until I drew closer that I noticed he was napping in the armchair. I tried sneaking away, but a floorboard betrayed me and he woke up.

He shifted in the chair, causing the notebook he'd been reading to slide off his lap. I picked it up and glanced at the page it had opened to before returning it to him.

"Your travel journal?" I asked.

"One of them." He traced his finger over the letters G.N. stamped in gold on the brown leather cover. The gold had dulled over the years, but the cover had fared worse. The corners were frayed and there was a large stain on the back. Inside, the pages looked as though they'd been dried off after getting wet. "I kept one journal for every journey we undertook. This is the first." He smiled wistfully as he removed his spectacles. "It was also my first time leaving England."

"How thrilling. You must have been excited."

"More anxious than excited, but it did turn out to be thrilling, even though we only went as far as Scotland."

"Would I be allowed to read it?"

The voice of Daisy calling out from down below stopped him from answering. "Yoo-hoo! Is anyone here?"

I leaned over the mezzanine rail and waved at her. "Hello! Would you like me to come down or will you come up?"

"That depends on whether tea is on offer."

I told the professor to remain seated while I made some tea. When I returned, I found Daisy and the professor in the larger reading nook, seated side by side on the sofa. She was looking close to tears and he was attempting to comfort her by patting her shoulder. He was relieved to see me.

I set down the tray. "You were as cheery as a summer's day when I left. What happened?"

Daisy showed me the professor's journal. "I read a few pages of this while we waited."

"And something in it made you sad?"

"Yes!"

I glanced at Professor Nash, a little dumbstruck that his travel journal had started out so miserably. "What is it?"

"He writes so well! My story is dull by comparison."

"There, there," he said, patting her. "You'll get better if you continue to practice."

She sighed heavily, her spine curving as she slumped. "I suppose."

We plied her with tea and cake then encouraged her to keep going with her story. She stayed at the library instead of going home, preferring to help me, although her version of being helpful was to rearrange the books on the shelves into a color-coded system. I would need to spend another hour putting them back in the correct order.

As we were about to close the library for the day, Cyclops arrived. He touched the brim of his cap in greeting and apologized for arriving when we appeared to be finishing for the day.

"I was just on my way home, but thought I'd come past on the chance Alex and Gabe were here. I have some information for them."

"They've been gone all afternoon," I told him. "Do you want to wait and see if they return?"

Cyclops shook his head. "I'll telephone them later."

"I can make cocktails," Professor Nash piped up.

Cyclops chuckled. "Not tonight. Speaking of cocktails, you should all come to dinner soon. I'll check with Catherine and get back to you with a date."

"All of us?" the professor asked.

"All of you."

"Even me?" Daisy asked.

"Especially you, Daisy."

She looked taken aback.

Cyclops was about to leave when Gabe and Alex arrived. They brought dark clouds with them and dark news, too.

"McGowan is a legitimate doctor," Alex began. "He's been at Rosebank Gardens hospital for thirty years, just as he claimed. Back in the nineties, the General Medical Council received complaints about the therapies used at Rosebank. Some patients left there worse off than when they went in."

"That aligns with what we know about Robin Reid," I said.

"Records show that McGowan wasn't in charge of the hospital then. He was simply one of several doctors employed there. According to statements on his file, the therapies were considered dangerous. They went further than the standards of the time. For instance, the water in the ice baths was colder than recommended, or the electric shock treatment went for too long.

After receiving the complaints, the GMC ordered Rosebank Gardens to cease the treatments. According to the GMC's records, the hospital complied and there were no more complaints."

"So Stanley's orderly friend was mistaken," I said. "As a young doctor, McGowan was simply following orders."

Gabe removed a piece of paper from his inside jacket pocket with fingers stained black with ink. "Not entirely. We spoke to a clerk who'd been at the GMC for years. He told us about an investigation conducted by Scotland Yard."

Daisy gasped. "What was the hospital accused of doing?"

"Not the hospital. Just McGowan." Gabe showed us the piece of paper with two names written on it. "He was accused of causing the deaths of these patients in 1894."

The same year Robin Reid disappeared.

CHAPTER 15

Gabe explained that the mention of a criminal investigation on McGowan's file had led to them telephoning Cyclops at Scotland Yard. "The clerk at the GMC had no other information except these two names, written on McGowan's file with a note to say they'd referred the investigation to the Yard. The patients were under McGowan's care at the hospital, but the clerk assumed he was found innocent since no criminal charges were laid."

"Did you find anything?" Alex asked his father.

"Very little," Cyclops said. "After I spoke to you, I searched through the archived cases and found the old files written by the investigating team."

"And?"

"And the two deaths occurred a month apart. Both patients were receiving treatment at Rosebank Gardens at the time. Rosebank reported the deaths and a coroner's inquest found the patients died of heart failure."

"Triggered by their treatments?" I asked.

"The deaths were found to be a result of natural causes."

"How old were they?" the professor asked.

"Seventeen and nineteen."

"So young," Daisy murmured.

It was very unlikely two such young patients had died of heart failure so close together at the same place.

Gabe pointed to the piece of paper. "It was their families who brought the deaths to the attention of the GMC, but they couldn't do anything without the coroner declaring a crime had been committed. The clerk we spoke to had never forgotten the deaths. He'd always thought them suspicious. He said it was an uneasy time for the medical profession in general, and Rosebank Gardens in particular. The investigation even made the newspapers."

"We went to several newspaper offices after speaking to you," Alex told his father. "We looked through a pile of old editions from back then." That explained the inky fingers.

"There wouldn't be anything of note in them," Cyclops said. "Merely speculation."

"Sometimes speculation can be accurate," Gabe added with a wry tilt of his lips.

"Did they reveal anything?" I asked.

"Some vaguely worded accusations against the doctors and their methods, all of which were strenuously denied by the Rosebank Gardens director. Then it was all forgotten. No more deaths were reported, no more complaints emerged. The negativity simply ended."

Cyclops confirmed that he could find no more official reports either. "The question now is, did Robin Reid die at Rosebank from the same thing that caused those deaths?"

"Robin wasn't there at the time of his disappearance," I pointed out. "His father said he was admitted in 1891, not 1894."

"He was nineteen in 1894," Gabe said. "Old enough to admit himself without parental consent."

If no one knew he was in the hospital except the staff, it would be easier to cover up his death. All they had to do was hide the body. It was a sobering thought, one that we all reached at the same time, going by the grim faces.

Gabe retrieved a pencil from the desk and drew a rectangle on the back of the piece of paper. "The grounds surrounding Rosebank Gardens are sizeable but not vast." He drew more rectangles inside the first one, representing the main building with its wings, and the outbuildings. "But there are only a few places where I'd bury a body if I were trying to dispose of one." He marked them with an X. From what I could tell, they were located on all the rose beds.

"Well?" Alex asked his father. "Do you think you can get authorization to dig up the grounds?"

Cyclops shook his head. "There's not enough evidence. In fact, there's no evidence, merely speculation. As far as the police are concerned, those earlier deaths were a result of natural causes, not murder, and you have no proof that Robin is even dead. My superiors won't approve the destruction of private property based on what you have."

Alex swore under his breath. "So, what do we do now?"

There was only one thing to do, in my opinion. We'd lost sight of why we'd started this investigation in the first place. It was time to step back to see the broader picture again. "We should stop. We're only looking for Robin because we thought it might lead us to finding out if he met up with Marianne—my mother—after she left Ipswich, but aside from the dead letters, we've not uncovered any other connection between them. There's no reason to believe he's my father. It seems he may have died at Rosebank Gardens after secretly admitting himself, but we have no reason to suppose Marianne was ever with him."

Their long faces didn't lift after my speech. No one looked relieved at the notion of giving up. If anything, their faces grew longer.

Gabe studied the two names on the piece of paper before folding it and tucking it into his pocket. "You're right, Sylvia. The investigation has changed. It's no longer about the possibility that Robin fathered you. But that doesn't mean I want to give up. I want to find out what happened to him. If we're right, and he died at the hospital after being subjected to dangerous treatments, he deserves justice. All the youths who died because they were told they could be made into magicians deserve justice."

"His father deserves to know what happened to him," Cyclops added.

Alex nodded. "And the returned soldiers who are patients there now need to be removed from McGowan's care if he is still using those dangerous treatments."

I may have been the one to suggest we end our investigation, but I was immeasurably relieved to hear they wanted to continue. Gabe was right. Robin and the others deserved justice, and if Stanley was right and Dr. McGowan was still employing dangerous methods to treat shell-shocked soldiers, he needed to be stopped.

"Then we're all agreed?" Gabe asked.

We all chimed in with a "Yes," even Daisy.

Cyclops placed his hat on his head. "Find the evidence I need to satisfy my superiors. If you can't find it using legal methods... don't tell me how you got it."

Daisy collected her bicycle from beside the door. "This is more thrilling than anything I could have made up for my novel. It's almost as thrilling as your journal, Prof."

The professor pushed his glasses up his nose. "Oh, er, that was all a long time ago."

Cyclops opened the door for Daisy, but Alex grasped the handlebars and offered to steer it outside for her. He was a little too enthusiastic, however, and pulled it from her grip.

She huffed crossly as she jerked it back and wheeled it out herself. She cast a glare at Alex before turning a smile on Cyclops. "Do let me know the date for dinner, and please tell Mrs. Bailey how much I'm looking forward to seeing her and the girls again."

Cyclops touched the brim of his hat. "They'll be keen for it to be soon, I'm sure."

Daisy wheeled her bicycle away from the door before getting on and riding off along the lane.

Cyclops bid us all farewell, but Alex blocked his exit. "You invited her to dinner?"

"I did. And Sylvia and Professor Nash, too. Is that a problem?"

"No, but she seemed...eager."

"She did. So?"

"She doesn't like me, so why is she eager?"

Cyclops clapped his son on the shoulder and chuckled. "How did I raise such a fool for a son?"

"A fool?"

Alex crossed his arms over his chest and shot his father a withering glare, but Cyclops wasn't concerned. He simply continued to chuckle as he slipped past Alex and sauntered along Crooked Lane.

Alex watched him go with a frown. "Aren't parents supposed to be supportive?"

Gabe laughed softly.

"Why does everyone keep laughing at me? What's so funny?"

The professor cleared his throat. "Does anyone want tea?"

"I ought to do some work," I said. "Daisy tried to be helpful with the shelving."

"That was kind of her," Alex said.

Gabe understood my meaning. "We'll leave you to it. Tomorrow, I think we should confront McGowan again about those deaths. Getting him to talk is the only way we'll get the evidence Cyclops needs."

"He won't talk," Alex said. "He's too clever."

They left together, discussing ways they could trick, cajole, or force Dr. McGowan into telling them what happened all those years ago.

The shelves that Daisy reordered happened to include some books about paper magic. After returning them to their correct locations, I withdrew one that caught my eye. I'd read it before when I first learned I was a paper magician, but I'd been overwhelmed by the discovery and not taken it all in.

I sat in the reading nook and searched through it for the spell to make paper stronger. The spell to make paper fly was mentioned, but only in passing. There was no mention of combining the strengthening spell with the magic from a graphite or ink magician to make invisible writing.

I removed some paper from the top drawer and laid it on the desk without overlapping any sheets. Then I picked one up and read out the spell from the book. Nothing happened. I didn't feel anything or see any change. Should I see a difference if the paper was stronger?

I easily tore the piece of paper in half. It was all the proof I needed. The strengthening spell hadn't worked. I read it again, altering the pronunciation of the strange words. Still nothing happened and once again, I was able to tear it easily. I stared at the spell, trying to make sense of the words and how they might be pronounced, but the skill of linguistics was beyond me.

The Petersons would help me. They'd been very supportive so far and had offered to teach me the spell, although so far I'd not taken them up on the offer. I hadn't wanted to, at the time. I'd been too overwhelmed with the discovery of my magic to cope with memorizing the spell, too.

But it was time. I was ready.

I was in a research frame of mind, so went in search of books about magician lineages. I wanted to learn more about children born to parents who each possessed very different magical disciplines, that couldn't possibly have stemmed from the same source. While there were several generic books and some that were quite specific, none mentioned silver magic.

I returned the books to the shelves and said goodbye to the professor. Instead of returning home, however, I took a bus to the Petersons' paper factory in Bethnal Green. I was too late. The office door was locked, as were the side gates used by the workers. They'd left for the day.

I peered through the gate's wrought iron bars, but the courtyard was empty except for a lorry parked at the warehouse entrance. There were no workers loading or unloading, no staff crossing the courtyard. Even the pulping machine had ceased its incessant pounding for the day.

I was about to give up and try the house where Walter Peterson lived with his wife and children, when I spotted a man in a brown suit emerging from one of the buildings. I called out then waved when he looked my way.

He glanced around, then, realizing I was trying to catch his attention, approached the gate. "The factory is closed, miss. Come back tomorrow."

I recognized him as one of the Petersons' senior employees, although I'd never met him. He didn't seem to recognize me, however, otherwise he wouldn't have been so rude as to make a shooing motion.

"I'm a friend of Mr. and Miss Peterson," I said in my friendliest voice. "Have they left for the day?"

He came closer and squinted at me. Finally, he seemed to recognize me. "You're that girl who claims to have just discovered she's a paper magician."

I bristled. "You sound like you don't believe it."

He simply looked me up and down, taking my measure. The narrowed gaze and curl of his top lip told me what he thought of me. "It seems unlikely that you didn't know, unless you were adopted."

"I wasn't adopted, but— Never mind." I didn't need to explain to him. "Are *you* a magician?"

"No."

"Are you from a magician family?"

"No."

"Then you can't know what it's like to suddenly discover you are a magician and yet your family is no longer alive and you have no one to ask." It was more than I'd wanted to say, but it didn't stop him looking at me as if I were wasting his time. "So are Mr. or Miss Peterson still here?" I pressed.

"Come back tomorrow." He went to walk off.

I tightened my grip on the bars and gave the gate a shake, but that only confirmed that it was indeed locked. "Why are you being so antagonistic? I simply want to know if either of them are still here."

He stopped but didn't reapproach the gate. "I'm just trying to protect the Petersons from people who wish to harm them."

I barked a laugh. "I don't want to harm them. I simply want to talk to them. How could I possibly harm them?"

"By claiming to be a sibling they never knew and wanting part of this." He indicated the massive factory with its myriad buildings. The land alone would be worth a large sum, and the successful business itself would be worth a fortune.

I blinked at the man, quite lost for words. But my mind worked at rapid speed, several thoughts tripping over each other, until finally one broke free. It was louder than the rest, and it was startling in its clarity. "Why would you think I'm a sibling they never knew they had? It's such an odd conclusion to jump to."

He stared back, his icy-blue gaze challenging. "I didn't say you are, just that you're claiming to be."

"But I'm not."

"Very well. Now go on, clear off."

My fingers began to hurt, so I loosened my grip on the bars. I hadn't realized I'd been holding them so tightly. "There must be a reason why you accused me. Has it happened before? Did someone claim to be their sibling? A paper magician?"

"He wasn't a paper magician, as it turned out. But yes, it happened before."

"Surely something so strange is a one-time occurrence. So why are you accusing *me* when I've shown no sign of taking advantage of the Petersons?" When he simply muttered something under his breath but didn't leave, I pressed on. "Sir, why do you think I might claim to be their sibling? Please, tell me. I'm trying to find out more about my family, and if there's a possibility that you know something, I would be forever grateful to you for telling me."

Perhaps it was the desperation in my voice, or maybe he wanted to talk about it all along, but he finally gave in. "I've worked here for some time. I knew Old Mr. Peterson well. He was a good man, but he was a philanderer. He had several liaisons outside of his marriage. It's conceivable one or more of those liaisons resulted in a child. His wife knew about the mistresses. His children knew, too. You can't tell them anything they don't already know, so don't go thinking of blackmailing them."

I shook my head, over and over. "Did you ever meet the women? Could you describe any of them?"

"No."

"Did his children?"

"I doubt it. He kept that part of his life separate. Now, if I were you, I'd forget the Petersons. They have good lawyers. They won't give you anything."

"I told you, I don't want their money or any ownership of this factory. I just want to find my family."

Walter Peterson emerged from one of the buildings and upon seeing us, approached the gate. His broad smile plumped his rosy cheeks and crinkled the corners of his eyes. "Good afternoon, Miss Ashe. What a pleasant surprise."

His cheerfulness was infectious. I couldn't help smiling in return. "Good afternoon, Mr. Peterson. I hoped to find you here still. I'd like to ask you a favor."

"Is it a magical favor?"

"Yes."

His smile widened. "My favorite kind." He unlocked the gate and invited me through. "Shall we adjourn to the office? I have sherry."

The employee touched the brim of his hat. "See you tomorrow, sir."

"Bright and early!"

I watched the man saunter off, wondering whether I ought to ask Mr. Peterson about his father's mistresses.

"Don't mind him." Mr. Peterson nodded at the retreating figure of his employee. "Good fellow, hard worker, but he's a bit of a curmudgeon. Understandable, I suppose, considering he lost his son."

So many fathers had, and mothers, too.

Mr. Peterson continued to chatter about his week as we made our way across the courtyard. By the time we reached the office, I had decided not to ask about his father. I didn't want him jumping to the conclusion his employee had and think I was after money or a stake in the business. I'd wait until I got to know him and his sister better before broaching the sensitive topic.

Mr. Peterson showed me through to his office, a grand space with a solid mahogany desk, bookshelves and cabinets. Neat stacks of paper formed towers of different heights on the desk. They were different thicknesses and textures, too, but all fine quality.

"Go ahead and touch them," he said, smiling.

"Oh no, there's no need."

He flipped open the top half of a world globe resting on a brass stand, revealing a selection of glasses and decanters. It was a curious piece of furniture, designed to impress, but I was drawn to the paper stacks. I reached out and caressed one while he poured the sherry, only to find that he'd seen.

He handed me one of the glasses. "No need to be embarrassed, Miss Ashe. I know you have urges." He tapped a finger on the stack as he passed it to sit on the other side of the desk. "You chose well. This is our finest paper. Very smooth and lightweight, yet it won't tear. Not for some time, at least, until the magic fades." He sipped his sherry before settling into the chair, resting the glass on his paunch. "So, how may I help you?"

"Can you teach me to speak the strengthening spell? I can't get the words right."

The smile that was never far away appeared again, brighter than before. "It will be my pleasure."

We spent almost an hour perfecting the nuances of the spell before it finally worked for me. I knew the moment I'd succeeded, as surely as I knew when I felt any other sensation, like heat or cold, pain or pleasure. The magic swelled deep inside me then surged along my veins, warming them, leaving tingles in its wake. Every nerve came to life, aware of the magic's force, aware of the parts of me that it touched before it burst from my fingertips. The paper's surface glowed with soft light before fading away, leaving behind magical heat that I now knew the artless couldn't feel.

I looked up at Mr. Peterson, seated opposite, unable to contain my smile. I'd done it! I'd performed magic for the first time. It was exhilarating and intensely, deeply satisfying.

Mr. Peterson sat back in his chair. "My! What a performance! I'd not expected that for your first time." He picked up the paper but quickly released it again and shook out his hand. "Hot. Miss Ashe, you are a strong magician. Are you sure you only have one magician parent?"

I tried very hard to contain my smile, but it simply wouldn't be quelled. "I believe I might have two, although only one was a paper magician."

"Your father, you said?"

It would seem so. "I never met him. My mother didn't speak about him. In fact, sometimes I wonder if his name isn't Ashe at all."

"Truly? Well, that is unfortunate, but I'm sure your mother had her reasons for keeping it a secret." He slapped his hands down on the chair arms. "Now, this requires a celebration. We can't let your first time using a spell pass without marking the occasion with good food and company. My sister is coming for dinner tonight. Will you join us?"

"I don't want to intrude on your family time."

"It's no intrusion. My wife wants to meet you, and Evaline will be happy to see you again." He pushed himself to his feet. "Come. Join us."

"If you're sure..."

"That's the spirit. You won't regret it. Our cook is excellent."

I spent a pleasant evening talking about magic, the paper business, and giving the Petersons just enough detail about myself that I didn't feel too exposed. I hoped to prod Evaline and Walter into thinking their father might be my father, without having to broach the topic myself.

Walter's joviality didn't waver throughout dinner, however. Nor did his wife's, whose giggles became louder with each glass of wine she consumed. Evaline, on the other hand, became thoughtful when I mentioned that I knew nothing about my father. She made no suggestion that we might be half-sisters but if the connection did occur to her, I'm sure she would want to discuss it with her brother alone first.

The conversation moved on until it was time for me to leave. Not only had I enjoyed myself, but I felt a sense of satisfaction, too. I left feeling good about myself. For the first time, I *felt* like a paper magician. Before making the spell work, a part of me hadn't accepted that I was a magician. It wasn't until I performed the spell that I realized a piece of me had been missing.

Now I was satisfied on a base level, as if a missing part of me had been found and returned. That missing piece had shored up my foundation, allowing something to be built on it. I could build something marvelous, something I'd never dreamed of building before speaking the spell.

And I couldn't wait to begin.

I still wanted to know more about my parents, my family, but

I didn't *need* to know. Being me—a paper magician—was enough.

* * *

I COULDN'T WAIT to tell Gabe about the paper spell the following morning when he collected me from the library. I hadn't told the professor yet; Gabe should be the first to know. He'd hardly walked in the door when I blurted it out.

"Congratulations!" he said. "I can see that you're pleased."

"Very, although I'm not altogether sure why. I don't manufacture paper and have no real need for the spell." I shrugged, unable to describe the feeling to him.

It turned out that I didn't need to. "Your magic is a part of you, that's why. My mother explained to me that magic is a component of your character. If that component is suppressed, misunderstood or forgotten, then you're not really the person you were meant to become. It's like having a keen sense of humor yet being forbidden to laugh, or being intelligent yet never given the opportunity to learn, or having a wanderlust but never allowed to leave the village."

He understood me like no one else had, not even my family. In a rush of emotion, I stood on my toes and kissed his cheek.

But he moved at the moment of connection. I missed his cheek and kissed the corner of his mouth instead. My heart thundered and my face flamed. Silence enveloped us, thick and pulsating. I didn't know where to look, but I couldn't look at him, even though I desperately wanted to see his reaction.

Had he moved deliberately?

I dropped back onto flat feet and dared a glance at him. He watched me from beneath lowered lashes, his expression unreadable.

The awkwardness was too tense, so I forced myself to break the silence. "I'll let the professor know I'm leaving."

A few minutes later, Gabe and I walked side by side along

Crooked Lane, he with his hands behind his back and me tying a scarf around my head to keep my hair in place for the journey. Our entire conversation consisted of me asking where Alex and Willie were, and he replying that they'd slept in after a late night out. They wouldn't be happy that he left without them, but Gabe seemed unconcerned for his safety.

By the time we reached Rosebank Gardens, the tension had eased somewhat. The smile he gave me as he assisted me from the motorcar could be interpreted as friendly rather than intimate, but the caress of his thumb over my knuckles left no room for misinterpretation. He'd removed his driving gloves and I'd dispensed with gloves altogether because of the heat, so the touch of skin against skin sent my body into a chaotic jumble of warm tingles and quite shut down my mind.

It was the only logical explanation for what happened next.

Neither of us saw the attacker until it was too late. He came at us from behind. It wasn't until Gabe hissed in pain and lurched forward that we both realized he'd been stabbed.

CHAPTER 16

$\mathcal{I}$ shouted for help. There was little else I could do. Blood seeped through the tear in Gabe's jacket at his shoulder, soaking the fabric. I tugged at the jacket to remove it, but he wouldn't stand still. He spun around, searching for the attacker. Spying a patient holding a large knife sprinting up the driveway toward the gate, Gabe took off after him. He was too far away to catch, however.

Yet Gabe *did* catch him. He pinned him to the ground and wrested the knife from his grip. It all happened in the blink of an eye. He must have used his magic to slow time, because he couldn't have reached the attacker otherwise. He'd had too much of a head start.

My guess was confirmed when Gabe sucked in ragged breaths. Breathlessness and tiredness were common side effects of his magic use.

I ran to him with two orderlies and a nurse on my heels. I fell to my knees on the gravel beside him. "Are you all right? Let me see."

He didn't object as I assisted him out of his jacket, but he winced when he moved his arm.

The two orderlies hauled the patient to his feet. He wore only the hospital-issued striped pajamas, no dressing gown or shoes. He must have rushed out of the building when he saw us.

"Why did you attack me?" Gabe asked.

The patient lowered his head. He was a young man, no older than me, with a badly scarred face and a hollow socket where his right eye used to be. Without a mask to cover the wounds, it was difficult to look at him, but I made myself. Even he deserved that dignity.

"Who are you?" Gabe pressed.

The patient let out a low, keening wail. He struggled, but the orderlies had him gripped between them and he was no match for their superior size and strength.

"Where did you get that knife?" Gabe continued. "Is it from here?"

"Could be from the kitchen," one of the orderlies said. "We'll take him inside and telephone the police."

The patient's wailing grew louder and he began rocking back and forth until the two orderlies tightened their grip. They led him back to the building, part dragging, part carrying him. It was a pathetic sight, yet troubling, too.

Was his attack on Gabe random? Or was Gabe targeted? If he was targeted, why? What reason could he possibly have to attack Gabe?

Or was he acting for someone else? If so, who?

The nurse took over my attempts to stop the bleeding. She tore open Gabe's shirt, inspected the wound, then clamped her hand over the cut. "This needs to be cleaned and stitched. Come inside."

As she led us to the building, Dr. McGowan emerged. He stopped to speak to the orderlies then turned to us. His nostrils flared. "What did you do to him?"

Gabe merely glared back, so I took it upon myself to protest. "Nothing! We had just arrived and were coming to see you when he attacked. We tried asking why, but he wouldn't answer."

"Leave the questioning to the police."

Gabe indicated the end of the drive in the distance. "He was heading toward the gate."

"Trying to leave, probably."

"Or trying to return the knife to someone on the outside."

Dr. McGowan looked taken aback. "I'll ask the guard if he saw anyone acting suspiciously."

The nurse directed Gabe to a small room behind the front desk. It was the same nurse who'd fetched Dr. McGowan on the night we broke in. Her no-nonsense manner was comforting, particularly when I wasn't capable of thinking clearly. I was still reeling from shock.

She ordered Gabe to sit on the chair then rummaged through the cupboard for supplies. "Remove your shirt and I'll clean you up. Let's see how deep it is."

I helped Gabe out of his shirt, doing my best to match the nurse's clinical indifference. It was impossible, however. There was simply far too much to take in, with the sprinkle of dark hair on his chest, and smooth skin stretched over the hard undulations of muscle. A lot of muscle, that I found myself skimming lightly with the back of my fingers.

Seeing the blood on my hand shocked my mind back to the horror of the situation.

"I can see you won't be any help." The nurse somehow managed to both smile and glare at me. "Would you mind stepping outside, please."

I was glad to, only because my embarrassment was beginning to make an appearance in the form of my reddening face.

I waited in the corridor, grateful for the support of the wall at my back. The nurse closed the door, so I couldn't hear whether they spoke or if she worked in silence. The rest of the hospital wasn't silent. It was as if it had woken up from a stupor. Patients wailed and shouted, setting my nerves jangling again. Calmer voices tried to quieten the shouts, but to no avail. I thought about walking outside to get some fresh air and peace when the door opened and Gabe emerged. He wore his shirt, but his jacket was nowhere to be seen. We must have left it outside.

He thanked the nurse for stitching him up. He looked fine. His shirt was bloodied and torn, his hair messy, and his expression annoyed, but he was all right.

It could have been so much worse.

The nurse picked up the basin of bloodied water and followed Gabe out. "Keep the wound clean and see your regular doctor in two weeks to have the stitches removed. You're lucky it isn't deep."

I drew in my first proper breath since the stabbing. It was supposed to rally me, but instead it brought on tears. Great, gushing, gulping tears that streamed down my face and no doubt made me look like a pathetic, emotional fool. Yet I couldn't stop them.

Gabe gathered me in one arm and kissed the top of my head. He didn't say anything. He didn't need to. It was enough just to be held by him.

I was in no state to talk to him either. I could barely even think. All I could do was worry about dampening his shirt with my tears, which was ridiculous since it was ruined anyway.

He held me tightly until my tears abated enough that I could hear the steady beat of his heart. The comforting rhythm soothed me further and I managed to gather what little dignity I had left and pull away.

I wanted to say something, to tell him I was relieved he was all right, or that I was terrified of what could have happened. Perhaps even ask him if it hurt. But of course he knew how I felt. My tears told him that. As to whether he was in pain, that was obvious too, in the tightness of his features and the way he kept his left arm still.

Gabe opened his mouth to speak, but didn't get the opportunity.

"There you are." Dr. McGowan strode along the corridor

toward us, a grim set to his jaw and Gabe's jacket over his arm. "Scotland Yard will be here soon."

"Why not the local constabulary?" Gabe asked.

"Because the orderly who made the call mentioned you were the fellow who broke in here the other night, and the local police thought the Yard should be involved from the outset." He sounded irritated and harried. "You can wait for them in my office."

"I'd like to speak to the attacker."

"Absolutely not! The police will deal with him."

"You'll let them arrest him and take him away?"

"Of course. There's no question of his guilt."

"But his health—"

"Why aren't you pleased?" Dr. McGowan shook his head. "You should want him arrested."

"Prison might not be the best place for someone like him. I don't know. That's your area of expertise."

Dr. McGowan's chest swelled. "And it's my professional opinion that he should be placed in a maximum security prison where he can no longer cause anyone harm."

He led us to the outer office to be watched by his assistant while he did the rounds of the wards. It felt like an age, but eventually Cyclops arrived with a team from Scotland Yard. His eye quickly assessed Gabe then, in front of all his colleagues, he embraced him, careful to avoid the wounded shoulder.

His first words when he drew away were to tell Gabe he would be in trouble.

"Don't inform my parents," Gabe said. "There's nothing they can do from America."

"They won't hear it from me. I was talking about Alex and Willie. I telephoned your house before I left the Yard. They should be here shortly."

Gabe groaned.

Dr. McGowan entered. "Good. You're here." He tucked his

clipboard under his arm and pocketed his pencil. "Come with me."

Gabe tried to follow, but Cyclops stopped him. "Stay here."

"But—"

"No. Let me speak to the suspect alone."

Gabe didn't look pleased, but he didn't argue. "Ask him if someone put him up to it." It seemed he'd had the same thought as me.

We waited a mere ten minutes until Cyclops returned, shaking his head. "All he would say was that God told him to do it. I tried getting more out of him, but he wouldn't talk. He wouldn't even say where the knife came from. One of the orderlies had asked in the kitchen and they said it wasn't one of theirs. My men have taken it as evidence."

"And the patient?" Gabe asked. "Where is he now?"

"He'll be processed back at the Yard. His departure has caused a commotion in the wards." As he said it, I noticed the noise level in the hospital. The voices had been elevated ever since the incident outside, and had slowly increased until they were now echoing off the walls.

Dr. McGowan had disappeared, as had his assistant. We were alone in the outer office.

Gabe sat again and leaned forward, resting one elbow on his knee. He dragged his hand through his hair. He kept his other arm tucked into his side.

I took his hand gently, worried that the pain might have traveled down his arm. But the squeeze he gave in response reassured me that if he did feel pain, he was managing it.

"Where is he?" came a shrill voice with an American accent. "Gabe?"

Gabe groaned again.

"In here, Willie," Cyclops called out.

"Don't," Gabe whispered. "If we remain silent, she might leave."

Cyclops snorted. "She won't rest until she's seen you. Besides, she's your punishment."

"For what?"

"For not waking her or Alex and bringing one of them with you."

Willie rushed inside, followed closely by Alex. A series of emotions passed over their faces, from briskly assessing, to relief, and finally anger. Alex hung back by the door, scowling, but Willie surged forward with all the huffing and puffing of a steam engine.

She shook her finger at Gabe. "Why didn't you wake me? You should have got one of us. I knew this was going to happen one day! This or kidnap, or..." She threw her hands in the air. "You've become too careless lately. You can't take your safety for granted. Understand?"

"I do."

Willie's lower lip wobbled. "Good," she said, her voice barely a whisper. She sniffed then wiped her hand across her nose. "Your turn, Alex."

"I think you said everything I wanted to," Alex growled. He turned to his father. "The suspect?"

"On his way to the Yard," Cyclops said.

"Did he talk? Is he the one who was trying to kidnap Gabe?"

"If he was, he's in no state to tell us. His mind is gone. We might never know why he did it, or if someone encouraged him."

Willie swore loudly. "Why didn't you use your..." She looked around and, seeing that we were alone, whispered, "...your magic?"

"I did," Gabe said. "It just happened. Time slowed. I was able to catch him and stop him getting away."

"Why not before he stabbed you?"

"He came at Gabe from behind," I said. "Neither of us noticed him until it was too late."

Willie pointed her finger at Gabe again. "You didn't get a

single injury in the war and now this! You're usually more aware of your surroundings, especially since the kidnappings. You're usually alert to folk coming up behind you. Why not this time?"

Gabe went to fold his arms over his chest, but winced in pain. He let them fall to his sides. "I was distracted."

"By what?"

Alex looked at me, but Willie didn't reach the same conclusion. She waited for a response, but Gabe changed the subject.

"I think he came at me from behind deliberately. He knew I wouldn't see him coming. By the time the knife struck, it was too late for my magic to stop him."

"How could he know what you're capable of?" Alex asked.

"From the previous kidnappings. Whoever was behind them has realized how I'm getting out of the situations without harm. Or if they don't know, they have an inkling and suspected that if they were to succeed they'd have to take me by surprise. Thankfully the attacker wasn't accurate, and merely got my shoulder."

"Unless he didn't want to kill you," I pointed out.

They all looked at me.

"Perhaps the plan was to study your reaction, whether you needed to see the attack or whether other senses were heightened enough to take over and save you. Or perhaps the idea was to maim you and make you easier to kidnap."

Cyclops seemed impressed with my theory. "You may have a point, Sylvia. He was an easy target with his back turned. The attacker could have stabbed him in the neck, killing him almost instantly, but he didn't."

I swallowed the bile rising up my throat. My legs suddenly felt weak, and I sat again.

Gabe rested a hand on my shoulder. "I think we should take Sylvia home."

"It's you who should go home," I said, standing again.

"After I speak to Dr. McGowan. I want to finish what we came here to do."

Despite our arguments, Gabe insisted on tracking the doctor

down, but McGowan refused to see us. The patients were restless and he was needed, so he claimed. Whether that was true, or whether he was merely avoiding us, it was impossible to say.

Outside, one of the orderlies was throwing a bucket of water over the spots of blood on the gravel near the motorcar. I shivered and looked away.

Before driving off in his own vehicle, Cyclops told Gabe to expect a visit from Catherine.

"Do you have to tell her?" Gabe asked.

Cyclops's response was to give him an arch look before driving away.

Willie retrieved the crank handle from the Vauxhall. "S'pose this'll be exclusively my job for a while."

"I can still use my right arm," Gabe said.

Alex opened the door then indicated Gabe should climb in alongside me. He nodded pointedly at the seat then slammed the door closed once Gabe was inside. At the front of the vehicle, Willie shot Gabe a glare across the Vauxhall's bonnet before inserting the handle into the crank slot.

"I think they're cross with me," he mumbled.

The silence on the journey confirmed it. If there were any doubts, Willie's huffing noises as she stared out of the window made sure Gabe knew just how cross she was.

It was a relief when we arrived at the library and I could leave the tension behind, but since Gabe insisted on walking me to the door, and Willie and Alex refused to let him out of their sights, we endured more of their silent treatment along Crooked Lane.

Gabe drew me aside when we reached the library. "Sorry about them."

"There's no need to apologize for your friends. They care about you." I peered past him to Willie and Alex, standing side by side in similar poses with their feet apart and arms crossed over their chests. Their scowls matched, too. "I hope their anger doesn't last too long."

"So do I. It's already tiresome."

I wasn't sure how to part from him after such an intense and frightening incident. In a way, it had brought us closer, but awkwardness had settled once more and tied my tongue. I didn't know what to say, so I said nothing.

Gabe wasn't as affected as me. "You were so happy this morning…" It took me a moment to realize he was referring to me successfully using the paper spell. "I wish the day hadn't ended this way."

"I don't think anyone wishes their day ends with a knife in the shoulder, but I appreciate the sentiment."

He mustered a wan smile at my silly attempt to lighten the mood. "You still look shaken. Will you be all right?"

It was my turn to smile. "I should be asking you that question. But thank you, yes. I'll be fine. You?"

"Don't worry about me. The Bristows will pamper me, Mrs. Ling will cook my favorite dishes, and Catherine will make sure Alex forgives me for leaving him behind this morning."

"And Willie? How long will she be cross with you?"

He sighed as he cast a glance at his cousin. "Her anger could dissipate before we reach home, or it could last a week. She's as unpredictable in her temper as she is in everything else."

True to form, Willie marched up to us and jerked open the library door. "Quit yapping. Sylvia, get inside or I'll drag you in there myself."

I did as ordered, turning around to say goodbye once I'd crossed the threshold. Willie slammed the door shut before I had a chance to lift my hand in a wave.

Professor Nash rose from where he was seated behind the desk, a pile of books in his arms. "You mustn't let Willie upset you. She's very protective of Gabe and will want to be sure of you first."

I frowned, trying to make sense of what he was saying.

"It took her almost a year to accept Ivy, and even then, she continued to grumble about her from time to time."

Ohhhh. He thought Willie was cross with me for having feelings for Gabe.

The professor smiled brightly. "So, how was your morning, Sylvia?"

"I'll tell you over a cup of tea. Or perhaps several cups. I'll make a pot and meet you in the reading nook."

CHAPTER 17

$\mathcal{I}$ was too restless to return home after work, so I called at Daisy's flat. I found her sipping a cocktail, dancing alone to music playing on the gramophone. Late afternoon sunlight streamed through the large windows, burnishing her hair, which was kept off her face by a scarf rolled into a band. She looked like a modern, clothed version of Botticelli's Venus from his famous painting.

With one hand clutching her glass, she beckoned me inside with the crook of her finger. "Dance with me, Sylvia." She swayed her hips and flailed her arms in the air. She probably meant it to be a seductive move but she looked a little like she was drowning.

I suppressed a giggle, so as not to offend her. Lord, it felt good to smile after such a trying day. I didn't mind that she made me dance a few moves with her. It was clear that she was quite drunk. A drunk Daisy was just the distraction I needed.

She started to sing, however, and I was considering whether to remove the record when thankfully the needle got stuck. "Pooh," she said as she lifted the tonearm. "Never mind. You missed the beginning anyway, so I'll restart it."

Before she could, I asked her to make me a cocktail.

She waved at the drinks tray on the sideboard. "Help yourself. Everything you need is there."

"But I can't make cocktails as delicious as yours."

She abandoned the gramophone and set about mixing me a martini. When she finished, she popped in an olive and handed the glass to me. "Thank goodness you're here, Sylvia."

"Oh? Why?"

"I'm so dreadfully *bored*."

"Weren't you writing your novel today?"

She waved off the question and sat on the sofa, tucking one leg under her. She patted the seat beside her. "Tell me something interesting. You must have some gossip for me."

"I do as it happens."

Her eyes lit up. "Is it about Alex?"

"No. Do you wish it was about Alex?"

"Of course not. I'm quite over him. I never think about him anymore."

"So I see. My gossip isn't about Alex, it's about Gabe. And I'm still quite shaken about it, to be honest." I sipped the cocktail then took a large gulp. "I'm going to need a second one of these to settle my nerves."

I told her about the stabbing. She was a good listener and an excellent audience, interjecting with the occasional gasp then giving me a fierce hug at the end.

"You poor, poor thing. It must have been awful."

"It was, but he seems all right." I blew out a long breath and relaxed into the sofa as the effects of the martini kicked in. "I think I was shaken more than him."

"That's war for you. The men have become immune to life-threatening situations. Being stabbed is probably nothing to Gabe."

"He wasn't injured in the war."

"Oh yes, I forgot. He was so incredibly fortunate, wasn't he?"

I sipped my drink. Daisy still didn't know about Gabe's magic. The fewer people who knew, the better.

She downed the remainder of her drink then unfolded her legs from beneath her. "Drink up. You need a distraction. We're going out."

"Where?"

"There's a new Italian restaurant that's supposed to be good. It's a little early for dinner, but we can walk slowly. Oh, wait, I have a better idea. The restaurant is near that stationer's shop, the one belonging to Huon's nemesis."

"Petra?"

"Yes. We can while away the time and chat to her."

Petra's shop would probably be closing soon, but I agreed anyway. I enjoyed her company and was keen to invite her to dinner to get to know her better. If I was being perfectly honest, however, I had another motive for wanting to talk to her.

* * *

WE WAITED for Petra to finish serving a customer then joined her at the counter. I tried not to touch the stationery items arranged so beautifully alongside her writing tools, but it was hopeless. I could no more resist touching them than I could resist kissing Gabe back if he ever kissed me.

"This is a lovely surprise," she said, smiling. "Is this a social visit or business?"

Daisy rested her elbows on the counter and her chin on her hands. She was still quite drunk. "Social. We'd like you to join us for dinner."

"I'd love to. I'll finish up here, then telephone my mother to let her know I won't be home for a while."

Before she locked the cash register, I pointed at the bound notepads on the shelf behind her. "I'd like one of those please, Petra."

"Would you like it wrapped?"

"No, thank you." I handed her the payment then rested my palm on the notepad. It held no magic.

I tore off the top page then tore that in half.

"Don't waste it!" Daisy cried.

Petra frowned. "I could have given you a scrap from the rubbish."

I picked up both pieces and closed my eyes. I pictured the spell in my mind, and the outcome. I let the words I'd memorized at the Petersons' factory spill out of me, rolling my tongue over some syllables, feeling the strange sensation of the vibrations of others. I made sure the letter T was as sharp as it could be, and the P popped. When I finished, warmth burst from me and poured into the paper.

I opened my eyes and smiled at the two women staring back at me.

"Sylvia?" Daisy asked, sounding breathless.

I handed her a piece of paper and gave the other to Petra. Both dropped their pieces and wiggled their fingers. "Sorry," I muttered. "I forgot about the heat."

They gingerly picked them up again.

"Try and tear it," I said.

They couldn't. No matter which edge they tried, it wouldn't rip, not even a little. All they could do was fold it.

Petra removed a pair of scissors from a drawer and tried to cut her piece. Nothing happened. The scissors may as well have been as blunt as a hammer. "Good lord. These were just sharpened." To prove it, she cut through another piece of paper from the same notepad. When half of it fluttered onto the counter, she looked up at me. She smiled.

Daisy threw her arms around me. "You've done it, Sylvia! You've learned your spell. When?"

"Last night, but I forgot to tell you with all that happened today."

"What happened?" Petra asked. "It must be important if you forgot to tell your best friend about this."

"Oh, it was," Daisy told her. "Gabe was stabbed."

Petra gasped. "Is he all right?"

I nodded. "He has stitches in his shoulder, but he'll be fine."

"So why are you here? Shouldn't you be with him? If he required stitches, he must be in some pain."

"Oh. No. We're just friends, and he has his other friends with him. He doesn't need me. I'd only get in the way."

Daisy and Petra exchanged knowing glances and smirks.

Petra picked up the piece of paper from the counter. "I've never known paper to be this strong. How long will your magic last?"

"I don't know yet. I'll keep one of these pieces and test it every day."

"As will I." She returned the scissors and the torn paper to the drawer. "Who taught you?"

I told them about the Petersons, but didn't mention the philandering father. Then I got to the real reason for calling on her. "Tell me everything you know about invisible writing. I think you mentioned only a graphite magician can create it, see it, and read it. We paper magicians can't, but our magic paper is necessary."

"That's true." She fished a bundle of keys out of her skirt pocket and used one to unlock a cupboard behind her. She removed a box and opened the lid to reveal several pencils. She plucked one out and wrote something on the magic-infused paper. "Can you see anything?"

"No. It's blank."

She held up the pencil. "This has my magic in it already. I spoke the spell into these today for a customer who's coming in the morning. He's an artist and likes to have several pencils on hand for sketching."

"Your spell makes them stronger?" Daisy asked.

"Yes. The two strengthening spells, mine and Sylvia's, have now combined to make invisible writing."

Daisy studied the paper only to shake her head. "I'll have to take your word for it. Sylvia, can you see anything?"

I shook my head, too. If I'd not already known that invisible writing existed, I'd have thought Petra was pulling our legs. "What does it say?"

"'Huon Barratt is a moron.'"

Daisy giggled.

"Speaking of Huon," I said. "He wants to create invisible writing with ink. He needs a paper magician so asked me, but at the time, I didn't know any paper spells."

Petra made a face. "Don't help him. He'll use it for nefarious reasons, like gambling or duping people in some way."

"He won't. He said he'll act as go-between, writing secret notes then reading them to the recipient if they don't have access to their own ink magician."

I wasn't sure why I wanted to defend him. Petra was probably right and he'd end up using the invisible ink in some illegal scheme or other. The possibilities were endless, and no doubt his mind was already thinking of the various ways he could earn a fortune. I didn't want to be a party to anything illicit.

On the other hand, being involved in creating a new spell could be interesting. And if I didn't help him, he would go to another paper magician.

I picked up the piece of paper with both our magics in it. I could discern the magic in both, each having its own rhythm. Mine felt strong, like a full orchestral symphony rather than a single instrument performing a solo.

"You're going to help him, aren't you?" Petra asked.

"I might."

She sighed. "If you do, just make sure you charge him a fair fee. Don't do it for free. And make sure the paper magic can't be traced back to you. You don't want the police knocking on your door when his scheme is uncovered. I would love to see him thrown in prison, but I would hate for you to become embroiled in something illegal because he was too careless to cover his tracks."

"He hasn't suggested anything illegal to me. It's quite legitimate, if a little ... unsavory."

But Petra had a point. Could Huon be trusted? He might not be able to resist using invisible writing for more than letters between clandestine lovers. Petra knew Huon well enough to know that he would give in to temptation if there was a benefit to him. Indeed, even I knew him well enough to know that.

* * *

THE FOLLOWING DAY WAS SATURDAY. When I wasn't helping with an investigation, I spent most Saturdays helping Mrs. Parry, exploring London, or spending time with Daisy. But I knew I wouldn't settle until I'd seen Gabe, so I called on him in the morning.

Bristow opened the door with all the officiousness I'd become used to, only to ignore his butler's code of conduct and actually express an emotion. I think it was relief. "Thank goodness you're here, Miss Ashe."

Panic seized me and squeezed hard. "What's happened?"

"Lady Farnsworth is being difficult. More than usual, I mean."

"Willie? In what way?"

Her voice traveled down the staircase to me, sharp and clear. "You ain't going anywhere, Gabe! You're staying right here where Alex and I can keep an eye on you."

Gabe's response was low and inaudible.

Bristow's wrinkles folded with his cringe. "I'm sorry to ask you to enter the lion's den, Miss Ashe, but would you mind rescuing Mr. Glass?"

"I don't think Willie will listen to me, but I'll try."

"Having another person there might mellow her."

I doubted it, but I suspected Gabe needed to see a friendly face. If nothing else, I could be another person to talk to while he convalesced.

Instead, I found myself not only drawn into their argument, but taking Willie's side.

Gabe's initial reaction upon seeing me was similar to Bristow's, although his relief was coupled with genuine pleasure at seeing me. I expected to see him seated in the sitting room in a comfortable armchair, a pot of tea, some cakes and a book within easy reach. Instead, he was on his feet, pacing. Alex moved to block the doorway again after I'd entered the room, and Willie dogged Gabe's steps. She'd been railing at him, but fell blessedly quiet when I arrived.

With all their gazes focused on me, I self-consciously uttered the pleasantries one gave an invalid acquaintance. "How are you today?"

"Fine," Gabe said on a sigh.

"You look well. Can I get you anything?"

"I have everything I need." He indicated the book, teacup, biscuits and blanket, all neglected. "And more. Tea?"

"No, thank you. I just came to see how you are and to keep you company if Alex and Willie needed to go out for a while."

Alex grunted.

Willie looked smug. "Ha! See, Gabe? She agrees with us."

"I do?"

"You reckon Gabe should stay here and recover."

"Yes, of course."

"We said the same thing, but he won't listen to us. He wants to return to the hospital and question McGowan." That explained Alex guarding the door and Willie's lecturing.

"I wasn't suggesting going alone," Gabe told her. "You can come."

"You got to rest. So sit, drink your tea, and read a book."

He appealed to me. "Help me, Sylvia. Convince them I'm capable of having a conversation with McGowan without reopening the wound."

While he had a point, I did think he should spend the day recuperating at home. "McGowan can wait until tomorrow."

He regarded me, his lips flattening. "Very well. I'll stay here.

But if I have to put up with Grim and Grimmer, I'd like some company."

I smiled and sat in the other armchair. "I have nothing better to do today than listen to Willie's mature and reasoned arguments for you not leaving the house."

Even Willie snorted at that. "You been drinking already?"

Alex opened the drawer of the console table and removed a deck of cards. "Do you know how to play poker, Sylvia?"

Bristow reentered the drawing room. "You have guests, sir. Lady Stanhope and Miss Hobson. I told them you were unavailable today, but they're insisting. They seem agitated."

Lady Stanhope marched into the room before being invited. "We're ladies. We don't get agitated. We are upset." She strode across the room to Gabe and clasped his face between her hands. "You poor dear boy. I heard what happened and came here immediately."

Behind her, Ivy clutched her throat, tears welling in her eyes. She looked like she wanted to throw her arms around Gabe and cry into his chest. Then she saw me and her face turned to stone.

Willie groaned. "Speaking of drinking early, I reckon we're going to need it."

Bristow bowed. "I'll have Mrs. Bristow make more tea."

Willie opened the flap of her jacket and pulled out a silver flask from the inside pocket. She winked at me. "Let me know if you need it, Sylv. We'll get through this together."

She'd been neither quiet nor discreet. Lady Stanhope clicked her tongue in disapproval. Ivy pretended not to have heard.

She bent to kiss Gabe's cheek. "This is appalling. Absolutely appalling. The hospital's management should be held accountable, and all their patients removed from their care."

"The system is overrun as it is," Gabe told her. "Hospitals like Rosebank Gardens are needed to treat shell-shocked soldiers. Before the war, their work wasn't as...necessary." He watched her closely, but she gave no sign that she recognized the hospital name or that she knew her brother had been admitted in 1913.

"What did the doctor say?" she asked.

"Which doctor?"

"The one who inspected your wound."

"A nurse at Rosebank stitched it up. I haven't seen a doctor."

"Gabe! You have to see a doctor!"

"I assure you, she was very competent."

"How do you know? Can you even see the wound? Let me check it." She reached out to unbutton his shirt.

He caught her hand. "There's no need."

"You're so sweet to worry on my account, but it's not necessary. I won't faint at the sight. I was a nurse, remember? I've seen far worse."

"I said it's fine. The wound isn't deep. Barely a scratch, really."

She slowly straightened, her hand fluttering at her chest again. "Oh. I see." She looked around, taking in all of us, including Lady Stanhope, settling on the sofa. "I'll leave you in peace, although I'm not sure how much rest you'll get with everyone here." She smiled gently. "You're fortunate to have so many people to make a fuss over you."

Gabe got to his feet and smiled tightly. "Let me walk you out."

Ivy looked pointedly at Lady Stanhope.

Lady Stanhope remained seated. "I need to have a word with Gabriel. Run along, my dear. I'm sure your mother misses your company."

Ivy lifted her chin in defiance and walked ahead of Gabe. They were still within earshot when she said, "Do be more careful in future. Don't trust anyone, especially *new* acquaintances. One can only trust old friends these days."

I wasn't sure if that was a dig at Lady Stanhope or me. It may have been directed at both of us.

"Insufferable girl," Lady Stanhope muttered. "And what a

nerve, too! It wouldn't surprise me if her family is the reason behind this nasty incident."

The thought hadn't occurred to any of us, but now we all looked at one another. We'd assumed the stabbing was linked to the kidnapping attempts, but what if she was right? What if Mr. or Mrs. Hobson were so angry with Gabe for not supporting their business or their daughter that they'd decided to punish him in a more tangible way than simply putting out false statements to the press?

Gabe returned, pausing in the doorway as we all stared at him. "Have I missed something?"

Lady Stanhope repeated her theory for his sake, but Gabe refused to believe it. "They're not violent people."

"No, but the men they hire could be. Those sort of people—ones in trade—don't get their hands dirty. They pay others."

I suppressed a sarcastic laugh at the implication that *her* sort of people, the nobility, did all their dirty work themselves.

"It's best to be careful, Gabriel," she went on. "Don't trust them. Don't trust their conniving siren of a daughter either."

"Siren?" Willie asked.

"The creatures from Greek mythology who lured sailors with their beautiful singing voices."

Willie screwed up her nose. "I've heard Ivy sing, and she ain't that good. But I reckon you're right and she can't be trusted."

"She or her mother," Alex muttered.

"You believe this nonsense too?" Gabe asked him.

Alex shrugged. "It's a possibility that we have to entertain. It could prove fatal if we don't take it seriously."

"So, we are all in agreement." Lady Stanhope addressed Alex. "Make sure the rest of the staff know not to let the Hobsons in. Mr. Glass's safety must be your priority."

Alex's jaw firmed. "It is my priority already."

"And he is not staff." Gabe rang the service bell. "Now, if you don't mind, the doctor ordered me to rest."

"I thought you didn't see a doctor, only a nurse."

Gabe gave her a smile as Murray appeared in the doorway. "Thank you for coming."

She left the sitting room to the tune of the ringing telephone in the hall. Bristow appeared moments later and announced that a detective from Liverpool was on the other end.

Gabe went to speak to him and returned after a few minutes. "That was Detective Inspector Lafayette. He was part of the team that investigated the disappearance of a man named William Collins in 1893. He was alerted to our inquiry because the description we gave the Liverpool police matched William Collins perfectly."

"Not Bill Foster?" Alex asked.

"According to Lafayette, there was no one named Bill Foster reported missing, but he's convinced William Collins is Foster. So am I."

"Did he give you anything to go on? A family contact, place of work, friends who might know where he went?"

"He did more than that. He told me why he suddenly disappeared. We were right. Collins was on the run from the police."

"What crime was he accused of?"

"Murder."

CHAPTER 18

The man we knew as Bill Foster was really named William Collins. Born and bred in Liverpool, he'd lived an unremarkable life and was widely considered by friends, family and colleagues to be a good man. He drifted from job to job, taking work as a laborer where he could. Despite his lack of education or any great skill, he was well respected, and generally regarded as kind and helpful, often lending a hand to friends who needed it.

Then one day he'd got into an argument at his local pub. Witnesses couldn't agree on what started it. Some said he'd bumped a man and spilled his beer. Others said it was over a barmaid both men liked. His closest friend, who was drinking with him that night, said people often picked fights with William because of his size and the fact he was known to avoid physical violence at all costs. Local lads wanted to be the one who beat Big Will. Their mistake was assuming that William *couldn't* fight. Just because he chose not to, didn't mean his large fist couldn't pack a solid punch. That night, the lads wouldn't stop their taunting and pestering. They spat on him, spilled their beers over him, and pinched him while no one was looking. When he finally reached his limit, William Collins fought back.

Given what Bill Foster's landlady and lover had told us, I tended to believe William's friend's version. He was a good man pushed too far. He wouldn't be the first to retaliate against bullies with fatal consequences.

When he realized what he'd done, he fled Liverpool. Leaving the only home he knew might seem like a drastic move, but the punishment for murder was death. There was a chance he could get a reduced sentence due to the circumstances, but it was a chance he wasn't willing to take. Sadly, I agreed that a judge and jury would take one look at a man of his size and think him a thug.

William Collins headed to London, a large city that he could get lost in. He changed his name and found accommodation in a room rented by Mrs. O'Brien, and work as an orderly at Rosebank Gardens. He settled into a new rhythm, and even fell in love with his landlady.

Then war broke out. He was patriotic and he had experience with the care and transport of patients, and the unique difficulties associated with hospitals. He was needed and he wanted to help. He joined as a stretcher-bearer, so he didn't have to fight or kill. He could *save* lives.

But the only way to enlist was to give his name. William Collins would be hauled back to Liverpool to face trial if he signed up under that name, and Bill Foster didn't exist. He needed a real name that belonged to a real man of a similar age who wouldn't be enlisting. He knew one from the hospital. Robin Reid.

Dead men don't need their names anymore.

When Gabe finished recounting this information he asked Murray to fetch his jacket. "Alex, you can drive. Sylvia, you can borrow my mother's scarf for your hair."

"Oh, er..."

Willie rose, hands in the air. "Whoa, wait. Gabe, you ain't going to Rosebank. You're supposed to be resting."

"I have rested. Now I'm ready to work again."

"You ain't going back there. What if someone put the patient up to attacking you and they try again? Maybe he got in another patient's ear."

"I'm not going to Rosebank, but thanks for your concern."

She folded her arms over her chest. "Where are you going?"

"Come with me and I'll show you. If it makes you feel better, bring your gun."

She looked at him like he was a fool. "It always makes me feel better, and I always take it wherever I go."

"I'd suggest you get a scarf to cover your hair, too, but there's no point."

"I don't wear scarves." When she thought no one was looking, she touched the mop of hair tied up at the back of her head.

I leaned closer. "It looks as lovely as always."

She narrowed her gaze at me.

I followed Gabe out of the drawing room, quickening my steps to keep up with his long strides. He moved with grace and energy, not at all like a man who'd been stabbed the day before. It proved that his comments about feeling fine weren't merely for our benefit, and he was telling the truth. My heart lifted to see him as robust as ever.

* * *

HAVING BEEN FOILED by Mrs. O'Brien last time, we knew it wouldn't be easy getting answers. She would probably slam the door in our faces. Willie suggested using brute strength to force our way inside. Alex told her it was a terrible idea.

"She could have us arrested," he said. "Not to mention that we want her to talk to us, not hate us or fear us."

"You men stand back. Sylvia and I will do it. We're small and female. She won't see us as a threat."

He snorted. "Sylvia perhaps, but have you looked in a mirror lately?"

"We're not using force," Gabe told them as he closed the motorcar door. "Is one of you escorting me?"

Alex leaned against the Vauxhall, staking his claim as the lookout on the street, while Willie went first up the steps and knocked on the front door.

Mrs. O'Brien opened it. Her smile vanished upon seeing us. "I've got nothing to say to you." She went to close the door.

Willie thrust her foot into the gap then shrugged an apology to Gabe when he glared at her.

"We have something to say to *you*," he said.

Mrs. O'Brien pushed against the door in an attempt to close it. Willie pushed back.

Gabe continued. "We know Bill Foster's real name was William Collins. He was on the run from the Liverpool police who wanted to question him over the murder of a man in a pub."

Mrs. O'Brien stopped pushing.

"We know the death was unintentional," Gabe went on. "We know the man was bullying Bill, and that Bill hit back when he'd had enough. If you talk to us, we can clear his name. It may not mean anything now he's dead—"

"It means a lot." She opened the door wider, revealing a forlorn woman where before she'd been all bravado. "It means his spirit can rest in peace, and his family can finally learn what happened to him. Family was important to Bill, but he couldn't write to them after he left Liverpool. It was his greatest regret about running away. He knew they would have endured shame when he was labeled a murderer. But my Bill wasn't a murderer. He was kind and gentle. The man who died deserved what he got, in my opinion, but Bill didn't mean to kill him. He just didn't know his own strength." Tears filled her eyes. She fished in her apron pocket for a handkerchief but couldn't find one.

Gabe handed her his. "What can you tell us about Robin Reid, the man whose name Bill used when he enlisted?"

She dabbed at her eyes with the handkerchief. "He was a

patient at Rosebank Gardens where Bill worked. He died after a short stay in the hospital, and was buried in the grounds. Bill dug his grave all on his own. He said it was one of the hardest things he's ever had to do. He liked the lad. He didn't think he should have been in hospital at all, but the lad admitted himself. He thought the doctors could make him a magician." She shook her head sadly. "In those days, the hospital only took patients who were artless but had magician parents. They claimed they could bring the magic out of them with their treatments. My Bill knew it was all bollocks after just a few months working there, but what could he do? He was just an orderly and the doctors had all that learning... The problem was, the patients wanted to believe they could be magicians, so they endured the treatments as long as possible. It was all just so sad, especially when they started to die."

"Do you know how many died?"

"Three. I know for certain, because two were reported in the papers. There was a police investigation and everything, but the deaths were found to be natural causes." She shrugged. "The third was Robin Reid, although the police were never told about him. The lad admitted himself, never telling anyone he was going to Rosebank. My Bill said he never even told his parents. That's why when he died after the other two, they decided to keep it quiet. Bill was on duty that night and found him dead in the bed. He reported it to the doctor who was treating the lad, but was told not to tell anyone else. Next thing he knew, he was ordered to bury the body. The doctor told him not to say anything to anyone. He threatened him. Bill would've disobeyed him and gone to the police if he could. But he was afraid they'd find out Bill Foster didn't exist. He couldn't risk them notifying the Liverpool police." She dabbed at her eyes again. "He told me, of course. We told each other everything. It was me who urged him to say nothing and forget about it. And he did forget, for years. Then in '14, he told me he wanted to enlist, that it was his duty. He was patriotic, was my Bill. He loved this country and he wasn't one to shirk his duties. I tried to talk him out of it, but he was determined. He said he could use Robin Reid's name since he was still alive, officially, that is."

"Did Bill mention how Robin died?"

"He wasn't sure, but he knew it had something to do with the hospital's treatments. They were experimenting with some new therapies. Bill never told me what. Maybe he didn't know." She shrugged. "Bill wasn't there when the patients underwent their treatments, but he saw them before and after and he told me they changed dramatically. Fully grown men who were excited about the prospect of becoming magicians became frightened of their own shadows. Before their treatments, they'd share a joke with Bill but after, they'd scream if he came near them and cower under their bedcovers. Bill reckoned something terrible happened to them in those treatment rooms. Something that scared them and killed three."

Few of the returned soldiers spoke about the war, particularly in front of women. I'd caught snippets of conversation here and there, and seen some paintings and photographs, so I was aware of the mud and death, the bombed buildings and destroyed forests. But the fear of dying and the horror of having to kill others...that was something I could only imagine. I knew from seeing the men suffering shell shock that it must have been awful.

The hospital stay must have been an equally traumatic experience for Robin and the other patients for them to show similar symptoms to shell-shocked soldiers when they left.

Mrs. O'Brien handed back Gabe's folded handkerchief. "Tell the Liverpool police what you said about Bill not intending to murder that man in the pub. They'll believe you. Tell them to inform his family of Bill's war service. Give them my name and address, too, if they want to write. They should know that he had a good life here, a happy life."

"I will. Thank you." He tucked the handkerchief back into his pocket. "You mentioned the doctor who treated Robin Reid ordered his burial... I know it was a long time ago, but did Bill mention his name?"

"No, sorry."

"Thank you anyway. We appreciate your time and I'll give our contact on the Liverpool police force your details to pass on to Bill's family."

We went to walk off, but she called us back. "Bill didn't mention the doctor's name, but you can find out who he was. He became the hospital's director a few years later, so Bill told me." She searched the sky above our heads. "That would have been in 1911 or '12. Bill was annoyed about it. He didn't think that a man without scruples who'd bury a body without notifying the family should get promoted to director. Bill didn't think it was right. He called it an injustice."

Dr. McGowan. It had to be. If not him, then his predecessor. It would be easy to check.

We waited until we were in the vehicle with the engine running before we told Alex what we'd learned. Then we all spoke at once, and all came to the same conclusion.

"It's got to be McGowan," Alex said. "He lied to us. Not only can we say for certain that Robin Reid was a patient in '94, we can be very sure McGowan remembers him even now. It's not easy to forget someone dying in your care." He spoke with the quiet gloom of personal experience.

Willie reached over and thumped the steering wheel. "Come on! Let's go and speak to him!"

"I thought we weren't going back to the hospital today." He jerked his thumb at Gabe, seated behind Willie.

"I never said that."

"Yes, you did."

She waved a hand at the road ahead. "If you don't want to drive, I'll do it. I'm a better driver than you anyway."

"Ha!" Alex released the handbrake lever and pulled away from the curb.

Gabe had remained silent throughout the exchange between

his friend and cousin, but now he shook his head. "We're not going to Rosebank Gardens. Drive to Scotland Yard, please, Alex. I want to speak to your father."

Willie turned to look at him. "You reckon he can do something?"

"He wanted evidence and now we can give him Mrs. O'Brien. She's a credible witness. Her statement might be enough to persuade Cyclops's superiors to reopen Robin's case, and perhaps even the cases of the two confirmed deaths."

* * *

CYCLOPS HAD to meet with his immediate superior as well as the commissioner before he was given authority to question Dr. McGowan over the death of Robin Reid. It all hinged on Mrs. O'Brien's statement, however. Fortunately, with a little gentle coaxing from Gabe and me, she told Cyclops what she'd told us.

With the relevant paperwork in hand, Cyclops was given full access to the hospital's records, including the prewar ones stored in the attic. It was hot and airless, and the two constables Cyclops had brought with him were soon sweating. As the minutes ticked by, and they closed yet another drawer without success, the room became stifling.

Cyclops slammed the final filing cabinet drawer closed and rounded on Dr. McGowan. They were both aged in their fifties, but that's where the similarities ended. Cyclops towered over the smaller doctor, his scarred face and eye patch making him appear much fiercer than I knew him to be. It was no wonder Dr. McGowan shrank away.

"Where is it?" Cyclops growled. "Where's Reid's file?"

Until then, Dr. McGowan had been watching the search from the doorway with a calmness at odds with the situation he found himself in. From that calmness alone, I knew the police wouldn't find Reid's file. McGowan was far too sure of himself.

That all vanished when an angry Cyclops confronted him. Dr.

McGowan took a step back, only to find his escape route blocked by Alex. "I don't know," he said. "If there's nothing in those cabinets then he mustn't have been a patient here."

"Bollocks," Gabe said. "He was admitted twice. The first time, his parents brought him. His father is still alive and can testify to that. So why is there no record of him at all? Is it because you destroyed every reference to him after we searched the filing room the other night?"

"You mean when you illegally broke in and disturbed my patients. No, Mr. Glass, I did not destroy anything."

"Or perhaps you destroyed the file at the time of Robin's death in '94. It makes more sense to do it then, after you buried the body."

"How dare you! I am a respected medical professional. I've written articles for *The Lancet* and been a speaker at lectures around the country. Your accusations are offensive and only point to your lack of education and understanding of this hospital's purpose."

"What purpose is that?" Willie spat. "The purpose of experimentation to the point of killing patients?"

"Rosebank Gardens and institutions like ours are the last bastion of hope for some of these men."

"We know," Gabe said, calmly. "Despite what happened to me yesterday, I can see that the patients have a home here and that most of the staff treat them with kindness and respect, something they'd most likely not get out in the world. But it wasn't always that way, was it? In the early nineties, when you treated the artless descendants of magicians, you used therapies that were untried and dangerous. You experimented on those patients and three of them died, including Robin Reid."

Dr. McGowan gritted his teeth. "There were two deaths, both deemed natural causes by the coroner, and there was no one here by the name of Robin Reid."

"We have a witness who will testify otherwise."

Dr. McGowan spluttered and huffed before finally denying it.

"You can't possibly have a witness. Everyone who worked here then has gone except for me." He turned to Cyclops.

Cyclops confirmed Gabe's statement with a nod.

"Who? Who is it?"

"We're not at liberty to divulge that information," Cyclops said.

Dr. McGowan's nostrils flared. "Whoever it is, they're lying! They have to be. They can't possibly have witnessed anything."

"We know this hospital tried new therapies on its patients, but they caused such trauma that three died. Two of those patients were admitted to Rosebank by their families, but Robin admitted himself and told no one he was here, not even his parents. He'd already confided that to the staff, so when he died, his doctor ordered the body be buried to cover up the trauma he suffered. Were you that doctor?"

"That's absurd. Why would I, or anyone, do such a thing?"

"You didn't want the police looking into the death."

"Two suspicious deaths had already made the newspapers," Gabe added. "A third would have sparked outrage and closer scrutiny."

"Those two deaths were from natural causes," Dr. McGowan said. "Are you suggesting the coroner was incompetent?"

"More likely he was swayed, either by you or the director of the hospital at the time."

"I don't have to listen to your accusations. You have no proof." He pointed at Cyclops. "I'll speak to the police commissioner about this."

"Go ahead," Cyclops said. "He knows precisely what proof we have and gave his approval for this search."

Dr. McGowan scoffed. "Proof! You haven't got any. Whoever the witness is, they're lying. You can't even prove Robin Reid was here, let alone died under our care. If he did, where's the body?" His sharp gaze flicked from Gabe to Cyclops and back again. "You haven't got one, and without a body, you cannot say for certain that the fellow you're seeking is even dead. You have nothing, Inspector, so I suggest you and your posse leave before I have you forcibly removed." He pointed at the stairs. "Good day to you."

Cyclops hesitated before leading the way downstairs, with Willie bringing up the rear ahead of Dr. McGowan. Even she had nothing to say. As much as we all fumed, our hands were tied. We couldn't threaten or cajole him, couldn't counter his arguments with our own, and certainly couldn't arrest him. Because he was right. We didn't have Robin's body. Without the body, we didn't have enough proof.

He was going to get away with it.

CHAPTER 19

With Gabe's stabbing fresh in our minds, we were all on alert as we crossed the gravel drive to the Vauxhall. I climbed into the back seat while Willie retrieved the crank handle from the floor. She didn't crank the engine, however. She joined Gabe, standing with his back to the vehicle. He scanned the property, taking in the lawn, beds of roses, and the row of trees marking the eastern boundary. I didn't need to see his face to know what he was thinking.

There was too much land. The commissioner wouldn't authorize the entire estate be dug up to search for a body. Without any record of Robin Reid being in the hospital, there wasn't enough evidence to proceed.

Dr. McGowan knew it, too. As he stood on the hospital's front porch, there wasn't a hint of concern on his face as he watched us leave. We were an annoyance to him, just another thing he had to deal with in his busy day, nothing more.

Willie cranked the engine then tossed the handle onto the Vauxhall's floor. "Smug prick. Look at him! He thinks he can do as he pleases here and get away with it."

"He has gotten away with it." Alex indicated the lawn,

dotted with patients and staff oblivious to our reason for being there. "Where would we even start to look for a body?"

I hated that McGowan wouldn't be held accountable, but our investigation hadn't been entirely fruitless. "At least we can tell Bernard Reid what happened to his son."

None of them responded. With a sigh, I turned away to watch the scenery slip past as we drove along the drive to the gate, the police vehicle behind us. A white flash between the trees at the property's perimeter caught my eye.

"There's someone there!" I pointed at the trees.

Alex slowed down. "Are you sure?"

"I…I don't know. I saw a white coat or pajamas…something like that."

"Going in the same direction as us?" Gabe asked.

"I don't know. It happened so quickly. I might be mistaken, but I don't want to take that risk. Not after yesterday."

Gabe's hand covered mine, resting on the seat between us. "No one will try anything now. We have a police escort."

Willie removed the gun tucked into her belt. "I'll check." She opened the door.

Alex reached over and grabbed her arm. "Stay here. Gabe's right. No one will try anything now. It's too exposed."

"You reckon the attacker yesterday thought it through logically? You reckon the next one will? Some of these men ain't got all their marbles and don't know what they're doing. Don't assume they think like us."

"Stay here," Alex growled again. "If there is an attack, you'll be more useful near Gabe than halfway across the lawn. I'm driving, and Sylvia won't be able to fight off a strong man on her own."

"I still have one good arm," Gabe told him. "I'm not entirely useless."

Willie closed the door again. "All right. But drive faster."

Driving fast was all well and good, but we still had to stop at the gate. The guard on duty was frustratingly slow, and quite oblivious to our agitated state. He whistled as he ambled to the gate, a bunch of medieval looking keys jangling at his hip. The whistling became as jarring as fingernails down a blackboard and I wished he'd hurry up. Gabe's thumb tapping didn't help my nerves either.

I focused on the trees and shrubs skirting the perimeter. They grew along the fence, coming right up to the gate. It was ample coverage for an attacker to spring at us at the last moment before we drove away.

The click of Willie's gun cocking was almost drowned out by the guard, shouting at us to drive through.

Alex revved the engine.

Willie, Gabe and I kept our gazes on the trees. So, when the nurse burst out from behind them and slammed both hands on the bonnet, we weren't taken by surprise. I still gasped, however, and my heart tripped.

Alex pulled on the brake lever. "I almost killed you!"

"Careful!" Willie snapped. "Don't dent the bonnet."

The nurse sucked in great gulps of air, her chest heaving with her breaths. She must have run all the way from the hospital or lawn, and she wasn't a young woman. I recognized her as the nurse who'd stitched Gabe's wound. She'd also been the one to fetch Dr. McGowan the night we broke in.

Gabe got out of the vehicle. "Are you all right, Sister?"

Willie swore loudly and scrambled to get out, too. "Gabe, what are you doing? Get back in." She pointed at the backseat with her gun.

The nurse slapped a hand over her mouth, smothering her cry.

"Put that away," Gabe growled at Willie.

"What if she tries to stab you?"

"She's not going to attack me. Put it away."

Willie narrowed her gaze at the nurse.

The nurse smoothed her hands down her uniform and blew out a shuddering breath. "I am not going to harm anyone. You can search me, if you like. There's nothing on my person except this." She tapped the fob watch attached to her uniform at her chest. "I suppose the pin could be used as a weapon, but I don't think it would do much damage."

Willie tucked the gun back into her belt. "It could if you stabbed someone in the eye. Or the neck."

"Only if I managed to hit a vital vein."

"I reckon I'll still check you, if you don't mind." Willie ordered her to put her hands in the air then patted her down. It was clinical and methodical, yet she did it twice to make sure.

The nurse smiled as Willie stepped back. "Find anything of interest?"

Cyclops joined us. "Something the matter?"

Willie waved a hand at the nurse. "She followed us from the hospital. I'm making sure she's not carrying any hidden weapons. Can't be too careful after what happened yesterday."

"Why were you following them?" Cyclops asked.

The nurse was unfazed by his terseness. She glanced back along the driveway toward the hospital several times, however. "If he knew I was here talking to you, he'd dismiss me without references."

Gabe removed some bank notes from his pocket and handed them to the guard who pocketed them and walked off, whistling. "No one need know you were here, Sister…"

"Wallbank. Matilda Wallbank." She patted her cap, ensuring it was still in place. "I wanted to tell you about a conversation I had with Dr. McGowan soon after I started work here. I was admiring the gardens, and the roses in particular, and he happened to mention they'd all been established many years prior, when the property was still a private home. Except for one. He pointed out the garden bed furthest from the house. It was planted in 1894, he said."

We exchanged glances.

"Which one?" Gabe asked.

"It's to the west and set back compared to the others. You

can't miss it. All the other rose bushes are situated for best viewing and sunlight, except that one bed. It doesn't seem to belong there." She cleared her throat. "If I were looking for something that went missing in '94 and suspected someone buried it in the grounds to hide it, I'd look there."

So she *had* been listening at doors. I'd wondered if she was the same nurse who'd hurried away from Dr. McGowan's office the day we met him.

Cyclops thanked her and ordered his men to turn their vehicle around.

One of the constables removed his helmet and scratched his head. "We're going to dig it up now, sir? But we haven't got any shovels."

"There are shovels in the old stables," Sister Wallbank said.

Both constables sighed before returning to their vehicle.

Sister Wallbank refused Cyclops's offer of a ride. "I'd rather not be seen with you. I like this job and don't want to lose my place here. The men need me. If you don't find what you're looking for... Well, I need to look after myself, since I have no husband to provide for me." Her gaze flicked to Willie before she disappeared into the trees again.

Willie watched her go with a curious expression, until Alex ordered her back into the Vauxhall.

We returned to the hospital behind the police vehicle. The constables went in search of shovels, while we went in search of the garden bed the nurse referred to. It was easy to find, based on her description. The only view of it from the house would be from the service rooms. While I liked the thought of someone planting roses for the staff to admire, I doubted they would.

"What is the meaning of this?" Dr. McGowan marched toward us, the thick wave of gray hair at the front of his head bouncing with every step.

"We're digging up these roses." Cyclops indicated the area.

"You have no right to do that!"

Cyclops showed him the order again. "This gives me the

right. Would you like to save my men some trouble and point to the area where the body is buried?"

Dr. McGowan crossed his arms and shot a defiant glare at Cyclops.

The defiance didn't last long, however. The two constables returned with shovels, along with an orderly. I recognized him as the man Stanley Greville was speaking to the day we saw him here. The orderly touched the brim of his cap in greeting then set to work, digging. Alex and the constables removed their jackets before joining him.

A mere fifteen minutes later, a skeleton wearing striped hospital pajamas was revealed. When they uncovered the skull, I turned away.

Gabe rested a hand on my lower back. "Do you need to sit down?"

I shook my head. "Poor Robin."

Dr. McGowan grunted. "You don't know it's him. That could be anyone."

Cyclops crouched by the body and pointed to a gold tooth in the skull. "Robin's dentist should have records about his teeth. There will probably be other telling signs on the skeleton, too. A good pathologist can find all sorts of identifying marks on bones."

Gabe crouched beside him and pulled a cloth out of the top pocket of the pajamas. He unfolded it to reveal a handkerchief with "R. Reid" stitched into the corner. "There's also this." He straightened. "You were working here at the time Robin died, McGowan."

"That doesn't mean I killed him or authorized his burial! It was the director, or another doctor. It wasn't me!" The higher his voice went, the less I believed him.

"When did you become director?" Gabe asked.

Dr. McGowan frowned. "Why?"

"Answer the question."

"I don't remember."

"I know." Sister Wallbank had approached from behind us, walking so softly on the grass that no one heard her. "It was in 1911."

Dr. McGowan tilted his chin. "What has that got to do with anything?"

It meant he was the doctor Bill Foster mentioned to Mrs. O'Brien, the one who authorized the burial of Robin's body the night he died. Bill told her the doctor became the hospital's director in 1911 or '12.

Cyclops signaled to his constables. "Dr. McGowan, you're under arrest for the unlawful death of Robin Reid in 1894."

Dr. McGowan backed away, hands up to ward off the police. "No! You can't arrest me! I'm the most senior doctor here. This place is nothing without me. Important work is carried out here. Ask the Home Office! These patients need me to cure them."

"You're not curing anyone," Sister Wallbank snapped. She was obviously no longer worried about being dismissed, now that it was clear Dr. McGowan was guilty. "Mr. Jeffries is worse off than when he arrived, as are a dozen more you've put on that new drug. I researched it and found out it hasn't passed clinical trials yet."

"What do you know about medicine?" he sneered. "You're just a nurse."

"He's experimenting on the patients?" Cyclops asked.

She nodded. "I'll give you a sample of the pills before you go."

"You experimented on Robin and the others, too, in the nineties," Gabe said to Dr. McGowan. "Was that also drugs, or was it a particular treatment, as Bill Foster believed?"

"This is absurd. I'm a doctor! My work is innovative, so of course things go wrong, at first, but that's how we learn and improve. It's common scientific practice to experiment!"

"You experimented on *people*."

"Look around you, Mr. Glass. Look at those men with their damaged faces, their wits gone." He hammered his finger into his temple and bared his teeth at Gabe. "What sort of life are they going to have anyway? If I don't cure them, they won't survive out in the world. At least they can be of some use here, by helping me test the latest pharmaceuticals and therapies. Out there, they're of no use to anyone. Not even their families want them."

His tirade was shocking. He was playing God, deciding who should receive untested medicine and therapies. The worst of it was, he believed he was doing good, that the sacrifice of a few sick men was worth it.

Cyclops had heard enough. He didn't wait for his constables to handcuff Dr. McGowan. He did it himself. "Take him to the motor and wait for me there. I need a word with Sister Wallbank." Cyclops shoved Dr. McGowan toward one of the constables who marched him to the police vehicle.

"This is outrageous!" the doctor cried. "I'm a medical professional! Unhand me, at once!" When he realized he wouldn't be released, he shouted insults at Cyclops until the constable punched him in the stomach.

"Didn't your mother teach you that if you haven't got something nice to say, don't say anything at all?" the young constable growled.

Cyclops asked Sister Wallbank to fetch a sample of the medicine Dr. McGowan had prescribed to the patients.

"I'll keep you company," Willie said, falling into step alongside the nurse. As they walked off, Willie could be heard telling Sister Wallbank how impressed she was with the way she'd stood up to Dr. McGowan. "You're real fierce. Want to have a drink with me later?"

I couldn't hear the nurse's response.

Cyclops told his second constable to stay with the body until the coroner's officers arrived to transport it to the mortuary. The orderly agreed to help him fill in the grave site while he waited. With that organized, there was just one more thing to do.

"Now I need to inform Robin Reid's father," Cyclops said heavily.

"We'll come with you," Gabe said. "We started this investigation, so we should be the ones to see it to its full conclusion. If it's too much for you, Sylvia, you don't need to join us."

"I want to."

I stared at the pajama-clad skeleton again, a mixture of emotions tangling together inside me. Robin Reid wasn't my father. Aside from the letters from Bernard Reid to John Folgate, nothing connected Marianne to Robin and the date of his death was wrong. Besides, the Reids were woolen magicians, not paper. Finding Robin had also not led us any closer to discovering why my mother was so secretive about her past, although I'd begun to form an opinion about why we moved from city to city so often. Bill Foster, or William Collins, had left Liverpool to escape prosecution. Had my mother also been in trouble with the police? Was she trying to stay one step ahead of the law?

Surely if that were the case, we'd know. Cyclops would have found outstanding charges against Marianne Folgate, yet neither the London nor the Ipswich police force were after her. So, what was she running from?

Or, rather, who?

Despite my disappointment at being no closer to discovering more about my parents, I was glad Robin Reid wasn't my father. I didn't want to be related to Bernard. Robin's desperation to be a worthy son to his magician father had led him to try radical, untested cures, even after his first stint at Rosebank Gardens failed and left him quite altered. He'd done it to be loved and accepted by a family that wanted him to be something other than what he was.

I glanced at Gabe, wondering if he felt an affinity for Robin and his situation as the apparently artless child of a magician parent. But he was looking intently at me, his expression full of concern.

"We'll find him," he said.

It took me a moment to realize he meant my father. "Perhaps." I didn't tell him that it might be better that I didn't find him. If Evaline and Walter Peterson's father was also mine, and he'd not wanted to help raise me, then wouldn't it be better not to know for certain?

We left the constable and orderly with the body and trudged across the lawn to the Vauxhall. Alex kept close to Gabe's side, his gaze sharp as he took note of every patient, every orderly and nurse. I was reminded of something that had occurred to me earlier during the confrontation with Dr. McGowan.

"He chose which patients to give untested medicines to, which ones would endure which cures," I pointed out. "His choices brought death to some and had devastating effects on others. He was playing God."

Cyclops slowed his pace. "The attacker said God spoke to him and told him to stab Gabe." Their gazes connected over my head. "Sylvia's right. He could have been talking about McGowan."

"Possibly," Gabe said. "But McGowan would know that stopping me wouldn't stop the investigation. It would only bring unwanted extra attention to the hospital."

Alex agreed. "The attack was related to the kidnappings, I'm sure of it. Whoever instructed that patient to stab you didn't want you dead, just incapacitated. With your attention preoccupied, they must have thought it would be easier to kidnap you."

I chose not to remind them of our other suspects—the Hobsons. I suspected they didn't need reminding anyway, and simply chose not to mention them.

Once Willie rejoined us, we piled into the Vauxhall. It was a tight squeeze, with the addition of Cyclops, but we managed it, although Willie couldn't sit still. It was more from excitement than discomfort, however. She couldn't stop smiling.

"Does this mean you have a new love interest?" Gabe asked her.

"Maybe. Tilda—that's Matilda Wallbank—and I are going to

have a drink later." Her smile turned secretive. "I sure do like nurses. There's something about 'em. Ain't that right, Alex?"

"I don't know what you're talking about," Alex said from the driver's seat.

Cyclops, seated alongside him, faced his son. "You're seeing a nurse?"

"No."

"He is," Willie piped up.

"I'm not."

"What about the one you met at the dance hall? She was real pretty."

"I didn't pursue it further."

"Didn't you kiss her?"

"No."

"Why not?"

"Because I didn't want a relationship with her and kissing her would have sent the wrong message."

She rolled her eyes. "I don't know what's got into you. You've become a prude."

"I am not!"

"The old Alex wouldn't have cared about mixed messages. He would have kissed her, and more."

Cyclops turned in the seat to face us. "Leave him alone. Maybe his interests lie elsewhere now." He winked.

"You mean Daisy?" Willie blurted out.

Cyclops stared at her before turning back to face the front.

"Since when did that matter to him? Used to be that he'd kiss two girls in the same night and not care."

"I'm not like that now," Alex growled. "I've got more respect for women."

Willie snorted. "Respect is fine, but Daisy wants nothing to do with you, so you should have taken up the nurse on her offer, at least until Daisy sees sense."

"Can we stop talking about my love life now?"

"We ain't talking about your love life because you ain't got one."

* * *

INFORMING Bernard Reid that his son's remains had been found wasn't the difficult experience I thought it would be. He didn't break down or get angry. His eyes remained dry, his voice even. He was mechanical and unemotional, as he had been when we first met him. Our last encounter must have been an aberration.

Cyclops showed him the handkerchief to prove we'd indeed uncovered his son's body. "This was found in the pajama pocket. Do you recognize it?"

Bernard traced his thumb over the stitching. "My wife made it. She was very skillful with the needle. Very skillful. Some used to think she was a silk or cotton magician because her stitching was so fine, but she was artless. I never blamed her for that, of course. It's not her fault. I loved her anyway."

I wasn't sure if he was extending that feeling toward Robin until he went to close the door and I saw his chin tremble and his eyes fill with tears. It seemed he cared, after all.

We drove Cyclops back to Scotland Yard. Before he alighted from the motorcar, he invited me to join his family for a picnic the next day. "If the weather's as nice as it is today, we plan to go to Richmond Park. You're more than welcome to join us. Daisy, too."

I accepted on behalf of both of us.

* * *

I'D NEVER BEEN to Richmond Park. It was quieter than Hyde Park and Hampstead Heath, but just as pretty with its rolling green hills dotted with deer, and ducks and swans gliding lazily over the lake. We found a spot under a large tree and spread out the blankets. I'd brought a cake, but I wasn't sure it was needed. Catherine had packed two large baskets full of sandwiches, cold meats, and salads, and Gabe had another with Mrs. Ling's pies and some fruit.

Before eating, Ella and Alex picked up tennis rackets and hit a ball back and forth. She'd received tickets for Wimbledon's opening day from her parents as an early birthday present and had excitedly told Daisy and me all about her favorite players.

Catherine sat nearby, watching on. "Ella could have gone on to play at a tournament like Wimbledon."

Cyclops handed her a glass of lemonade. "She wasn't interested. She wants to keep tennis as a hobby, not a profession. You know why that is."

Catherine sighed. "Not this again."

"Not what again?" Gabe asked. He'd helped unpack the baskets and spread out the blankets and cushions. I was relieved to see he moved easily and didn't seem in pain from his injury.

Cyclops shook his head at Gabe in warning, but Lulu, the boisterous youngest child, didn't heed it. "She wants to join the police force."

"But she's a woman," Daisy said.

Cyclops filled another glass with lemonade and handed it to her. "The Met have just had their first intake of females. They're called WPCs, and they work with female and child victims, mostly. Ella won't be patrolling in bad areas or after dark. It'll be safe."

Clearly this was an ongoing discussion in the Bailey household, one that I suspected Catherine would ultimately lose. "I don't like it," she said. "I know some of the things you see every day, Nate, and what Alex saw, too, when he served, and I don't want my little girl experiencing that."

"She's not little anymore. She's twenty-two. If any of us are equipped for police work, it's Ella. Do you agree, Gabe?"

Gabe nodded. "She'll cope well."

"You got to let her join, Catherine," Willie said. "Women can't hold other women back. It ain't right."

Catherine bristled. "I'm not holding her back, I'm just concerned for her. It's a mother's prerogative to worry about her children."

Mae had been plucking daisies to make a chain, but now turned to her mother. "You shouldn't worry about Ella. She's very capable."

"That's nice of you to say, Mae." I gathered from Catherine's tone, that the sisters didn't often say kind things about each other.

"If you want to worry about one of us, worry about Lulu. She *stole* my diary and read it. That's an arrestable offence, but Father wouldn't put her in cuffs. Honestly, what's the point of having family members work for Scotland Yard if they won't arrest people who do the wrong thing?"

Lulu had been lying on the grass with her eyes closed, but sat up when she heard her name. "Mae has been walking with a boy." She poked her tongue out at her older sister.

Catherine scolded her youngest for tattling, but Cyclops frowned at his middle daughter. "Who is the boy? Do we know him? Who are his parents?"

Mae glared at her sister. Lulu smiled smugly.

By the time their argument fizzled out, Alex and Ella had rejoined us. We tucked into the food, chatting as we ate. Catherine asked Daisy how her novel was coming along, and Daisy sighed heavily.

"I've come to the conclusion that I'm not a writer. I couldn't get past the first chapter. Not only was the chapter rather boring, but I got bored sitting all day."

"What will you do next?" Ella asked.

"I don't know, but I hear you're thinking of joining the police force as a WPC."

Ella frowned at Catherine. "My mother won't let me."

"I could be swayed," Catherine said.

Ella brightened. "Really? Father, can you bring home an application form tomorrow?"

"I wish women could join the police force when I was younger," Willie said. "I'd have made a great detective."

"They can't be detectives," Ella told her. "Just constables."

Willie pointed her egg and cucumber finger sandwich at her. "You can be the first."

Ella liked the sound of that.

"I wonder what the training entails," Daisy said. "Perhaps I should apply, too."

"No!" Alex all but shouted.

Everyone stared at him.

"Why not?" Daisy asked. "Do you think I'm not capable of being a policewoman?"

"I, uh..." Alex appealed to each of us in turn. "Gabe, you agree, don't you?"

Gabe plucked a grape off the bunch. "Don't drag me into this. I think a woman should do as she pleases." He popped the grape into his mouth. "Who wants to race paper boats?"

Lulu squealed with delight. "Did you bring enough paper for everyone?"

"Wait," Alex said. "You misunderstand. I think women should choose any career they like, too."

"Except policewoman," Daisy shot back.

"No."

"Just me, then?"

"Yes. No. That's not what I meant." Alex looked stricken.

Daisy waited for an explanation, but Alex didn't give one. He simply took the piece of paper Gabe handed him from the stack he'd brought along in the bottom of the picnic basket.

Daisy shook her head when Gabe offered her a sheet. "I don't know how to make paper boats."

"Me either," I said, taking a sheet anyway. "But my paper planes used to beat my brother's all the time, so I'll give this a try."

Gabe began folding his sheet in a rather complicated way. "I should warn you, I've been the champion at paper boat racing since I was twelve. No one has managed to beat me."

"It's true," Cyclops said.

"And he never lets us forget it," Mae responded.

"He's very annoying," Lulu said with a roll of her eyes.

"I think he cheats," Ella added.

Gabe got to his feet, boat in hand. "You're all jealous."

Gabe, Willie and the three girls raced to the lake's edge where they waited impatiently for the rest of us to join them.

Catherine fell into step beside me. "They do these races at every summer picnic and it always brings out their competitiveness. You would think Willie was fifteen again from the way she behaves."

Willie shouted at us to hurry up or forfeit.

"*You* forfeit," Gabe said to her. "I'm going to beat you anyway."

She pushed him. He pushed her back and she lost her balance. If he hadn't caught her, she would have fallen into the lake. The three girls fell over each other, giggling.

I looked around to see where Daisy had got to and found her and Alex a few paces behind. For a moment, I thought they'd become friends, but then I realized he was doing all the talking and she was pretending not to hear him. She focused directly ahead, arms crossed over her chest. As they passed Catherine and me, I heard him tell Daisy that he said what he'd said because he knew firsthand how dangerous policing could be.

She finally stopped and rounded on him. "So you think I wouldn't cope with the danger? You think I'd be afraid?"

"No. I don't want you to join because I'd worry about you."

Even Daisy's stubbornness melted in the face of the sweet sentiment. She lowered her arms and muttered, "Oh." She shuffled her feet. "You don't have to worry. I'm not going to apply. Not because I'm afraid, you understand."

"I believe you. You're one of the bravest women I've met."

She blinked wide-eyed at him.

He continued to the water's edge, folding his paper into a boat shape as he went. She trailed after him.

Catherine and I shared a smile and continued on. I hung back a little, however, and put the finishing touches on my boat. It even had a little mast. I stopped at a patch of daisies and plucked a flower off its stem and placed it inside the boat. As I did so, I whispered the paper strengthening spell.

I joined the others and set my boat on the water. "How is a winner determined?"

"The one that travels the furthest before sinking," Ella said. "Everyone places their boat in a row at the same time. It has to be at the same time, or it's not fair. Ready?"

Alex handed his boat to Daisy. "You place ours."

"Ours?"

"Hurry up," Lulu whined.

Daisy hastily put her boat in the water at the end.

"Now you give it a little push," Ella went on. "But not too hard because…" She pointed to Daisy's boat, taking on water over its bow. "That happens."

Daisy sat back on her haunches. "Oh no! I'm sorry, Alex. We didn't get very far."

He laughed. "Never mind. We were never going to win."

"You're conceding to Gabe already?"

"Not to Gabe."

Willie let out a *whoop* as a breeze pushed her boat ahead of the others. She traipsed along the edge of the lake, treading on reeds and getting wet. She stopped to remove her boots and socks then rushed to catch up to her boat as it floated away. Ella's boat soon caught up, and she followed Willie at the edge of the lake.

"I'm coming for you," she teased.

Willie dipped her hand in the water and splashed Ella. Ella removed her shoes to wade into the shallows and splash her back.

Mae wrinkled her nose. "It's muddy and reedy, and there are

probably creatures swimming around wanting to nibble your toes."

"You're such a princess," Ella shot back.

Gabe leaned closer to me. "Those two always want theirs to be fast so they make them lightweight. But it's not about speed, it's about stamina. Look. They're already taking on water."

Both Ella and Willie's boats listed to the side as their bottoms became too soggy to keep them afloat. Catherine and Cyclops's boats had already sunk, while Lulu's and Mae's were half underwater. Gabe's and mine sailed along nicely until they were the only two left floating.

"Are you sure this is your first time making a paper boat?" Lulu asked me. "You're very good."

Mae rolled her eyes. "She's a paper magician, silly. Of course hers is going to win. It's the fun of the race that matters, not the winning."

"Nah," Willie said. "It ain't the winning that matters, it's seeing Gabe lose." She beamed at him. "Best boat race we've ever had."

Gabe watched his boat slowly sink, inch by inch, until it disappeared from view altogether. Then his face changed to a look of pure horror. "Oh God. What's that?" He pointed at the calm lake surface. "Willie, get out of the water!"

I'd never seen Willie move so fast. Or, at least *try* to move fast. Her foot got stuck in the mud and she ended up tripping over and fell face-first into the reeds.

Everyone burst out laughing.

A bedraggled Willie traipsed out of the lake, dripping from head to toe. She shook herself out like a soggy dog and snatched up her shoes and socks. "Lucky for you, you're injured." She poked a finger into Gabe's chest. "I won't push you in the water. But I will do this."

He arched his brows at her. "What?"

She threw her arms around him and gave him a fierce hug, then slipped a damp sock down the back of his shirt.

"You're a child," he told her as he untucked his shirt and let the sock slide out and fall on the ground with a wet plop.

"And you're a loser at paper boats."

"It wasn't a fair race," I pointed out.

Gabe gave me an innocent look, but it was all for show. He'd chosen an activity he knew I would win, even though it would see him lose a crown he'd held for years. It was a selfless act and I wasn't entirely sure I would have been as kind if the situation was reversed.

"It doesn't matter," Lulu said. "He finally lost!" She picked up her skirts and skipped after her parents, walking hand in hand ahead of us.

Ella flung an arm around my shoulders. "I knew your paper magic would be useful."

"That's not all she can do with it," Daisy said, falling into step beside her. "She's about to help Huon Barratt invent invisible ink. Imagine the possibilities!"

"Invisible ink," Gabe said flatly. "With Huon."

"Yes," I said. "Why do you say it like that?"

"Like what?"

I shrugged. "Like you're a little annoyed."

"I, er…"

"Nobody trusts Barratt," Alex filled in when Gabe didn't go on. "He only cares about himself. Gabe doesn't want him taking advantage of you. Of your magic, I mean, and your generous nature."

"I like him," Willie announced. "He's fun."

"The last man you called fun, you ended up marrying."

She tossed a rude hand gesture in his direction then set off at a run, barefoot with her boots in hand.

"Oh, you're in trouble now, Willie!" Alex shouted as he ran after her. Not wanting to be left out, Mae and Ella picked up their skirts and ran off too.

"She really is a child," I said, laughing. "As quick as one, too."

When Gabe didn't respond, I glanced at him, worried that his wound was troubling him after all this activity.

But he simply regarded me thoughtfully. "Be careful with Barratt, Sylvia."

"I can handle Huon." Indeed, I felt as though he was one of the few men I could handle. It was his lack of subtlety that made him easy to fend off. I always knew what he was thinking the moment he thought it. I also suspected he was a good man, underneath it all.

"I just don't want you getting hurt," Gabe said.

I reassured him that I'd be fine and left it at that, even though I could have gone on to say that he was more capable of hurting me than Huon ever could be. Saying so would only ruin the perfect day.

So instead, I removed my shoes and ran after the others. "Come on, Gabe, or you'll lose for the second time today."

Look For:
SECRETS OF THE LOST LEDGERS
The 5th Glass Library novel

Did you know the Glass Library series is a spin-off of the Glass and Steele series? Go back to where it all began with book 1, The Watchmaker's Daughter by C.J. Archer.

A MESSAGE FROM THE AUTHOR

I hope you enjoyed reading THE DEAD LETTER DELIVERY as much as I enjoyed writing it. As an independent author, getting the word out about my book is vital to its success, so if you liked this book please consider telling your friends and writing a review at the store where you purchased it. If you would like to be contacted when I release a new book, subscribe to my newsletter at http://cjarcher.com/contact-cj/newsletter/.

ALSO BY C.J. ARCHER

SERIES WITH 2 OR MORE BOOKS

The Glass Library

Cleopatra Fox Mysteries

After The Rift

Glass and Steele

The Ministry of Curiosities Series

The Emily Chambers Spirit Medium Trilogy

The 1st Freak House Trilogy

The 2nd Freak House Trilogy

The 3rd Freak House Trilogy

The Assassins Guild Series

Lord Hawkesbury's Players Series

Witch Born

SINGLE TITLES NOT IN A SERIES

Courting His Countess

Surrender

Redemption

The Mercenary's Price

ABOUT THE AUTHOR

C.J. Archer has loved history and books for as long as she can remember and feels fortunate that she found a way to combine the two. She spent her early childhood in the dramatic beauty of outback Queensland, Australia, but now lives in suburban Melbourne with her husband, two children and a mischievous black & white cat named Coco.

Subscribe to C.J.'s newsletter through her website to be notified when she releases a new book, as well as get access to exclusive content and subscriber-only giveaways. Her website also contains up to date details on all her books: http://cjarcher.com

Follow her on social media to get the latest updates on her books:

f facebook.com/CJArcherAuthorPage
X x.com/cj_archer
instagram.com/authorcjarcher